the TECHNO MAGE

S.W. Raine

The Techno Mage

Published by: S.W. Raine 2020
Cover Design by: Fiona Jayde Media
Editing by: Renee Dugan

ISBN: 978-1-7348795-0-6

For more information visit:
http://swraine.com

To Holly for guiding me on the right path,

and

to my husband Thad for putting up with my
insane career choice.

CHAPTER 1

The sound of metallic tinkering and sudden hisses of steam filled the repair shop. Sweat beaded across Ikarim's forehead as he pulled back from the gigantic motor he'd been repairing. The heat inside the building was stuffy, even with the high bay door opened. He removed his oily, rust-stained fiddler cap and wiped his brow with the back of his bare forearm. Despite it being the cleanest part of his body, a streak of dirt still smeared above his green eyes.

He glanced at a tall and lanky young man who pulled on a thick rope with gloved hands and levied another hunk of machinery about the room as if it weighed practically nothing. Ikarim shook his head and chuckled to himself; even with his toned form, he would never have been able to make it look that effortless. He combed

1

his fingers through his messy blond hair, secured the hat back on his head, and returned to his work.

A small copper bell, attached to a string running to another area of the building, chimed. Ikarim looked up to the device, then turned to the lanky man, puzzled. "Isn't it a bit early for a break?" he mused out loud.

The thin man shrugged, just as confused.

"What? I cannot allow my beloved employees another well-deserved breather?"

The voice was gruff. Both young men turned their attention to an elderly man who stood on the landing, one hand braced on the railing for steadiness, the other on the brass Derby handle of his cane. He had once been a tall man; his height now crumpled with age. A black top hat adorned with a pair of goggles sat atop his head. His finely-waxed white handlebar mustache was shaped in an uprising swirl, his goatee beard expertly trimmed. He turned to move closer to the staircase, and the monocle over his left eye shimmered iridescently. Despite his age, his visible blue eye was still fierce, revealing a youthful fire still alight in the old man's soul.

"*Doktor* Gesselmeyer," Ikarim greeted, setting his massive wrench down.

"Is everything well?" the lanky man asked as he moved toward the Scientist.

"Everything is well, Arteus. I simply came to inform you I will be running errands and will be

2

late returning home. Could you lock up shop for me, my boy?"

"Yes, *Vater*. Of course."

"And can I trust you to have this piece finished by tonight? The *Kapitän* will pay extra if it is in top shape by morning."

"Of course, *Vater*. We have everything under control."

"And will we have an infusion ready by morning as well?" asked the old man.

"I will make certain that Mags has it ready," Ikarim piped in.

"Where is Mags?" Arteus asked, craning his long neck to catch a glimpse of the Alchemist.

"Ah." Gesselmeyer pulled away from the railing and limped to the door with the aid of his cane. "The *Dame* Wiegraf is currently dealing with another suitor arranged by her father. Fetch her in ten minutes when your break is over."

As the old man left the bay, Ikarim's eyes met his friend's, whose lips were twisted as he bit at the inside of his cheek. Ikarim attempted a reassuring smile; he knew the mechanic was worried about his father, who always seemed to return from his errands the worse for wear—as if a dozen years had passed each time.

Ikarim's gaze dropped in defeat, and he shuffled over to a rusted bench in the corner of the bay. Two rolled up, woven cloths were neatly tucked beneath it. He grabbed a handkerchief from his overall pocket and wiped at the grime on his hands before he pulled them out, shooting a quick glance back to Arteus, who watched his father from the tiny bay window on the landing.

While the young man lingered at the door, Ikarim sat and partially unraveled the smaller cloth next to him. Inside were various tools: screwdrivers, wrenches, pins, needles, hammers, pliers. The bigger cloth contained a strange jumble of brass blades, which he carefully placed in his lap. Ikarim took a tiny screwdriver and tinkered with a few blades, careful not to scratch them in the process. He found himself smiling, taking joy in his craft.

"You have been working on that for ages," Arteus stated. "Are you almost finished?"

The screwdriver almost slipped from his hand. "Yes," he replied, his startled heart racing.

"Will you ever tell me what it is?"

"No," Ikarim replied with an ever-so-faint smirk. "It's a surprise. You'll see soon enough." Arteus watched in silence until Ikarim added, "Break is almost over. I should go get Mags."

"I'll get her," Arteus chipped in eagerly.

Before Ikarim could retort, the mechanic had already vanished beyond the bay opening. He slowly shook his head in amusement and returned to dabbling with his work.

***

Arteus left the building and stepped into the midday sun. He dusted himself off to try and appear presentable, fiddling with the trank of his oversized utility gloves as he turned the corner of the building.

A medium-size airship was anchored to the nearby dock, its gleaming metallic panels almost blinding. It had thick wings beneath two large parallel propellers in the back, and a long sleek body to help it glide through the air. Fine flags rippled and tossed from its two large masts, broadcasting the Royal Guard's official navy-blue-and-white emblem for all to see. In the distance, Magaliana, sporting Arteus' tan overalls which were entirely too big for her petite frame, stood with her arms crossed over her chest while a soldier in red spoke with her.

Arteus paused, his heart sinking. When the young woman's blonde dreadlocks swung back and forth from the motion of her refusal, he released a breath he didn't know he held and sped up toward her.

"Mags!" he called out. The couple turned their attention to him. "Break time is over."

The soldier's lips moved—perhaps a plea to reconsider—as he turned his attention back to the Alchemist. Magaliana shook her head once more. The soldier reached out to grab her hand, but she took a step back, waved goodbye, and spun around so quickly her waist-length dreads

5

whipped around her. An irritated frown painted her porcelain features as she marched away from the man, but when her eyes met the mechanic coming to her rescue, she gave a genuine smile. A warm flash waved over his face and he was sure his cheeks were pink by the time she reached him.

Arteus respectfully removed his cap and quickly attempted to flatten his disheveled chestnut-colored hair. "I... didn't mean to interrupt..." he stuttered sheepishly.

"Of course you did," the young woman replied as she looked up into his brown eyes. "Break time is over. Besides, we were finished talking," she added, glaring over her shoulder. She continued toward the building, and Arteus gladly followed.

"Your father has resorted to soldiers now for potential suitors," he observed, disheartened, slowing his pace to walk in step with her.

"Indeed. I can tell him one million times that I do not want to marry, but he insists. He says, 'I cannot allow my only daughter to be taken care of by anything less than a real man.'" Magaliana's posture straightened and her chin rose high and proud, imitating her father's broad shoulders as she walked with her arms out. When she spoke his words, her tone lowered, forcibly manly. Arteus snickered in amusement, his cheeks still rosy.

"On a different subject," he said after he

cleared his throat, an attempt to remove the ever-present lump that formed when he was near Magaliana, "*Vater* had to run errands and wanted to be certain that an infusion would be ready by morning."

"Of course. I'll get right on it," she said as they entered through the front of the building.

***

The afternoon turned into evening, and the trio cleaned the shop after they finished their work. Ikarim made his way to the dock and boarded the small dirigible to begin his routine, while Arteus extinguished the lanterns and locked the doors behind them.

After ensuring the balloon had sufficient inflation, Ikarim turned the control wheel and glanced behind him to make sure that the tail obeyed. He then looked to Arteus, who was supposed to pull the anchor up but instead lingered on the side of the ship. As usual, his attention was glued to Magaliana, who had walked to the edge of the dock to look out over the horizon from their small floating island. Ikarim parted his lips to redirect the attention of his love-struck friend, but nothing escaped him as his gaze followed toward the Alchemist, then past her.

Clouds stretched for miles at the dock, akin to water from a lake. The whimsical puffs were fluffy with tints and hues of purples, pinks, and oranges. The scene before them was beautifully painted, and he wondered if it was just as breathtaking in the Lands Below as it was in the Upper Lands. Magaliana crouched down on the edge of the dock and swept her delicate hand into the clouds. A thin layer dissipated like smoke from her touch.

"Mags!" Ikarim finally called out.

Magaliana slowly stood and wrapped her arms around herself, turning to make her way back toward the dirigible. Arteus offered her a gloved hand to the hull, but she declined with a slight wave and climbed aboard herself. Once she was seated, he slid in after her and hoisted the anchor, but Ikarim didn't depart. Instead, his gaze remained on Magaliana.

Her green eyes were back on the horizon, pensive. She had never been so unsettled after speaking with her suitors before. Something was wrong, but he didn't want to disturb her thoughts, so he turned back to the control wheel. The dirigible pushed off with Ikarim at the helm, sailing mere inches above the sea of clouds.

It was Arteus who gently broke the silence. "What's on your mind?"

Magaliana never shifted her gaze. "Petty Officer Hogarty said that the Carronade fired today."

Ikarim's eyes fell to a tiny mirror vibrating at his side. He tweaked it to see his friends in the back. He had overheard an extremely dangerous word: Carronade. "Where did it fire?"

"He said that it hit Portugal."

"Ouch," Arteus piped in. "Didn't *Prinz* Francisco head down to the Lands Below on a mission a few days ago?"

"*König* Rodriguo won't be happy..." Ikarim frowned. "Another pointless war for power."

Magaliana wrapped her arms around her legs as she curled up in her seat, and Ikarim focused back on the horizon. The trio were silent for the remainder of the trip back to Gesselmeyer's mansion, their somber thoughts preventing conversation.

CHAPTER 2

Once at the mansion, the trio went their separate ways. Ikarim washed the oil, grime, and sweat from his hair and body before he slipped into some clean clothes and headed down the cluttered hall to continue working on his project in the drawing room. He tilted his head in consideration as he paused before the main library. Did the library hold any information on the Carronade? Curious, he entered the grandiose room.

Fine wooden shelves and towering cases were filled to the brink with leather-bound books. Aged notes spilled out from every shelf and large stacks of heavy tomes sat unsorted on the dusty floor. Not a single inch of wall on all three levels was visible; everything was hidden behind bookshelves accessible by spiraling staircases, small patios, and rolling ladders.

Ikarim grabbed the lantern hanging by the

doorway and found the wind-up key beneath the metal frame, cranking it three times as the lantern clicked and ticked. A floating sphere inside the glass globe came to life and cast a warm glow. Ikarim brought the lantern with him as he stepped inside the room and studied the book spines on the shelves, flipping through a few weathered titles he hoped contained information on the Carronade, but they mostly offered nothing on the subject.

He perused more until he arrived at a fine, hand-carved desk in the far-right corner of the library. A display sat atop the oaken surface; a clunky black screen with thin knobs situated atop of a large metal box, connected to a typewriter via a mess of wires. Ikarim set the lantern down, reached behind the box, and pulled the small lever. The sound of the box hissing echoed around the vast room. When he cranked the lever on the side of the screen, the piece of technology chugged along like a train and steam escaped from the back.

A blinking cursor appeared on the otherwise-blank screen. Ikarim allowed one index finger to hover across the surface of the typewriter before he finally pressed a key.

C_

The cursor continued to blink after the input of the letter, so he clanked away and entered the rest of the word.

CARRONADE_

He pressed Enter and the word vanished. Ikarim frowned. Had the machine run out of steam?

"Ike!" Magaliana called. "Dinner!"

Ikarim turned his attention toward the sound of his friend's sweet voice. His lips parted to reply, but no words escaped him as the screen flashed and averted his attention. It was filled with words and numbers. Names and coordinates. Abbreviations and dates. He shook his head in confusion, the information too much to process. His attention was once again pulled away from the analytical engine by Magaliana's terrified shriek.

"*Doktor* Gesselmeyer!"

Ikarim's heart skipped a beat. He spun away from the machine and knocked the lantern off the desk, shattering it across the floor. Wincing, he rushed from the library, down the hall, and toward the front door. Magaliana's voice sounded so strained, as if something had happened.

She and Arteus were already there when he skidded to a halt; Arteus was by his father's side as he tried to help him, while Magaliana stood back, hands covering her mouth.

Gesselmeyer, despite his old age, returned to them as if a dozen years had gone by, his body so weakened he could hardly limp, even with the aid of his cane. His body shook from a nasty coughing fit, his skin ashen.

"Come, *Vater*. Let's get you to bed..."

"*Nein*." The old man's voice was hoarse and barely above a whisper between coughing fits. Arteus paused, concern written all over his face, until Gesselmeyer's cough finally subsided. "No. I just need..." He trailed off for a moment. "Food. Dinner. Bring me to dinner."

Arteus eyed the old man with uncertainty, but eventually replied, "Yes, *Vater*," and helped Gesselmeyer lean on him for support as they slowly walked toward the dining room.

Ikarim's attention lingered on the old man, ready to jump in to help at a moment's notice. When they had disappeared around the corner, he turned to Magaliana. Shock froze her in place, and he hated to see her in such a state. He pulled her toward himself to hold her close, and she leaned into his shoulder and frame. Her hands moved away from her mouth and gripped at the fabric of his white shirt instead.

"I've never seen him so frail..." she whispered.

"He'll be fine." Ikarim tried for a reassuring tone. "With some delicious food and a little rest, he will be good as new."

Magaliana pulled away and stared at him with uncertainty, as if searching for the lie. Ikarim did not break; he tried hard to believe the words that escaped his own mouth.

"Ikarim! *Dame* Magaliana! Come. Let us eat dinner," Gesselmeyer called, his voice weak.

Ikarim gave a feeble, albeit soft smile and motioned with his head in the direction of the dining room.

Decorative wooden fretwork adorned the burgundy-colored walls, and gold-framed paintings depicting various everyday events and activities hung above the panels. They both made their way to a large mahogany table that seemed better suited for dozens of guests, where silver trays were loaded with seasonal vegetables, mutton, bacon, cheese, and eggs. Arteus sat close to his father in a bid to keep a keen eye on the old man's frail and fragile form. Ikarim abandoned his habitual place around the table to do the same, as Magaliana filled the plates and served them.

The trio were silent, unlike Gesselmeyer, who was quick to speak up despite his grave condition. "I will have none of this," he huffed with difficulty.

"*Vater...*" Arteus started.

"*Nein*, Arteus. There will be no worry, frustration, or somber faces." The Scientist took a moment to catch his breath while the trio exchanged concerned glances. Gesselmeyer spoke up once more. "Arteus, an anecdote, if you please."

Arteus' eyes widened as they shot back to his father. A fist adorned in a tightly fitted leather glove rose to his lips as he cleared his throat. He stuttered and frowned while he searched deep

14

for something to say; an amusing tale about a baker that he had encountered when he was younger came about at long last. Magaliana piped in with a tale of some shenanigans her elder siblings had gotten into. As time passed, there were smiles and laughter all around.

The joy immediately faded once Gesselmeyer, his meal barely touched, made his intention to retire early for the night. The trio exchanged concerned glances once more—Arteus while biting the inside of his cheek—before he helped his father to his feet. Magaliana began to gather the leftovers to take to the kitchen when Gesselmeyer stopped her.

"Please," he croaked. "Finish your meal. Do not stop on my account."

Magaliana slid back into her chair obediently, her gaze on her plate. Arteus helped support his father's frail body as he led him to his room.

Once alone with the young woman again, Ikarim cleared his throat to break the tension. "Everything will be fine."

The Alchemist did not look at him. After a long pause, she continued with the dishes. Ikarim sighed. Unwilling to press the issue, he stood and padded away in silence to fetch a broom to clean the shards from the shattered lantern in the library.

A haunting glow emanated from beneath its debris. With another lantern in hand, Ikarim approached the mess. Crouching, he set the second lantern next to himself and carefully lifted the lid. The orb's faint glow became slightly brighter. Ikarim picked it up, dusted it off, and inspected it closely for damage before he placed it in his trouser pocket. He would see to it that Magaliana gave the orb another infusion so that it would shine as good as new and be placed into another lantern. Ikarim got back to his feet and swept a large area of the wooden floor before he brushed it into the dustpan.

His eyes travelled back to the analytical engine. Curiosity stirring, he placed the dustpan on the floor and leaned the broom against a bookshelf before he returned to the steam-powered machine. An endless list of names and numbers filled its screen: places such as Bangui, Kowloon, Gibraltar, Bridgetown, and Chungho, with the country's initials next to it, coordinates, and dates that seemed to go in chronological order.

A loud hiss of steam from the chugging screen startled him. Ikarim reached for the lever behind the box and pulled. Instantly, the words and numbers vanished, plunging the library in darkness once more, illuminated only by the new lantern's glow. Ikarim picked up his supplies, disposed of the shattered glass, and made his way to the kitchen where Magaliana was almost finished with the dishes. Without a word, he grabbed a few of the clean ones and put them away. He felt Magaliana's green eyes on him, but she did not retort to his actions.

His mind spun. What did all those locations mean? And what did they have to do with the Carronade?

Ikarim hung the last of the brass pots on the wall over the long counter while Magaliana dried her hands after wiping everything down. She hung up her apron, whispered a half-hearted goodnight without making eye contact, then turned to leave.

"Wait," Ikarim said. Magaliana paused but did not turn to face him. He reached into his pocket and pulled out the orb, which still had a faint glow to it. "Think you can infuse it again? We'll put it into a new lantern for the library."

The Alchemist finally turned around, her eyes on the item in her friend's hand. "I can..."

She delicately took the orb and inspected it in their common silence. Ikarim stared at her, in her rosy flowered dress and white bandana to keep her dreadlocks out of her face. He noted by the slight furrow to her brow that she was still concerned for Gesselmeyer.

"Mags... You know that you can talk to me, right?"

She nodded, then turned and walked away. He hated when she didn't want to burden anybody with her emotions.

With a deep inhale and exhale, Ikarim left the kitchen and stopped by Gesselmeyer's room on his way to his own. The old man was fast asleep, as was Arteus, curled up on the floor next to his father. Ikarim lingered for a moment, disheartened, then quietly left them to their rest.

CHAPTER 3

Ikarim was in the dining room, the eggs on his plate cold and uneaten. He hadn't slept very well; his mind raced all night with concern for Gesselmeyer and scenarios regarding the list from the library. It didn't make sense. He didn't understand it.

A rustle followed by a soft thud broke his train of thought, and his eyes rose to the figure leaning against the doorframe, cane in hand.

"*Guten morgen*, Ikarim."

Gesselmeyer didn't look quite as worse for wear as he had the previous night, but Ikarim still detected a more decrepit appearance than should have been present. He was surprised to see the man standing.

"Goodness, boy. Don't look at me like I have risen from the dead. You can't get rid of me that easily," Gesselmeyer chuckled, limping to the dining room table with the aid of his cane.

19

"Sorry..." Ikarim muttered, rising from his chair to help the old man into his own. "Would you like some eggs?"

"*Nein.* I have little appetite this morning. And by the looks of it," he pointed to Ikarim's breakfast, "...neither do you."

Ikarim returned to his seat with a sigh, his attention on his food until he felt a pair of eyes boring into him. Embarrassed, he sank deeper into his chair and glanced back up to find the Scientist watching him intently.

"Well, go on," Gesselmeyer said. "There is clearly something on your mind."

Ikarim inhaled and exhaled deeply, his mind reeling. He didn't even know where to start, but eventually was able to form a coherent thought. "I went to the library last night. Earlier, Mags said that Portugal was fired on by the Carronade, which made me curious. I tried finding information on it, but the books were no help. So, I used the analytical engine and found a list of names, coordinates, and dates."

"Ah," Gesselmeyer simply said.

"What does it all mean?"

"Those are my archives. I have been keeping track of every shot fired by the Carronade since the beginning."

Magaliana, attempting to wrap a single blonde dread around the rest of her hair, paused upon entering the dining room. Her eyes were wide as she stared at the Scientist, much like

Ikarim had.

"*Guten morgen, Dame* Magaliana," said Gesselmeyer.

"*Guten morgen,*" she muttered, dropping her gaze to the ground.

She returned to struggling with her hair when another set of hands found hers. Arteus, with pink cheeks and trembling gloved fingers, helped tame Magaliana's hair. He didn't seem at all surprised that his father was out of bed.

When Gesselmeyer continued, Ikarim's attention fell back onto him. "I've only heard rumors of how the Carronade truly functions. Theories. I've researched the physical damage to the areas and have calculated the densest haze versus the least to pinpoint the exact location of the blow. I am still trying to analyze what the haze is made of, how it affects the body, why the coordinates were chosen—"

"You went to Portugal?!" Arteus gasped, his face drained of color.

"I did."

"*Vater*! You willingly endanger yourself in the haze for science?! For theories and rumors?!"

"Art..." Ikarim cautioned his friend, something he found himself doing often.

"What about your work here, *Vater*? What about the shop? What about your numerous creations? What does a dangerous cannon's

21

residue—which could potentially kill you—matter to your work here?"

"Enough!" Gesselmeyer scolded.

"Art..." Her hair finally tied, Magaliana turned around to look up at the angry young man and gently placed a lithe hand in the middle of his chest. But her actions did not calm him or even distract him as they usually did.

"*Vater*, I forbid you to—"

"That's enough, Arteus!" Gesselmeyer stood up on shaky legs. "My business is my own. Now, prepare the airship. We are running late."

Ikarim blinked and peered at the mechanical timepiece that graced the wall near the window—a mass of copper gears and pipes, pressure gages, and needles he had fabricated for the Scientist's birthday years back—while Arteus and Gesselmeyer glared at one another. They weren't late at all, but Ikarim figured that theory was posed as an end to their argument.

Arteus spun on his booted heels and stormed out. Neither Ikarim nor Magaliana moved or made a sound until Gesselmeyer snapped at them, "Well?! Get going, the both of you!"

Magaliana rushed out of the room with a squeak. Ikarim slowly strolled out with dishes in hand but paused at the door. He glanced over his shoulder and caught a glimpse of the old man sliding back into his chair with a loud and exhausted sigh. Ikarim rarely saw Gesselmeyer angry, and he especially never saw the old man lose his temper with his own son.

Ikarim inhaled deeply, swallowing the tension, and pushed on to get his affairs ready for the trip to the shop.

***

Dusting her hands off, Magaliana stepped out of the dark infusion room connected to the main office. Deep in thought as she mentally ticked off another item from her to-do list, her green eyes casually moved to the large windows—then did a double-take and gasped.

A large airship approached on the horizon, its white-and-bronze panels reflecting the clear blue sky. Giant twin rotors flanked the sleek body while dozens of swollen white sails—attached to the rear fins—billowed from its momentum. Narrow, tapered pennant flags flown from the masthead bore the official royal colors of navy blue and burgundy; the only ship more important was that belonging to Queen Victoria herself, with flags of white, navy, burgundy, and royal purple. Three smaller zeppelins followed the airship, their flags announcing that they were of the Royal Guard.

Magaliana rushed out of the building in excitement and wonder. Arteus and Ikarim were already there, just as much in awe.

While both mechanics helped the royal airship and one of the zeppelins set anchor at the dock of the floating island, Magaliana prowled the length of the largest ship, taking in every detail. It was the most amazing thing that she had ever seen.

She came to a stop as a tall, dark-haired, weathered man in a well-decorated scarlet uniform appeared at the entrance of the royal ship. His tunic—with golden pattern braids that pulled away from the cuff lace, and thick braided shoulder boards—differed from the rest of the Royal Guard.

"Brigadier General Franklin Darley," Gesselmeyer greeted in a thick English accent as he limped heavily to meet with the man.

The General turned his dark eyes toward the Scientist. His distinct lack of emotion made the scars running down his cheeks all the more intimidating. He marched down the boarding plank, accompanied by two soldiers. Two more disembarked from the zeppelin and joined them. Magaliana followed at a distance, curious, settling near Ikarim and Arteus.

The Royal Guard halted before Gesselmeyer, all four soldiers standing at attention behind their superior. A white gloved hand rose in salute before he offered the old man an arm to shake. "Doctor Handsel Gesselmeyer. I thought you were an alchemist, not a mechanic."

"Scientist," Gesselmeyer corrected. "I leave the alchemy to *Dame* Wiegraf and the mechanics to these capable gentlemen." He gestured to the trio. "I simply supervise."

"I trust you supervised them well enough to have the captain's motor ready in time?"

"The *Kapitän's* motor is ready, as are your infusions. Arteus, Ikarim, please show these gentlemen to their belongings."

They nodded and led the way, leaving Magaliana by herself. While Gesselmeyer and the General spoke, one of the soldiers broke off from following the mechanics and headed toward her. Magaliana frowned.

"Lady Wiegraf." He politely removed his black cap in her presence, revealing his blond hair.

Frustrated, she swiftly turned away to face the magnificent airship, instead. "Please," she huffed. "If my father sent you..."

"He did not..."

Magaliana slowly and suspiciously glanced over her shoulder. The soldier's thin lips curled into a confident smile as he tucked the cap under one arm.

"...But he did ask me to bring you this." He reached into his uniform breast pocket and offered her an envelope.

Magaliana recognized the official Wiegraf seal, and she bristled with anger. Spinning back around, she snatched the letter from his hand.

"You lied! My father did send you!"

He forcefully stopped her from storming off with his fingers wrapped around her wrist. Magaliana whirled back around in an instant, glaring him down. The soldier quickly released her, his blue eyes apologetic. "Please, Lady Wiegraf. Your father did not send me. It was I who sought your father and asked."

"I do not wish to marry," she snapped, rubbing her wrist. "You should know this. The entire world knows this!"

"What is marriage without friendship first? I did not ask his permission to marry you. I asked his permission to court you. Of course, I would need your permission as well—"

"Permission denied," she cut him off, storming away once more.

"Lady Magaliana." The soldier followed her, his voice soft. "I am not yet requesting permission to court you. Today, I came to simply speak with you."

The Alchemist rolled her eyes and came to a stop, inhaling and exhaling deeply before she turned to face the soldier, one hand impatiently on her hip. "Then speak."

The smile returned to his lips. "How about I start by giving you my name? Sergeant Jerry Cambridge, at your service." He bowed.

"Sergeant Cambridge!" a voice called from nearby. They both turned their attention to the General as he approached. Cambridge stood tall and saluted. "Sergeant, we could use an extra set of hands."

"Yes, Sir!" His eyes met Magaliana's one last time before he placed his cap back on his head, nodded politely, and stepped away.

A sigh silently escaped her at Darley's interruption. She was furious with both her father and Cambridge, but the Sergeant was especially more tenacious and bolder than all her other suitors. She muttered in thanks and shifted her gaze away from the General, uneasy when he lingered.

"How much do you know about airships, Lady Wiegraf?" Darley suddenly asked.

Magaliana glanced over her shoulder to the General, who proudly looked upon his vessel. "I..."

She knew a surprising amount on the subject and devoured the fascinating knowledge whenever she could. Her attention followed the General's and she smiled, her rigid posture becoming more at ease. She parted her lips to speak again, but it was the General who spoke instead. "Allow me to give you a tour."

Brimming with excitement, Magaliana turned her gaze to him, caught off guard by a faint smile on his stony features. He swept an arm open in gesture for her to follow and board the airship.

"Thank you!" she whispered, elated at his offer.

As they approached the thick wooden plank, Magaliana's heart raced in anticipation. She had forgotten about Cambridge. Once she boarded, it was as if she entered a whole new world. It took a moment for her eyes to adjust to the difference of lighting compared to outside.

"Welcome aboard the HRM SS WINDIGO." Darley stepped past her and she followed down the small, dimly-lit hall, illuminated every couple of feet by infused orbs much like the ones used in lanterns. He informed her that the ship held one hundred and eighty-five men aboard. Magaliana tried not to make eye contact with most of the ones they crossed paths with. Sleeping quarters and washrooms were constant on both sides of the corridor until they arrived at a small set of steep, narrow stairs. Darley climbed down first and helped Magaliana below deck into what he introduced as the operations room.

The air was stuffy and warm. Chairs were bolted low to the ground, and consoles with large radar displays surrounded the area. The tour continued into another hall, and Magaliana stayed on the General's heels, drawing the attention of more soldiers than she wanted. Once they stepped into the empty galley, she breathed in relief.

"Please. Have a seat," he said.

Magaliana sat at the corner of one of the tables. It was a little warmer in the galley due the proximity of the kitchen, which smelled of delicious vegetables from the upcoming lunchtime stew. While the General stepped toward the counter where two chefs buzzed about on the other side, she glanced about the galley and took it all in, amazed at the enormous construction.

It didn't take long for Darley to rejoin her. He offered a small loaf, and only sat down opposite of her once she graciously accepted. "How are you enjoying your tour, Lady Wiegraf?"

"I very much enjoy it, thank you."

She set Cambridge's envelope on the table and separated the loaf down the center.

"Do you get many suitors from your father?"

"Too many," she sighed. Not wishing to continue with that portion of the conversation any further—even if he did save her from Sergeant Cambridge—she tore a small piece of the loaf, shoved it into her mouth, and turned her attention to the chefs in the kitchen. "How do two chefs cook for almost two hundred people?" she asked once she swallowed her bite.

The General humored her silent request to avoid the subject of suitors. "We have four chefs, actually. Two do breakfast, the others do lunch, and a combination of the four prepare the evening meal." He went on to explain the unofficial seating rule in the galley, and that the senior and junior mess rooms next door down the corridor also doubled as briefing rooms when needed.

When they finished their bread, the tour continued. They passed through the engineering control room, walked by the laundry room, senior and junior recreational lounges and the gymnasium, and arrived at a stairwell. Darley climbed first, then helped Magaliana into the hangar.

A gasp escaped her at the grandiose sight. She was aware that the airship was large, but never expected it to be so enormous that it could fit other ships inside. Lost in admiration, she walked around the hangar. Her hand tentatively reached toward the frame of one of the four small dirigibles, but she resisted.

Darley took her to the upper deck, where she squinted from the sunlight in the blue sky. The summer breeze, despite being warm, was a welcomed sensation from the clingy stuffiness inside the ship. Gesselmeyer's shop was cast in a whole different perspective, and she couldn't help but grin in delight. It was short-lived, however, when she noticed that everyone on the floating island had finished getting the captain's motor aboard. She figured that her tour would be over, and her suspicion was confirmed when the General spoke.

"Looks like everything is ready." He stepped over to the railing at the edge of the deck.

Magaliana's gaze fell in defeat. It was fun while it lasted, but she was going to have to return to reality. The letter from her father suddenly felt heavy in her hand. "Why were you sent to pick up the *Kapitän's* motor?"

"I offered." He turned to face her. "The shop was on the way to my next destination, and we could easily fit the motor on the WINDIGO. Also, I owed him." Magaliana almost missed the twinkle in his dark eyes; the only indication of his amusement. "Come, let us get you back to the Doctor."

They returned to Gesselmeyer. Darley thanked the Scientist and handed him a leather pouch filled with a rather hefty and heavy sum, which Arteus took and held for his father. The soldiers and General gave a salute and turned to leave. Cambridge pulled away and Magaliana shot Ikarim a pleading look as the Sergeant approached, but both mechanics were ushered away by Gesselmeyer to give her privacy.

"Lady Magaliana," he started, respectfully removing his cap once more. "With your permission, may I return in three days' time? We could have a picnic and talk about whatever you wish."

"No, Sergeant Cambridge," she replied with a sigh. "I am not interested."

"Then perhaps we could invite your two friends? That way, we will not consider it an attempt at courtship, but rather the intention I had meant it to be all along: one of friendship. I would love to get to know your friends."

"You would love to know them in order to know me," she stated, unimpressed.

Cambridge grinned as he glanced toward his ship, then back at Magaliana. "Think what you want. I will see you in three days' time. Be ready."

With that, he placed the cap back on his head and bid the young woman farewell, returning to his zeppelin. Ikarim and Arteus aided both ships with their planks and anchors while Magaliana stared out at the horizon in annoyance, the letter her father had written clutched in her hand.

"Mags!" Arteus called out once the ships had set sail. Magaliana blinked and turned to find him approaching while Ikarim and Gesselmeyer returned to the building. He stopped before her with flushed cheeks—as he always had in her presence—and looked down to her. "Are you all right?" he asked with apparent concern.

She nodded and cast a glance over her shoulder at the ship which contained Cambridge.

"Another suitor from your father?"

"Yes. And a letter!" Magaliana said in exasperation, waving the letter around.

"What does it say?"

She broke the seal and unfolded the letter inside, scanning over the contents. "He is begging me to reconsider marriage, and to do so hastily. The usual."

She tore the letter in half, then into smaller pieces. The warm breeze carried the confetti away from her palm before she headed toward the shop with Arteus in step. As he opened the door for her, Gesselmeyer stepped out instead. He adorned his top hat and looked to his crew.

"*Vater*?" Arteus started, unease in his voice." Where are you going?"

"To run errands."

His expression immediately flashed with anger. "To the hazed lands? *Vater*, I forbid you!"

"*Nein*, Arteus. I am truly running errands." Gesselmeyer casually replied. "And even if I were to return to the hazed lands, you cannot forbid me from doing my job."

"It's dangerous, *Vater*! Don't you care that you are putting your own life at risk?"

"Art..." Magaliana tried, hesitant. "Please, stop." She didn't want another argument like the night before.

"Listen to *Dame* Magaliana, Arteus. Lock up if I have not returned in time." Gesselmeyer nodded to the trio and limped away to his own dirigible. Magaliana and Ikarim silently watched Arteus for any reaction. He remained still, biting at the inside of his cheek, his attention focused on the door in frustration. Finally, he stepped past his friends, entered the building, and disappeared down the hall. Magaliana's concerned gaze turned to Ikarim.

"I thought he'd be angrier—" A loud crash from the bay area interrupted Ikarim, and he heaved a sigh. "... and there it is."

Magaliana slowly shut her eyes. She was just as worried about Gesselmeyer's so-called 'errands' as Arteus, and their arguments were on the border of getting out of hand.

A strong and calloused hand gently squeezed hers. Her eyes immediately opened to find Ikarim's attempt at a convincing smile before he released her hand. "He'll be all right, don't worry. Go get some infusions ready, I'll help him clean up."

Magaliana slowly padded toward the infusion room but paused upon hearing the muffled conversation between both mechanics. Through Arteus' frustrated tone, she could make out concern over Gesselmeyer willingly endangering himself. She overheard her name coming from Ikarim, mentioning her dislike of their arguments. When she didn't hear a reply from Arteus, she faintly smiled at the image of him blushing in embarrassment. Having eavesdropped enough, she continued into the room.

CHAPTER 4

They had only been home for a few
minutes, and Arteus was already pacing
the mansion hallways. His father hadn't returned to the shop before they closed, and the
longer he was out running his 'errands', the
more Arteus believed he had been lied to and the
old man really did go to the hazed lands, despite
his son's protests.

He approached a dead end down one of the
numerous halls where a window overlooked the
colorful evening sky and twinkling lights from
the Lands Below. A small and rickety table sat
beneath it, decorated with a white doily and a
glass vase containing blue hyacinths that Magaliana picked a few days prior. His cheeks grew
hot and his heart fluttered at the thought of her.
He ran his gloved hand lightly over the flowers,
and something out the window caught his eye.

His attention focused on the snail pace of the approaching aircraft, and the anger returned when he recognized his father's dirigible.

Arteus rushed outside, ready to anchor the vessel and confront the old man. "Where have you been?" he snapped, pacing the length of the dock.

Impatiently waiting for the slow aircraft, he frowned; something wasn't right in the way the airship crawled. He parted his lips to inquire about the speed, but nothing came out as dread washed over him at the sight of the old man.

Gesselmeyer looked like a corpse. He was so frail as he slouched in the pilot's seat, struggling for breath between raspy coughs.

"*Vater!*" Arteus darted to the anchor rope that hung on a post nearby, and attempted to fashion a lasso to pull the vessel in. Gritting his teeth and fumbling in his panicked state, he finally succeeded and swiftly made his way to the edge of the dock. It took a few frustrating tries before he hooked on to one of the ship's cleats. His wiry frame pulled the ship in with ease, and once it was along the dock fenders, he tightly secured his end of the rope to the dock post and jumped aboard the dirigible, nearly losing his footing from the sway. Grasping onto the vessel's edge, he regained his balance and climbed over to his father.

"*Vater*, why? Why did you go back? Why did you not listen to me? I forbade you!"

The old man appeared to have no energy to even speak.

"Oh, *Vater*..." Arteus bit his tongue from any more words; Gesselmeyer could not fight back.

He easily scooped his father's frail form into his arms and climbed out of the dirigible, rushing back to the mansion to find Ikarim and Magaliana standing at the door—Ikarim's face clear with concern, and Magaliana with her hands over her mouth in horror.

"Mags, get me a heated pot and bring it to *Vater*'s room. Ike, I need—"

"*Nein*... Arteus..." the old man tried between shuddered breaths.

"*Vater*, you need to rest!"

The Scientist said nothing more as a chest-racking cough escaped him, and Arteus carried him to his bedroom. Concerned that he would damage his father's frail form, he set him onto the large bed with excessive softness, but the old man continued to cough, wheeze, and breathe heavily. Ikarim busted in with a few extra blankets, and Magaliana stood at the door with the heating pot full of hot coal. As he and Ikarim placed the warm covers about the old man, Magaliana stepped inside and shoved the pot beneath the blankets by his feet.

The trio watched Gesselmeyer in silence for what seemed like ages before Ikarim finally spoke. "Come, Mags. Let's get dinner ready. Call us if you need anything," he added to Arteus before they left him alone with his father.

"Arteus—" Gesselmeyer started but was cut short by another coughing fit.

"*Vater*, please save your strength. Don't talk."

"Arteus, I must tell you..." Gesselmeyer's words were slow and drawn out, a labored breath in between each.

Arteus reached for the pot's handle and gave it a jiggle to produce embers for more heat. "I'm sure it can wait until morning, *Vater*."

"*Nein*, Arteus." His voice was barely above a whisper. "I must tell you the truth."

He sat at the edge of the old man's bed and awaited this 'truth'. Gesselmeyer pulled his hands out from beneath the blankets and brought his shaky fingers to Arteus' gloves, trying to remove them. Arteus frowned and pulled his hands away, adjusting them back on properly. "*Vater*, why are you taking off my gloves?"

"Let me see your hands."

"You know I do not enjoy showing them off..."

"I don't want to hear it. Show me."

Arteus flinched and reluctantly removed one of the black leather gloves from his hands. Beneath, rather than skin and bone, was a uniform arrangement of metal and wires similar to human anatomy. He pulled off the other one, and a sigh of contentment escaped Gesselmeyer amid a few wheezes when he touched Arteus' hands. He ran his shaky, fragile fingers over each metal extremity, then reached for the cuff of his son's sleeve and tugged at it. Arteus got the hint; he unbuttoned it and rolled the sleeve to his elbow so the old man could see the continuation of metal and wire up his arm.

"My finest work," he whispered, shaky fingers continuing up Arteus' forearm to the wires coursing with blue liquid. "And your leg?"

Arteus patted his left leg below the knee. "As good as the rest."

"Arteus, I have to tell you... This pains me, but you must know."

"Yes, *Vater*?"

"You are not my biological son." Arteus stiffened, and Gesselmeyer continued through ragged breath. "I was in England for a conference one day long ago. On my way back, I stopped at a town's junkyard for some cogs, springs, and coils for my projects. As I left, I spotted something I never thought I'd ever come across in a pile of junk..." A powerful coughing fit attacked him, his grip tightening on Arteus' metal arm before his eyes finally set back onto his son. "It was you! A baby, silent and observing, with an arm torn at the elbow, a leg torn at the knee, and another arm torn from its socket."

Arteus frowned, racked with disbelief. He couldn't wrap his thoughts around this new reality, it just didn't make sense. "*Vater*, you said I got into an accident with a rotor blade..."

"Cover up story. How does one explain to a child that he had been abandoned during the war and left to die?" Arteus was unable to answer, so Gesselmeyer continued, "With no children of my own, I instead returned home with nothing but a child. I fixed you up, my boy. I clothed you, fed you, and came up with repairs for your body. My best work. Why do you hide them after all this time? Why..."

Arteus pulled his arm away and quickly rolled his sleeve back down. Sadness washed over him at Gesselmeyer's weakened frown, and he turned his eyes away from his ill father. "I don't want her to see me like this. I am a monster."

"You are no monster!" Gesselmeyer scolded as Arteus slid the gloves back over his metal fingers. "You are a man!" He gasped for air. "Nothing will change that! Ever!"

"*Vater*!" Arteus said desperately, trying to calm the old man down.

"Prosthetic limbs do not make one a monster, Arteus!" he said through a coughing fit. "*Dame* Magaliana knows this!"

Arteus' cheeks flushed. They remained in silence for a time, save for the old man's raspy breaths once the coughing fit subsided. At last, weakly, Gesselmeyer spoke once more. "You are my son."

"I know, *Vater*. I know."

"I love you, and Ikarim, and *Dame* Magali- ana as my own."

"*Vater*, shh..." Arteus gently covered the old man's hands back beneath the covers.

"I am so tired... I am so sore..."

"Sleep, *Vater*. Shut your eyes and sleep. We will speak of this more in the morning when you've regained some strength."

Gesselmeyer slowly shut his eyes. He took one final agonizing breath, and then there were no more.

Arteus fought back tears as he leaned in and gently placed his lips upon his father's forehead. Slowly, he pulled back and rested his head on the old man's chest as he allowed a few sobs to escape.

Ikarim and Magaliana sat at the kitchen ta- ble in silence in the light of a lantern, their meal uneaten, when Arteus eventually made his way back to them. Tears stained his cheeks, and his eyes were so puffy he could barely keep them open. Magaliana shot up from her seat and launched herself at him, wrapping her arms tightly around his thin waist while she cried, stricken with grief. It took him a moment, but he carefully placed his hands against her shoulder blades to comfort her. Ikarim slowly made his way over and placed a hand on both their shoulders. Sorrowed, nobody said a word.

Arteus finally pulled away once Magaliana's sobbing hiccups subsided.

"What are we going to do?" she asked.

Arteus didn't know. He had never really considered it, before.

"We have a funeral," he finally said. "Right here." He turned away from his friends and shuffled off down the hall. "With lots of fire," he added, over his shoulder.

Arteus allowed more tears to fall as he returned to Gesselmeyer's room. His gaze fell on his father as he slowly shut the door behind him.

"Why didn't you listen?" he whispered. "Why didn't you heed my warnings? Did I not matter, *Vater*? Did your projects hold more importance than your family?"

He sat on the edge of the bed once more and lowered his hand to gently stroke Gesselmeyer's thinning white hair while he studied every inch of the old man's face. He barely looked like the Scientist Arteus knew and loved. He significantly aged each time he went to the hazed lands, and Arteus wondered—if his father hadn't passed away—how many more times he would have gone before he would be completely unrecognizable upon his return.

The sound of cracking wood outside broke him out of his thoughts. He made his way to the bedroom window and found Ikarim and Magaliana tossing old planks into a pile. He turned back to the bed. "It's time."

A wooden crate was set up like a coffin atop of the pile of planks, dry sticks and newspaper stuffed inside of it like a nest. Small infused orbs flickered about like lightning bugs. Arteus emerged from the mansion with the old man wrapped in a white sheet and gently rested him onto the bedding.

Magaliana stepped forward with her alchemy jar, the flame already dancing inside, and nestled it within the twigs. Ikarim lit a corner of paper and placed it on the kindling. It crackled and hissed from the dryness, and the trio stepped back. The flames engulfed the crate and the entire funeral pyre was soon ablaze.

Magaliana slowly slid her tiny hand into Arteus' gloved one. Uncomfortable, he swallowed hard. Would she discover his secret? The thought was short-lived when she wrapped one arm around each of their waists. They all watched as the flames worked to reduce everything to ashes in the flickering light of the infused orbs and millions of stars.

The fire died down some hours later. The trio sat nearby; Arteus had found bottles of gin and sherry in the house, and it seemed like the perfect remedy for the night.

"*Vater* told me something before he passed away," Arteus said, his cheeks hot not from Magaliana's presence for once, but from the effect of the alcohol. "He told me that I was not his biological son. He found me as a baby, brought me here, and raised me as his own. He insisted that he loved me as his own. And you, Ike. And you, Mags," he added, taking another gulp of his drink.

"He was like a father to me, as well," Ikarim said. "I was six years old when the war ended, and the world split into the Upper Lands and the Lands Below. My father didn't want us living in poverty beneath the Upper Lands like scum, so one day he took my mother, my brother, and I to the elevator that connects the London from the Upper Lands to the London Below.

"We waited in line for hours. I saw many fights, saw many people crying—children and adults alike. A lot of men were yelling and screaming at the military. The price to the Upper Lands was rising with each hour, apparently. I remember my parents arguing about splitting up, about who would be left behind. My father was going to stay behind while my mother was to go up with my brother and me. The closer we got to the London elevator, the plan suddenly turned into my brother and mother staying behind instead. I don't know what happened after, but I remember getting on the London elevator with my father. He told me to keep quiet and stay by him.

"When we reached the Upper Lands, the guard at the gate and my father began arguing. Apparently, by the time we paid and left the Lands Below to the time we reached the Upper Lands, they had instilled a tax. My father couldn't afford the tax. They forced us apart. I remember they shoved my father back into the elevator. I fought the guard when he tried to get me into an airship that would take me away. I cried and screamed and kicked and scratched. I don't know for how long. But then there was this tall man with a top hat and a monocle. He spoke to one of the guards, paid a sum, and picked me up. I immediately stopped crying. He took me home with him, and here I am, bidding farewell to the man who saved me."

Arteus raised the bottle of gin in the air—a toast to Gesselmeyer—before he brought the bottle to his lips and took a long swig. Ikarim did the same with the bottle of sherry. Arteus passed the gin to Magaliana, who simply held the bottle.

"I didn't know *Doktor* Gesselmeyer as long as you both have," Magaliana admitted. "I was kicked out of the house, so to speak. I had many arguments with my father about marriage. My father is a notable and respected German Lord. He married my mother, daughter to a notable and respected Lord of English non-nobility,

45

strictly for political reasons. But he fell in love with my mother. I was the third born. My elder brother married an Irish Duchess, and they married my elder sister off to a Dutch Lord.

"When I turned sixteen, my father arranged a meeting with a Soviet Lord. He was so old and looked horribly mean. I refused. I was beaten for my disobedience, but I stood strong. My father ignored me and arranged for our wedding within that week. Thankfully, the Soviet Lord died. Rumors were that another German Lord poisoned him. An Archduke made his intentions known, and my father tried to arrange us, but I put up such a fight that the Archduke no longer wanted me. I did the same to the five other arrangements my father had made. He was furious with me. He said that he did not want his youngest daughter to not be taken care of, and that I must marry. We argued for what seemed like forever.

"He said that if I was so confident about taking care of myself, then to do it. He bet that I couldn't even last a week. I left... I had a miserable first few days. Nowhere to sleep, nowhere to eat... I was sitting in a corner, tinkering with a sphere I infused with alchemy, when *Doktor* Gesselmeyer found me. We talked. He was such a nice man. He offered me a place to work and a place to stay, and here I have been for four years."

Ikarim raised the sherry bottle and took a drink before he handed it to Arteus, who did the same. Magaliana still held the bottle of gin. They all glanced to the dying embers as a strong gust of wind swept up the ashes and scattered them across the sky into the nothingness, the open space in between the Upper Lands and the Lands Below.

Ikarim got to his feet. "Come, Mags. Let's retire for the night. We will have a long day ahead of us," he said as he helped her up.

Magaliana finally downed what little gin remained, and her attention settled to the horizon beyond the docks. "It's a clear night. I wonder if anybody will realize the loss of a great man..." Her attention shifted to Arteus as he remained seated. "Please come inside, Art."

"I'll be in later," he said.

Ikarim pulled Magaliana away, and Arteus was left alone with the remainder of his father's ashes, allowing more tears to flow as he brought the bottle of sherry back to his lips.

CHAPTER 5

It had been three days since Gesselmeyer passed away. Ikarim bought proper mourning attire for both himself and Magaliana, as they had none. Although she ached with grief, Magaliana coped. She kept herself busy while she cleaned, helped the cook with the meals, and made sure Arteus ate despite his grief.

She wiped her hands on the gray apron about her waist as she stepped out of the drawing room but paused when she caught her reflection in the mirror above the fireplace. She turned to the looking glass and judged her appearance; although the black flaxen dress was beautiful—and fit her well, much better than Arteus' borrowed clothes—it was still a reminder of a loss.

She fussed with the gray bandana in her hair which kept the long dreadlocks out of her face. Tearing her attention away from the mirror, she continued into the hall, where she found Ikarim and Arteus approaching the front door. How unbearable it had to be for Arteus to be expected to return to work after such a short mourning period, while she, as a woman, was supposed to mourn much longer. She didn't think it fair; she wished he could mourn his father for as long as he needed.

"Are you heading to the shop?" she asked.

Ikarim nodded. "There will be a mountain of work waiting for us."

"May I join?" Neither mechanic replied, looking to one another, so she begged with a slight quiver in her voice, "Please, I... I can't stay here alone. Besides, if there are any infusion orders, it'll keep my mind off of things."

A gentle smile made its way to Ikarim's lips. "Of course you can come. We'll wait."

Magaliana clasped her hands together and tried to keep the tears that threatened to well up at bay. With a quick glance to Arteus—who looked away with rosy cheeks—she made her way to her room, removing her apron and bandana. Within a few short minutes she was ready and met her friends by the dirigible, set to take off.

The air was fresh and cool in the early morning, a pleasant change from the warm breezes in the midday heat they had been subjected to for the past few weeks. Magaliana mentally went over a checklist of things that needed to be done, but Arteus broke the silence as they neared the shop. "A ship..."

Magaliana froze. They weren't ready to deal with sky pirates without Gesselmeyer.

Thankfully, the zeppelin's sleek metal design screamed military; though the rogues, mercenaries of the world, were also known to fly whatever ship was available to them. Magaliana reached for the spyglass. "The flag bears the colors of the Royal Guard."

"I didn't think we had any more military orders after the General's..." Ikarim mused.

As they pulled in, a soldier stepped away from the locked door of the repair shop.

"Cambridge," Magaliana whined, sinking into her seat and briefly debating if she would have actually preferred the sky pirates.

Two more soldiers helped anchor the trio. Ikarim and Arteus slid out of the dirigible and met Sergeant Cambridge.

"I was a little worried when the shop was locked. I thought perhaps something bad had happened," Cambridge said in relief, stepping past both mechanics and holding out a hand to aid the young woman. "Is everything all right, Lady Magaliana? Are you well?"

She sighed and climbed out of the vessel with the aid of the Sergeant's offered hand. "I am well, Sergeant Cambridge, thank you." Ignoring the pleased smile that spread on his thin lips, she wiped at the black, flaxen mourning dress to make herself look presentable.

His smile quickly vanished. "Who..." he glanced at Ikarim, Arteus, then back to Magaliana. "Who died?"

"My father," Arteus growled.

Magaliana swallowed hard and tried not to let her annoyance at the tactless question get to her. "*Doktor* Gesselmeyer passed away a few days ago."

"Oh, Lady Magaliana! I am truly sorry for your loss." He led her to her friends. "Your father was a great man," he added to Arteus. Magaliana couldn't release the Sergeant's hand quick enough when she rejoined her friends.

"He was," Arteus agreed with a glare.

"If there is anything I can do... I can do anything from lending a helping hand at moving things, aiding with paperwork... I can even see if you can receive loaned funds from the Queen herself for the funeral."

"That won't be necessary," Arteus growled.

Magaliana stepped forward to be the mediator in case Arteus' temper got the best of him. "That won't be necessary in the sense that there was already a funeral. A private funeral. Ike, Art, would you excuse us?" She glanced back to them over her shoulder.

Ikarim nodded and placed a hand on Arteus' shoulder while he continued to glare at the Sergeant. Ikarim managed to pull him away, and

Cambridge nodded to the two soldiers who accompanied him. "Make yourself useful, men! Follow these lads and help out."

"Yes, Sir!" both soldiers replied as they followed the mechanics. Magaliana was left alone with the Sergeant.

"Lady Magaliana, despite the circumstances, might I say that you look gorgeous in a dress."

"You most certainly may not, Sergeant Cambridge," she huffed. "This is not the time or place."

"Oh, but it is. Remember? I said that I would come back in three days' time for a casual picnic with you and your friends."

Her stomach dropped. She had completely forgotten. "On a ship of the Royal Guard, and in uniform?" she eyed him suspiciously.

"Yes," he smiled. "I could get called away at a moment's notice, but I'm allowed breaks every now and again. However, I know that with the current events, your friends will be busy." Magaliana frowned and opened her mouth to retort, but Cambridge silenced her with an index finger to her lips. "And, of course, you are also busy, which is why the picnic will be pushed back to another day. In the meantime, my men and I are fully at your service."

"Until you get called away." Magaliana pulled away from his touch and crossed her arms gravely over her chest.

Cambridge chuckled. "Should the circumstance arise, yes. I would be a man searching for new employment were I to refuse the Queen's call." Magaliana smirked at his remark, and immediately regretted it. "Oh, Lady Magaliana. I saw that attempt at a smile. It was little, but it was satisfying. I wish you would understand that there is no ill or other intention whatsoever in my attempt at friendship. Now, tell me: how can I be of service?"

***

Sergeant Cambridge's soldiers were put to work with a bit of heavy lifting. While Ikarim laid on his back to better reach a valve on the large engine he worked on, he overheard Arteus ask the soldiers questions about death certificates and the possibilities of what could happen to the shop or the mansion.

Ikarim tackled a few more tasks, then wiped his filthy hands on his handkerchief and dug into his trousers for his scratched rose-gold pocket watch. Despite its rough appearance on the outside from excessive handling and falls, the watch face was as pristine as the day Ikarim cleaned it, fixed it, and installed new cathedral hands years prior.

Break time had come and gone. A saddened sigh escaped him as his eyes travelled to the bell that usually alerted them. It was heartbreaking to think that the old man was no longer there to keep track of time for them, or to give them extra breaks for no real reason other than love.

He glanced about to track down Arteus, who was still working with the soldiers, then headed for the bench where he kept his side project.

Everything was spread out and he was deep into his careful work when he overheard Arteus thank the soldiers for their help and information and say he had nothing further for them to do. Pulled from his focus, Ikarim looked up. Arteus rubbed his temples as he approached, removed his cap, and ran his gloved hands through his hair with a sigh, sliding onto the bench next to him.

"Are you all right?" Ikarim asked.

"No," Arteus admitted, "but I suppose that I will be... Eventually." He glanced over at Ikarim's project, which was much sturdier and steadier and put-together than the last time he saw it. "What is it?"

"Wings." Ikarim set his screwdriver down and lightly spread out the metal sheets like feathers, to form two magnificent brass-colored wings attached to a disk with cogs, coils, screws, and bolts.

Arteus' eyes lit up. "Such stunning craftsmanship! Ike, they're...!"

"Give them to Mags," Ikarim said with a smile, and gently placed the wings into his friend's lap.

"I... I can't," he said, flustered. "You made them."

"I did make them," Ikarim chuckled, "but for no real purpose. I think that Mags would like them and would love to receive them from you. And I know that you want to give them to her," he grinned.

Arteus picked up the finely-crafted device, scrutinizing it inch by inch. "It's perfect, not a single defect," he said in awe, placing the wings back in his lap. "I love her," he eventually admitted.

"I know."

"But she can't possibly love me back."

Ikarim raised a brow. "Why not?"

Arteus shot him a look; one that was supposed to mean everything, but in the end, meant nothing at all. "You've seen me, Ike. You know what I look like." Arteus raised his hands and wiggled the cybernetic fingers hidden beneath leather gloves. "And that's not even all of it. She can't possibly love me back, she is the daughter of a German *Herr*, and I am... Well..."

Ikarim frowned. "Art, you are not a monster. You never have been, and you never will be. You have a heart of gold, and I only ever see my friend, the son of a great German Scientist, with amazing prosthetics." Arteus turned his head away. "Are you so ashamed of how you look that what's inside no longer matters? I have known you for most of my life. You are physically and mentally strong, and I've always looked up to you. Your cybernetics are most definitely nothing to be ashamed of. Be proud of who you are, inside and out. *Doktor* Gesselmeyer loved you enough to give you what you no longer had—a home, and limbs—and he worked hard at making them perfect for you. Being ashamed is like saying that you do not approve of *Doktor* Gesselmeyer's love, of his hard work."

Arteus glanced back to Ikarim for a moment in silence, eyes filled with uncertainty.

"Go on!" Ikarim urged with a grin. "Give Mags the wings. I suppose it's time for Sergeant Cambridge to leave now, anyway. We've got work to do."

Arteus nodded. Ikarim covered the wings with the cloth and returned them back to his friend. They left the bay area and headed out to rescue the Alchemist from her suitor.

Magaliana was speaking to one of the soldiers while the Sergeant returned from his ship with papers in hand. "Here you are, Lady Magaliana, give these to—Ah! Arteus, just the man I needed," he said as they approached, and held out the papers for Arteus to take. "It isn't much, but these are instructions and directions for most of the answers you seek."

Arteus took the papers with his free hand and scanned them over quietly.

"Thank you, Sergeant Cambridge." Magaliana broke the awkward silence. "We appreciate the help."

Cambridge smiled. "Anything for you. For all of you." He looked to Ikarim, then back to Arteus. "I aim to please, and I'm here to help. And please, call me Jerry."

Ikarim caught the unimpressed glance Arteus shot at the Sergeant from over the papers, and smirked.

"I suppose I shall take my leave, or did you need more help?" Cambridge asked.

"No, we're good," Arteus replied dryly.

"Very well. We will postpone that picnic to another time. Keep in touch, my Lady," Cambridge said to Magaliana. "Arteus, Ikarim, if you ever need anything, I am but a message away." He saluted, turned, and led the soldiers away.

"Thank you, Sergeant Cambridge," Magaliana said. "For everything."

The Sergeant waved off her words as he approached his ship. "It's Jerry!"

Once the military zeppelin left port, Magaliana inhaled deeply and let out a long breath. Taking the papers from his friend, he caught Arteus' attention and motioned to him. "Go on."

Arteus swallowed hard as he held the wings to his chest. "Mags, I… I have something for you. Here," he started, his face beet red.

Magaliana glanced at Ikarim with a raised brow, and he gave her a single, comforting nod.

He took the cloth from Arteus and watched his friend slide the young woman's arms through the straps, trembling so badly Ikarim thought he would drop the wings, but he managed.

Once in place, Ikarim pulled out his pocket watch as his friend tightened the fit around Magaliana's shoulders and flipped the damaged hunter's case open to reveal the reflective interior. He handed it to the young woman, who took it and raised it so that she could see over her shoulders.

She gasped. "Art, they're beautiful!" She snaked her arms about his waist and rested her head up against his chest. Arteus awkwardly wrapped his arms around her beneath the wings. "Thank you," she whispered as she got up on her toes, placed a kiss on Arteus' chin, then pulled away and turned to Ikarim with a smile. "Look, Ike!" She lifted her arms gracefully on each side and spun slowly, showing off the wings.

"Very nice," Ikarim said with a faint smirk.

"Art is so nice to me."

"That he is," Ikarim agreed.

"All right. I think I'm overdue for creating an infusion or two—or even three—so I better get to work." Magaliana handed him back his pocket watch, then spun around once more before she headed back toward the shop. Ikarim couldn't help but smile; he knew that she would love them.

He turned his attention to Arteus, whose eyes lingered on the woman. Ikarim patted his back in amusement. "What are you going to do?"

Arteus blinked, then slowly pulled his eyes away once she was inside. "I'm sorry, what?"

Ikarim smirked, then grew serious. "What are you going to do with the shop," he specified.

Arteus breathed in deeply and exhaled, shaking his head. "I don't know. We could keep it open, or we could sell it."

"Do what's right for you. Don't worry about us."

Arteus nodded, his expression slightly exasperated. "I need to... I need to think." He turned suddenly and headed to the edge of the floating island.

"Let me know if you need anything..." Ikarim called out after him.

He glanced to the shop where Magaliana disappeared, then back to the other mechanic, watching him pace the length of the dock a few times. Ikarim wanted to help, but there was nothing he could do. He had to let his friend grieve and let him make important decisions.

With a conflicted sigh, Ikarim headed back to the shop.

CHAPTER 6

The sun had passed the midday point, roasting anything in its reach despite the cool morning. Ikarim sat in the shade by the side of the building as he placed the finishing touches on the repairs of a crane. He paused for a moment and glanced about suspiciously as there was a certain buzz about the air that had him feeling that something just wasn't right. Nothing seemed out of the ordinary, however, and his gaze fell back to his work. He soon frowned and got to his feet, looking out over the horizon. Nothing. He headed to the docks to see if anything was happening in the Lands Below, but the clouds were white, thick, and fluffy, and covered his view.

Suddenly the pillow-like surface stirred. A red flag made its presence known, decorated with a black winged skull inside of a large cog wheel. It rose higher and higher until the wooden ship it belonged to surfaced from the sea of clouds. Ikarim's eyes went wide and his stomach sank as two more emerged.

"Sky pirates..." he hissed to himself as he slowly backed away. He then spun around and ran back toward the building at full speed. "Pirates!" he hollered as loud as he could so that Arteus and Magaliana could hear him. "Pirates!"

They were not prepared for pirates. They never had been. They had always relied on Gesselmeyer's way with words and negotiation skills the very rare times they'd had to deal with them.

Ikarim didn't get very far. Something heavy fell atop of him, causing him to trip and crash to the ground. He cried out in shock, surprise, and pain as his body rolled from the momentum until he came to a halt, entrapped in thick netting. Dizzy and discombobulated, he called out to Arteus.

Three tall ships, built for both sea and air, floated in the sky, surrounding the shop. A motley crew of pirates and bandits disembarked—some helping with the anchors, while others ran toward the building.

Arteus opened the door and shot from a small Enfield revolver. He stopped one pirate as the group then scattered and fired their own guns. Ikarim flinched and gasped as a bullet ricocheted off Arteus' metal arm, hitting another marauder. Not wanting to stay in the crossfire,

Ikarim reached for his boot, pulled out a hidden knife, and promptly began cutting at the web. He quickly glanced toward his friend when he heard the man roar in anger; the bandits piled atop the slender mechanic, and though he flung a few away with ease, they eventually proved just a little too much and Arteus crumbled to the ground beneath them.

Ikarim gritted his teeth and hastened his attempt at freeing himself from his entanglement when a figure loomed over him.

"What have we here?" came a voice.

Ikarim tore his eyes away from his blade to an older, rugged-looking gentleman with slicked back blond hair. Dark eyes peered down at the mechanic past his sharp nose. A woman's scream pulled Ikarim's attention away from the matter at hand.

"Mags!" he gasped in alarm as he turned toward the repair shop.

Magaliana struggled as she kicked and screamed while she was pulled from the building by her arms. Arteus gave a panicked cry from beneath the bodies piled atop of him. They dragged her to the man who stood before Ikarim and shoved her down at his feet.

"We found her using alchemy," said one of the goons.

Magaliana crawled toward Ikarim and tried to help him get free, but the pirate leader snatched a large hand around her dreadlocks, stopping her in her tracks. She cried out in surprise and pain, and immediately released the net as she grabbed her hair at the base of her head to ease the pain. Ikarim tried to reach for the intruding hand to help release her, but she was forcefully pulled to her feet and spun around to face the leader.

"Don't you touch her, you piece of...!" Arteus tried, but his threat died as he cried out in pain.

"Mags? Is that your name?" he asked her. He pulled Magaliana's hair this way and that to get a better look. "Such a pretty face. Such fierce green eyes, so full of life." Ikarim caught Magaliana's murderous glare. "And an alchemy user, at that. That'll fetch me quite a price on the black market."

Ikarim froze at the man's words, before he doubled up his efforts to escape. He couldn't let them take Magaliana.

As she tried to escape the pirate's clutches, Arteus cried out in anger. He flung off some bandits from the pile and, with a few less atop of him, tossed off more until he eventually stood up. They were relentless, but Ikarim knew that his friend was angry and would do anything to protect Magaliana. The young man charged at the pirate leader just as Ikarim finally freed himself. With a knowing smirk, the leader shoved Magaliana into Ikarim, pulled out a Howdah pistol from the various weapons about his belt, and shot Arteus.

Ikarim and Magaliana both cried out in shock. Arteus skidded to a halt, his eyes wide, as blue liquid drizzled down one of his mechanical arms. The group of marauders knocked him back down and piled atop of him once more. Shoving the gun back into its holster, the leader stepped over to Arteus as he wiped his hands on his black slacks before tweaking the cuffs of his crisp white shirt beneath a brown pinstripe vest. He shrugged to adjust his intricate shoulder pads, then crouched to address his victim.

"A man in my business has to know weaknesses of even the largest and strongest monsters. You're no monster, but you're unnaturally strong. So, I simply shattered your liquid infusion, rendering whatever's attached to it useless. You'll regain movement when the initial shock wears off, but your cyborg arm will be just that—an arm."

Standing back to his full height, the head pirate turned to face Ikarim and Magaliana. Ikarim, knife at the ready, stood protectively in front of the woman.

"So. We have an Alchemist and a Strong Arm. What about you?"

"I'm nobody," Ikarim replied with a glare.

"I don't believe that. Your friend looks like a nobody," he started, nodding in Arteus' direction, "but was actually hiding that he was a Strong Arm. And this young lady knows alchemy. That's rare, for a woman, even in the Upper Lands. So... What about you? What part do you play in this trio?"

"I'm nobody," he repeated. "Just a mechanic." Even if he was special, Ikarim knew better than to advertise his abilities, at this point.

The leader crossed his arms over his chest. "There's no reason to put the word 'just' in front of the word 'mechanic.' Mechanics are well regarded and beneficial to working airships! Which is perfect, because I have a rather serious problem and will need the three of you to help me."

Ikarim growled. His words had backfired against him. "I don't help your kind," he finally said.

The pirate chuckled. "My kind? What exactly is my kind, might I ask? I am a man, like you. But I am one shunned by the rich society of the Upper Lands, and one too good for the Lands Below. I am simply trying to make a living of my own means." He then addressed his men. "Lock them up in the hold and lock her up in my quarters," he added as he pointed to Magaliana. "Take what you think we need, and what you think we can sell. Hurry, I'm sure the military is hot on our trail."

Ikarim swung his blade out at one of the bandits that had reached for Magaliana. He wouldn't let them touch her. "I won't help you!"

he hissed, struggling to keep the pirates at bay, but was unsuccessful and was eventually over-powered.

The older man shrugged nonchalantly. "I could torture you until you comply, but I think, based on your reaction—based on *his* reaction, actually—" he stated as he nudged his head toward Arteus, "that you will do what is necessary to keep... what's her name... Mags safe from harm."

Ikarim shot the man such a glare as he was dragged away that the pirate leader grabbed at his heart mockingly, as if to pretend that looks really could kill. He then waved goodbye with a mock pout.

Grunting could be heard in between Magaliana's upsetting screams as both Arteus and Ikarim struggled with a large number of pirates.

"Let her go!" Ikarim demanded, but every time he tried to escape his captors to help the woman, their grip on him became more power-ful and painful.

The wind was knocked out of Ikarim as he got shoved down into the hold. Arteus was forced in moments later, but he grabbed onto the wooden deck with his one good hand. Shots fired, and Arteus fell as blue liquid streamed from his other arm. There was laughter above as they locked the metal grate.

Arteus cried out Magaliana's name in a panic. Ikarim crawled over to the mechanic, concerned. He tried to calm his raging friend, but Arteus ignored him in favor of yelling at his paralyzed arm, trying to get it to work.

"Art, that's enough," he tried, but the young man didn't listen. "Art!" he said forcefully, shaking him by the shoulders to get his attention. "Do you hear me? That's enough!"

"No!" Arteus snarled. "You might have given up on her, but I haven't!"

"I haven't given up!" he said, exasperated. "But there's nothing we can do from down here! We need to regain our focus."

Arteus glared at Ikarim before he shut his eyes and sighed. "Then what's the plan?"

"I don't know, yet," he replied, studying their surroundings. "But if he wants to play this game, we'll play with him. Match his wits."

Arteus breathed deeply before he nodded. Ikarim helped him sit up, then glanced about for said plan.

CHAPTER 7

It seemed like forever before the ship finally moved, and the tension building in Arteus was enough to drive him insane. He had to save Magaliana, whatever the cost. He had regained movement in both arms, but as the pirate leader said, he had lost his strength. He huffed in frustration as he paced through the hold, while Ikarim inspected every inch of it for a plan.

Marauders rushed about on deck in haste for departure. Orders were shouted and sails hoisted as the wooden vessel creaked under pressure. Heavy footsteps thudded above their heads and eventually came to a stop; their captor slowly crouched closer to the metal frame, fingers entwined and a sneer on his face. "How are your arms doing?"

"Come down here and I'll show you," he growled.

The pirate chuckled. "I see morale hasn't improved."

"Come and say that to my face!" Arteus felt a hand to his shoulder: Ikarim's signature move to get him to calm down.

"I would invite you both on deck for a discussion, but you, Strong Arm, might need to remain down here and cool off a bit more."

Arteus glared as Ikarim stepped past him and paused at the foot of the ladder. "No, he stays with me. I promise I'll keep him in check."

"Good lad." The pirate stood up and motioned to a few of his goons to unlock the grate.

Ikarim was the first out of the hold, and as Arteus climbed behind him, they quickly restrained him by the arms. He searched his friend's face for help; Ikarim was far better with words than him.

"That won't be necessary!" Ikarim appealed. "Let him go."

The leader nodded and they released Arteus. Rubbing his metal arms, he glared at the man who separated him from the Alchemist. "Where is Mags?"

"She is unharmed. She is well."

"Where is she?" Ikarim repeated. "We don't talk unless we're together. The three of us."

The pirate casually fiddled with the cuffs of his shirt. "I commend you for thinking that you have the upper hand and are in any sort of position to be making demands, but you're not. I will take you to her, regardless, as that was my intention. Contrary to your beliefs, I am not a monster, I am human. We are not enemies—yet—and I want you to be comfortable and treated more as guests than livestock. I'm sure you can agree."

"You just got done locking us up as livestock," Arteus growled.

"Precautions, lad. Precautions. Follow me."

He led them up a ladder to the stern, to the Captain's quarters. The door was unlocked and swung open to reveal Magaliana sitting in front of a large chest against the back wall, arms wrapped around her legs, her cheeks stained with tears. She looked like a terrified and lost angel with the wings still on her back.

"Mags!" Arteus shouted.

She scampered to her feet and launched herself at Ikarim, wrapping her arms tightly around his neck. Arteus steadied his friend as he almost stumbled backward from the force of her momentum, then ran his fingers through her dread locks while she trembled, relieved that she was in one piece.

"What a lovely family portrait," the older man drawled. "Reunion time is over, I'm afraid. Step inside, please."

They shoved the trio inside the quaint cabin. Thick, burgundy curtains hung around the bed, haphazardly tied with string against the posts. A folding, cross-framed chair with low relief carvings sat near the large chest, a fancy cushion loosely resting on the webbing between the side rails of the frames. A tiny barrel was wedged next to it, acting as a nightstand.

"Are you hurt, Mags?" Arteus asked.

She shook her head. "No, but... Your arms!"

Arteus froze. With everything that happened, he had forgotten his shirt was ripped and torn and revealed his cybernetics to everyone, Magaliana included.

"They're fine," the pirate leader said, unconcerned, as he shut the door behind him. "The sudden loss of infusion rendered his prosthetics temporarily paralyzed, but he can move them now—clearly—and the wires are nothing you and your friends can't fix, I'm sure." Arteus glanced away from Magaliana, ashamed, which the older man noticed. "Don't tell me, despite this huge display of affection, that she never knew about your prosthetics!"

"What do you want with us?" Ikarim asked, and Arteus appreciated the change of subject.

"Please, have a seat," the man offered.

"We'll stand, thanks."

"Suit yourself." He took a step back toward the side room, then paused. "Ah! Where are my manners? The name is Benedict Keenan, Captain of the Doom Crusaders." He gave a quick bow. "You are currently aboard my ship, the *Raider*. She is the most notorious of my fleet."

"I've heard of the *Raider*," Magaliana chipped in. "Carrack type, three square-rigged masts, impressive forecastle and aftcastle... And able to carry a crew of fifty."

Keenan clapped slowly. "Well done, lass! I was expecting more along the lines of notoriety of piracy, but that was even better than I had imagined." He ducked into the side room, pulled out a plain wooden chair with a weathered leather cushion, and placed it in front of the door. "So now that I have introduced myself and we know that the Alchemist's name is Mags..." he took a seat, "what of you both?"

Arteus stiffened. He didn't want to give his captor the advantage. He shot Ikarim a warning glance when his friend turned to him, but Ikarim shook his head faintly, reassuring him that he had everything under control. "My name is Ikarim. This is Art."

"Well, then. Ikarim, Art, shall we talk business?"

"I suppose we don't have a choice."

"Oh, you have a choice. It might not be a choice that you like, but fewer problems will be had with your full cooperation." Keenan stretched his arms forward and cracked his fingers as he locked them together. "I have a ship in need of repair. A band of rogues heavily damaged it."

Arteus raised a brow. "If this is your biggest and most notorious vessel of a rather large fleet, why are you concerned about one tiny ship?"

"Fair question. Under any other circumstance, that is the way I would treat it, but this specific ship is special. It holds... sentimental value, if you will. It was the first one I captured. I gave it to—well, it doesn't matter. The point is that the ship is back in my possession and is in terrible need of repairs."

"What's your price?" Ikarim crossed his arms over his chest.

"Your life intact?" Keenan answered as if it was a self-explanatory question. "Your stay in this very room as opposed to the hold? Three meals a day? The young lady's virginity untouched?" he added, much to Arteus' dismay. "I could go on..."

Ikarim frowned, then glanced back at Arteus, whose attention shifted from glaring at the Captain for his comment about Magaliana. They stared at each other for a moment in silent conversation; Arteus knew he needed to cooperate, to control his temper. They all needed out of this alive.

He dropped his eyes in defeat, and Ikarim turned back to Keenan. "Once we fix your ship, will you let us go? Without shoving us overboard?"

"No," he answered, but continued before Arteus lost his temper, "because I want you to upgrade this ship afterward. I want it better. Faster. Deadlier. After that, you may leave. You have my word."

"The three of us," Ikarim bargained. "Together. Safe."

"Assuming all goes according to plan, yes."

"And if it doesn't?"

"Then you best hide when things get dangerous." Smirking, he got to his feet and returned the chair to the side room. "You will remain here unless summoned. There are books, paper, and ink in here," he pointed to the side room, "blankets and pillows in the chest... Only one bed, unfortunately. Two of you will have to sacrifice comfort for the chair and floor, unless the lass wants to spend her nights with me..."

Arteus growled and lunged at the Captain, but Ikarim grabbed both of his shoulders and stopped him. "Art, no!"

"Ah." Keenan raised an index finger. "One other thing, Strong Arm... Control your temper. As I see it, you will be the reason our contract doesn't go according to plan."

Arteus glared and spat in the Captain's face. Ikarim pulled him back with all his might, and both landed onto the floor. Benedict wiped his face with his pristine sleeve, looking displeased for the first time. "There will be guards at the door. Fair warning."

Benedict opened the door and stepped out, but not before shooting Arteus an annoyed look. Then he slammed the door shut and locked it, trapping the three inside the room.

"Art, what were you thinking!?" Ikarim hissed as he stood.

"I want him dead!" he jumped to his feet.

"Art..." Magaliana soothed.

"Don't make a move out of line," Ikarim scolded. "Don't risk your life... Don't risk Mags' life. From now on, we do nothing without all our input. Is that clear?"

Arteus stared spitefully at the door, insulted over the statement of being the deal breaker and eager to defend Magaliana's honor by breaking Keenan's face for his comments about her.

"Is that clear?" Ikarim repeated with emphasis on each word.

Magaliana was the first to nod. Defeated and powerless, Arteus agreed as well. Ikarim shut his eyes and exhaled deeply.

They were all in this together.

CHAPTER 8

The night was hot as the ship peacefully glided through the air, and the Captain's quarters were stuffy despite the small, open windows. Magaliana sat in the chair by the chest flipping through a book of notes, the cabin lit by two lanterns hooked to the ceiling, while both young men were in the other room.

Ikarim had snooped around, taking in every detail, his mind racing with possibilities and scenarios. His exploration eventually led him to the side room, where leather-bound books filled the built-in shelf against the far wall, and maps—both rolled up and unfurled—lay in disarray on the large table. In his hunt, he came upon a small chest beneath the desk, which contained an airwave receiver. With Arteus' help, he tried to get a working signal for most of the evening.

He was tired. More often than not, he found himself zoning out, his gaze on nothing in particular outside the large open window. He had already contemplated climbing out, but by the time his feet hit the quarterdeck, the guard at the door would have alerted everyone.

An irritated hiss from Arteus woke him from his reverie. While the Strong Arm struggled to get a signal, Ikarim stepped back into the other room, catching Magaliana mid-yawn as she shut a book. "You should sleep."

"I don't want to." She hugged herself. "I'm afraid to."

"Don't be. We'll watch over you, won't we, Art?"

Arteus abandoned the small airwave receiver and leaned against the doorframe, his gaze traveling from Ikarim to Magaliana. He watched her for a second, then nodded. Though Ikarim couldn't see it due to the flickering lantern lights, he knew his friend was blushing.

Ikarim offered his hands. "Come." Magaliana's delicate hands slipped into his, and he led her to Arteus, who unfastened the straps of her metal wings and removed them from her back. Ikarim helped her onto the bed and sat on the edge with his back against the wall, stroking her hair while she curled up and placed her head in his lap.

His attention was focused on Arteus, whose eyes were glued on the Alchemist. He wondered what was going through his friend's mind. The entire situation was hard for the hot-headed man, but he needed to make sure Arteus didn't make a move out of line... For Magaliana's sake. For all their sakes.

Arteus eventually disappeared back into the side room and returned with the airwave receiver which he placed on the chest as he sank into the chair. Magaliana's wings rested in his lap, and he ran his gloved fingers gently across the surface of the craftsmanship, deep in thought.

Once Magaliana's breathing was steady, indicating that she had fallen asleep, Ikarim finally spoke. "What's wrong?"

Arteus shot him a glare, which caught him off guard. Had he done something wrong?

"I love her," Arteus mumbled, his glare vanishing as his sad gaze fell onto Magaliana.

"I know."

"She saw me. My arms."

"Art..." Ikarim sighed. Magaliana stirred, and he waited until she was still again. "Art, she doesn't care about your arms."

"How do you know?"

"I just know. She would never consider you a monster. She's not like that."

"You seem to know her better than me..." he frowned.

"Is that what this is about? About how close we are?"

78

"She always runs to you," Arteus said, his eyes still on the Alchemist. "Always. I do everything for her, but she still runs to you."

"Art, listen to me and listen well." Ikarim leaned forward, speaking lowly. "Not that this is the time or place for this conversation, but I led her to you. I gave you those wings so that you could give them to her." Arteus' gaze dropped to the metal wings in his lap, and Ikarim relaxed back against the wall. "I know that you love her, I let you fetch her from her suitors." He continued to run his fingers through her dreads. "I love her, too."

"Ike!" Arteus sighed in exasperation.

"Just as much as you do," he added, his eyes back on his friend. "But you are my best friend. My brother. And I want nothing more than your happiness, at the expense of my own selfish wants and needs. So I always lead her to you. Because if you are happy and she is happy... It's all that really matters to me, in the end, above all else."

Magaliana stirred and Ikarim soothed her. Arteus watched with a sorrowful expression.

"She does not hate you, Art, you're not a monster," Ikarim added with a yawn. "She loves you for you. She doesn't care about your arms. If anything, knowing her, she's probably quite curious about them."

The dim, flickering flames from the hanging lanterns extinguished and plunged the room in darkness, ending their conversation. Ikarim heard a sigh escape his friend before the static from the receiver ceased. He started digging through the chest for blankets and pillows. Eventually, Ikarim drifted off.

He felt movement.

Ikarim's eyes shot open and his heart raced. Where was he? He glanced down into his lap to find Magaliana stirring. His heart sank when he remembered where they were.

The sun rose on the horizon, illuminating the cabin enough to see everything. The pirates were already out and about from the sound of thuds and scuffs outside the Captain's quarters.

Magaliana shot up in a panic, gasping. Ikarim pulled her into him and wrapped his arms about her shoulders. Her tense body relaxed and she wrapped her own arms around his neck.

"Did you sleep well?" he whispered.

She gave a faint nod as she pulled away. "Did you?"

He rubbed his stiff neck. "I suppose it was better than if we had slept in the hold..."

Magaliana cast him an apologetic look before her eyes roamed around the stuffy room. "Where do you think we are? Still in Germany?"

Ikarim shrugged. "We could be anywhere, at this point."

She slid off the bed and tiptoed between Arteus' feet on his nest of blankets on the floor, leaning against the chest and peering out the tiny, open window.

Arteus sat up, awake, his eyes on Magaliana. She turned away from the window and gave him a weak smile. "Good morning, Art."

"Did you get any sleep?" Ikarim asked.

Arteus did not answer. Instead, his gaze fell to his ungloved hands.

"Art? What's wrong?" Magaliana asked.

Without raising his eyes, he held out his cybernetic hands for her to take. After a beat, she slid hers into his. The metal digits closed about hers slowly, and he gently pulled her down to him, then released her and opened his arms as wide as he could. Vulnerable, he finally met her gaze. "What do you think?"

"Art..." Ikarim started. Was he seriously still on about their conversation from the previous night?

Magaliana didn't answer. Arteus rolled up his tattered sleeve and shoved it in her direction. She flinched, then slowly dropped her eyes to the cybernetics. Once she finally touched them to inspect, he momentarily closed his eyes.

"What do you think?" Arteus repeated.

"I..." Magaliana started.

"Do you consider me a monster?" he pulled his arm away from her.

"Art, stop," Ikarim warned.

"Of course not!" Magaliana breathed. "Why would you ever think that?"

81

Arteus grabbed the wings nestled on the chair's cushion and lightly ran his metal fingers over each feather. "Are you aware that Ike made these?" He continued when Magaliana nodded, "He gave them to me, to give to you."

"I know."

"Turn around."

Magaliana slowly obeyed, her eyes finding Ikarim's. Ever-so-gently, Arteus slipped her arms through the straps, excessively careful as if he was afraid to break her now that he was exposed. Once the wings were adjusted onto her shoulders and back, he took Magaliana's hair in his hands and wrapped one dread around the others to keep them out of her face.

Magaliana's eyes never left Ikarim. She looked concerned, almost afraid. A trembling cybernetic hand swept down to her shoulder as Arteus turned her back around to face him. His cheeks were flushed, and he swallowed hard, clearly nervous. Then he trailed softly up her neck, cupped her cheek, and leaned in to kiss her.

Magaliana stiffened, and Ikarim parted his lips to stop the nonsense. He knew that she was too nice to say no. And when did Arteus suddenly get so brave, anyway?

It was a loud knock at the door that interrupted everyone. Magaliana swiftly pulled away and got to her feet as all three shot their attention to the door.

"Breakfast!" a pirate called out, setting plates onto the Captain's desk via the window in the side room. Ikarim looked to Arteus, who averted his eyes and hung his head in shame.

"Let's eat," Magaliana said, breaking the awkward silence. She stepped past Arteus and into the side room. Ikarim helped his friend return the blankets and pillows to the chest while she returned with two plates, served them both, then returned to the side room and stayed.

"Art..." Ikarim wanted to ask his friend why he acted the way he did, but he dropped the question when Arteus sat in the chair and began fiddling with the receiver. He was embarrassed enough, and he'd probably ignore the question, anyway.

The food on their plates was half-eaten when a voice over the airwaves captured their attention.

"... to Handsel Gesselmeyer—... The entire shop was ransacked, and—... Three hostages—..."

Ikarim frowned and Magaliana shot out of the side room, concern clear on her face. Arteus continued to play with the knob to get better reception.

"... Magaliana Wiegraf, the daughter of *Herr* Wiegraf—..."

The Alchemist brought both hands to her mouth to keep her fear silent and rushed to Ikarim's side. Arteus hissed his discontent as they continued to listen.

"... German Imperium and Queen Victoria's Royal Guard are doubling up efforts for her retrieval—... Offering a hefty reward to the one who returns his daughter—... I will stop at nothing until we find her—..."

There was nothing but static for a few more seconds. Arteus went to adjust the knob, but not before somebody else spoke.

"Copy that, Sergeant Cambridge."

"Do you think Keenan knows?" Magaliana whispered in horror from behind her hands.

Large, loud thumps approached and the lock jangled louder than ever before the door slammed open. There stood Captain Benedict Keenan, a wild look about his features. He pointed at Magaliana as his dark eyes settled on her.

"YOU."

He knew.

CHAPTER 9

Ikarim and Arteus sprang to their feet to protect Magaliana, blocking the Captain from reaching her.

"Don't fight, you won't win," Captain Keenan pulled out and the room flooded with pirates. Magaliana screamed and jumped back against the chest; the mechanics were outnumbered and dragged out, but not without a struggle.

"Throw them back in the hold," Keenan ordered, stepping back inside his quarters.

Like a trapped animal, Magaliana lunged at the Captain, scratching his cheek deep enough to draw blood. He easily overpowered her with a snatch of her wrists, shoving her back onto his bed. She cried out as she landed on the metal wings. Before she could move, he had climbed atop of her and pinned her arms to her sides with his knees. She screamed and squirmed, crying out for help. A rough hand muffled her, and a blade aimed straight at her right eye faster than she could blink. Her body became rigid with fear—even her mind froze at the thought of her imminent death.

"That's clever, you know," Keenan stated, inches away from her face. "Mags," he added for emphasis. His breath was sour. "Took me a moment, but I figured it out. I want you to confirm, however. No lying. And no screaming when I let go, or I really will hurt you. Understand?"

Magaliana whimpered beneath his large hand and crushing weight, but she nodded as best as she could. When the Captain released her mouth, she gasped for air and sobbed.

"Are you really *Dame* Wiegraf?" he asked.

Magaliana nodded, sobbing harder.

"Do you know how much your father is offering for your safe return? That kind of price could buy me ten new ships..." Keenan trailed the blade down to her tear-stained cheek. Magaliana panicked, her thoughts whirling, her body rigid again. "Magaliana Wiegraf." He allowed the name to roll off his tongue. "There's only one problem with turning you in. You see... Your father has a treaty with Queen Victoria. And then there's that Cambridge fellow. With me being a pirate, the Imperium siding with your father, and that Sergeant from the Royal Guard, turning you in would result in my immediate arrest. But..." he added, pensive, with a mischievous smirk, "there is a man that would have better use of you than I, and he could pay me well. Not as much as your father is willing to offer, probably about half that... And, in all honesty, five ships are better than none at all and a free trip to the gallows, don't you think?"

He pulled away, and she curled up like a terrified and beaten dog. Sheathing his knife, he paced a bit, then disappeared in the side room. "Mister Newal!"

The door opened, and a towering, dark-skinned pirate stepped inside, looking to the Alchemist before the Captain handed him a folded note upon his return.

"I want a meeting with the Techno Mage." The pirate raised a brow at his Captain's strange request. "Are you questioning me?"

"No, Sir."

"Then go."

The dark-skinned man nodded and shut the door behind him.

"The Techno Mage doesn't exist," Magaliana squeaked, still cowering.

Benedict turned to her. "What?"

"The Techno Mage doesn't exist," she repeated. "He's nothing but a myth. So is his ship."

Keenan smirked. "I love that you are so well educated. And being the daughter of *Herr* Wiegraf, now I understand why. The *Faugregir* may be a myth, *Dame*, but I assure you that all the textbooks and military documents are wrong. The Techno Mage is quite real."

"I thought you wanted repairs to your ships, not five additional ones."

"By selling those five, I can repair all of my ships. Don't let common sense distract from your intelligence, that was rather insulting."

"What will you do with me until then?"

"You, Magaliana Wiegraf, are staying locked up here where I can keep a close eye on you, and where, as long as you obey, you will be unharmed and well fed. If you put up a fight, you'll end up bound and gagged. I want you separated from your friends. The Strong Arm particularly will end up getting you killed, and I can't have that." He opened the door and added over his shoulder, "Not until I have my payment."

He locked the door behind him. Alone and frightened, Magaliana allowed her emotions to flow and cried her heart out.

***

The grate slammed and locked above them as Ikarim and Arteus tumbled down painfully into the hold.

"Mags!" Arteus called out as he scrambled to his feet. "Mags! I'm coming!"

He rushed up the ladder and slammed his hands against the cover. Nothing happened. With no physical sensation in his cybernetic arms, he wailed on the metal with all his might and even tried to pull the bars apart so that he could escape and reach Magaliana, but without infusions, he remained severely weakened.

He called out the Alchemist's name in desperation, then spun toward his friend. "Ike! Help me!"

"I can't do anything, Art!" Ikarim replied in exasperation. "I don't have nearly as much strength!"

"We can't just leave her!"

"We can... For now."

Arteus shot him an incredulous look. Was he serious? "I'm not giving up on her," he huffed and turned back to the grate.

"Art, I haven't given up on her. The Captain won't hurt her, especially now that he knows who she is. Don't be the one to endanger her."

The Strong Arm's entire body flashed hot with rage. He jumped down the ladder directly in front of Ikarim, glaring at him.

Ikarim raised his hands defensively. "Remember what the Captain said—"

"I'm very well aware of everything that he said." Arteus cut him off—but Ikarim was right. His temper was a threat to Magaliana's safety.

Lowering his head, he stood where he was, silent, unmoving. He could hear Magaliana crying, and his hands clenched into fists. Then the cries turned to screams. Arteus gritted his teeth and rushed up the ladder to try to break through the grate again.

The screams became more and more desperate, as did his movements. He heard commotion up above in the form of voices and heavy footsteps in between Magaliana's cries.

There was a gunshot. Then there was silence.

Ikarim rushed to the grate next to Arteus, fear clear in his features. Arteus yelled at the top of his lungs in a panic, then whimpered when the Captain began shouting.

"Let that be a lesson to you all! If ever any of you even touches a hair on her head, you'll find your brains splattered over the ship as quickly as him. I will not hesitate. Do I make myself clear?!" Arteus and Ikarim kept their eyes focused past the grate as a few acknowledgements rose from the other pirates. "Good! Throw him overboard and get to cleaning this mess. I want my quarters and this deck spotless within the hour!"

With moans and groans, the pirates got back to their business. Arteus scanned every ugly mug that walked by the grate until a figure paused over the hold. The Captain, blood splattered over his shirt and face, peered down at them, his hardened eyes locking with Arteus. He shoved Magaliana forward for both men to see. The clothes she wore—her mourning clothes—were mostly torn off her body and blood splattered over her face and skin.

Arteus' eyes went wide and his heart sank. He couldn't protect her. Her fearful green eyes found them both before Keenan forced her away.

Arteus frantically tried to break through the grate. He even tried to frantically grab the Captain's ankle when he stepped by. Where was he taking her?

He yelled in anger a few times, then slid down the ladder to the ground in defeat. Ikarim sat next to him in silence, both utterly helpless.

CHAPTER 10

Two days had passed since she was separated from her friends. Captain Keenan
had given her some of his own clothes to wear—
a long, pristine white shirt and a belt. As much
as she hated to let his clothing touch her body, it
was either that or allow glimpses of her skin
through her torn flaxen dress. She had even
fashioned one of the lighter-weight blankets
into a wrap about her waist to act as a skirt.

The Captain himself would bring her meals
and sit with her and try to make conversation.
But Magaliana would not speak or touch her
food, unwilling to accept anything from her captor. She had barely slept, her mind not allowing
a moment of reprieve. Every time she had tried,
nightmares plagued her, or she would be startled awake by footsteps and voices outside the
cabin door.

Magaliana had just donned her wings—her last remaining shred of hope—in the glow of the sunrise when the door unlocked and the Captain stepped in with a wooden tray of eggs, porridge, bread, butter, and fruit.

"Eat up, *Dame*," he said as he kicked the small barrel into the middle of the room and placed the tray atop of it. "The Techno Mage replied with his coordinates, and we are almost there."

Magaliana eyed the Captain suspiciously. She knew that the Techno Mage didn't exist, so who did Benedict believe this mythical person to be? She quietly sat on the edge of the bed but did not eat when Keenan filled her plate.

"*Dame* Magaliana, please. You have to be in your best shape to meet with him, or I won't get my payment."

"I would rather die." The hatred in her voice was feeble and frail, much like her spirit.

"You have not been mistreated. You could very well have been locked up in the stocks, but instead you have clothes, books, a bed, and the freshest and finest food aboard this ship. Trust me, not even my own men eat this well. We did have that little mishap, but that has been dealt with, and the example has been set..." Benedict continued to eat while Magaliana ignored her angry stomach and got back to her feet, longingly looking out the small window over the chest. "We are currently above the Pacific

Ocean. We are headed for an uncharted island, as per the coordinates. We should be there soon, so please eat at least a little something. I'll have a basin brought for you to clean yourself up when I am done."

"What about my friends?" she whispered. It was the most she had uttered in two days.

"Frankly, they weren't even thought about as part of the bargain." When Magaliana's eyes welled up with tears, Keenan continued as his eyes fell on his food. "But we'll see what I can do. Now, I'm afraid I must insist. *Eat*."

Magaliana reached for a slice of cantaloupe—her weakened body trembling—brought it to her lips and nibbled on it like a mouse.

"Good girl," Keenan added as he chewed a mouthful.

He left the quarters after he ate. During that time, Magaliana only had a slice of cantaloupe and two slices of an apple, even when he'd mentioned that the porridge would give her strength.

Another pirate entered the room soon after, and she backed away in alarm and dread, vividly recalling what happened two days prior. This man paid her no heed, however, resting a basin of cold water—which sloshed over the edge and onto the floor—and a rather dingy sponge by the door before he walked away. Magaliana wrinkled her nose at the water and gave it as wide a berth as she could on her way into the side room, ignoring the Captain's orders.

Her mind raced as she glanced out the large window. She was anxious, yet curious about who Keenan had really contacted. There was no physical proof that the Techno Mage existed. Her attention turned to the leather-bound books on the built-in shelves, and she tilted her head, curious. Would there be information in his notes?

"Land, ho!"

Magaliana glanced up from her research only to meet Captain Keenan's eyes. "Come, *Dame.*"

The door was unlocked and opened, and Magaliana reluctantly peered out into the main cabin. After a beat, the Captain offered his hand for her to take.

"Come on, we don't have all day."

When she still did not move, he sighed audibly and seized her hands, pulling her to her feet. She whimpered but had no energy to scream. Her legs threatened to give out from beneath her, so the Captain hauled her over his shoulder and climbed the ladder onto the upper deck, setting her down near a solid wooden post. She was overcome by lightheadedness and her balance wavered, but the Captain caught her and held her steady. She slowly turned to find a compass sitting in a carved cavity in the wood, revealing the direction they faced. Her eyes moved to the horizon, but all she could see were the rain-filled clouds below on an endless sky.

"As you know, *Dame*, because you are a smart and scholarly young woman, a carrack is firstly and foremostly a ship built for the sea. And since we will be landing by an island, it will get pretty bumpy. Make sure you hold on tight." He took a breath, then bellowed to the rest of his crew, "To your stations! Prepare the masts!"

The pirates scrambled about in semi-orderly fashion, calling out from their respective stations to inform their Captain that they were ready for the next order. Magaliana gripped the post as tightly as she could while Benedict lifted a hidden compartment above the compass which contained a few buttons and a lever. He pushed the lever forward, and the ship plunged into the clouds.

Magaliana could hear nothing, nor could she see anything. It was as if time stood still. The clouds became a thick fog, their wetness like a mist. She turned her head up and barely found Keenan's face hidden in the brume, his gaze focused ahead, determined. His eyes momentarily fell to hers before they glanced back ahead.

And then, as suddenly as they had plunged into the clouds, they fell out. A dark and gloomy island appeared beneath them, the water around it violent and savage.

"Report!" the Captain barked.

"There are no ships," came a voice from the crow's nest.

"No ships...? Do we have the correct coordinates?" he mused to himself, then shouted to his crew. "Keep your eyes peeled, men! Report the tiniest suspect activity. Do you see anything, *Dame*?" he asked quietly.

Magaliana's eyes searched the thick canopy and jagged cliffs. Other than the angry ocean and the island, she saw nothing. No pirate ships, no airships, no blimps, not even a raft.

"Fire!" called out a pirate. "I see a campfire!"

Magaliana craned her neck and squinted out toward the island as Benedict released the lever. He pulled a metal spyglass from his belt and stepped away from Magaliana to get a better view.

"Be prepared to land!" he called out as he collapsed his spyglass and shoved it back in its holster.

"Land?" Magaliana squeaked in alarm. "Land where? The ship will be battered like a rag-doll by the ocean, and the island is covered in trees and rocks!"

"Have a little faith in mine and my crew's abilities, *Dame*," Benedict smirked.

The ship dipped and pivoted, and Magaliana gritted her teeth when her feet almost flew off the deck. The Captain pinned her between the post and himself while he navigated. Giant waves crashed aboard as they drew nearer, the salty spray drenching the crew on the main deck. Keenan called for the bilge rats, and a dozen men ran below deck.

The tide slammed into the airship, shaking it violently as they descended, battering harder until, finally, the bottom of the vessel touched the surface. Magaliana's fingers practically dug into the post despite being safely pinned as the carrack shook with the force of the most powerful earthquake. Benedict continued to bellow orders. Through the chaos, she barely heard her friends, their cries from the hold practically drowned out by the ravaging crashes against the *Raider*.

Her heart sank. "Ike! Art!" she gasped and tried to run to them.

Keenan pulled her back. "Not a good idea, *Dame*."

"But my friends!" she pleaded. "They'll drown!"

"Not my concern." He gritted his teeth as another forceful wave hit the ship.

Magaliana spun around in her tight confines, her arm and hand poised and ready to slap some sense into the man, but he grabbed her wrist and shoved her into the tower. His eyes left the shaky horizon for a second. "If they drown, it will be from their own ineptitude, and not from the water level on my ship. Again, you underestimate my crew."

"Sir!" called a voice from above. Keenan's eyes swiftly left her for the horizon, then he frowned. Magaliana realized that the ship was still and quiet—save for Ikarim and Arteus' shouts. Curious, her gaze followed the Captain's.

The island was within reach, but there was a radius of the ocean around the *Raider*—usually so rough and rugged—that was calm.

"Steer her in!" the Captain ordered, his voice startlingly loud. "Steady the sails!"

The ship gently rocked across the smooth surface as the waters outside its orbit continued to ravage. They steered the vessel in safely and moored as close to land as possible. The crew prepared two small yawls while Benedict released Magaliana, pulled the spyglass from his belt, and glanced around the island. "There's a man..."

"The Techno Mage?" asked one of the pirates.

"We'll soon find out," he muttered only loud enough for Magaliana to hear. "I want cannons at the ready! Remain at your stations!"

Magaliana took the spyglass from him as he gave his orders, and glanced out toward the campfire. Dressed in a black uniform and top hat, a handsome figure sat on a large rock by the flickering flames. A white, glowing sigil encircled an area at his feet.

"He's using alchemy..." She frowned. How had he managed to make the transmutation circle glow?

Suddenly, his ice-blue eyes rose and looked directly at her, gloved hands adjusting the chain that linked both sides of his cape. A smirk crept to his lips, numerous studded piercings on his face glittering from the movement. She blinked and pulled the spyglass away, taken aback at how he somehow knew to look directly at her.

Keenan stepped away from Magaliana and pointed to two pirates on the main deck. "You two. With me." He then turned to her. "Shall we?"

CHAPTER 11

Oars in hand, Benedict's focus was beyond the Alchemist sitting across from him, to his ship. He wasn't thrilled with the situation; he knew of no man who could calm the ocean, yet there it was, a section tranquil and quiet while the rest of the waters raged on the horizon. The boat glided peacefully over the surface as he rowed, helped to shore by his men once they were in wading distance.

He set the oars down and jumped out, splashing in the ankle-deep water. He offered Magaliana his hands to aid her to her feet, but she stared at the man on the rock in fear. Benedict sighed. He didn't have time for this. Placing one foot back in, he scooped her into his arms with slight difficulty due to her metal wings and lifted her out of the boat, setting her down once he reached dry sand. "I trust I don't have to drag you, *Dame*. There's nowhere for you to go.

You've witnessed the waters, and if you run into the forest, well, that's out of my hands. Even I have better sense than to attempt to deal with the locals."

He approached the figure with a frightened Alchemist on his heels and his men behind him, guns drawn and ready.

The man smiled warmly and opened his arms in greeting. "Captain Benedict Keenan." His tone was much softer than any would imagine. "How nice to finally meet you."

"I wish I could say the same," the Captain retorted. "Who are you?"

"I'm the Techno Mage."

"Prove it," said one of the other pirates.

The man's attention shifted and a smirk crept to his lips. He focused back on Captain Keenan. "How many people do you know can calm the waters of the Pacific Ocean?"

"I know of none."

"Is that not proof enough?"

"How do we know it's really you, and you're not just some henchman for the real Techno Mage?"

The man dropped his gaze and removed one of his gloves. His attention remained on his bare hand as he turned it over a few times, then raised it for the Captain to see. Keenan raised a brow as the man traced invisible designs into his palm, then slid off the rock and slammed his hand down into the glowing sigil at his feet. An explosion roared behind them, and the Captain flinched, spinning around to find one of the yawls demolished with nothing left but splinters of debris on the shore.

Bewildered, Captain Keenan whirled back to face the Techno Mage, his own gun pulled from his belt and aimed directly at the man's head.

"Don't worry, you won't need it." The Techno Mage put his glove back on, infuriatingly calm. "Only two of you are returning to the ship."

Magaliana's legs gave out, and she collapsed at Keenan's side. He didn't catch her this time. He glanced down to make sure that she was still somewhat all right, then looked back to the Mage. "Shall we move on to business?" he asked, holstering his weapon.

"Of course," the man replied with that irksome smile.

"This is the *Dame* Wiegraf. She is the daughter of *Herr* Wiegraf. She is my prisoner." Magaliana shot him a spiteful glare from the ground, but he ignored it. "*Herr* Wiegraf is offering a large sum as a reward for her safe return."

"How much?"

"Enough to buy ten new ships for my crew."

"My, that is quite a large sum," the man mused.

"My problem is that I can't claim the reward."

"Ah, yes." He grinned in amusement, leaning back against the large rock. "Because you're the infamous pirate Captain Benedict Keenan. Her safe return would result in your immediate arrest."

"I see that we're on the same page. So, I was thinking of a trade with somebody who is off the grid."

"Name your price."

"The *Dame*, in exchange for half of what *Herr* Wiegraf is offering."

"I'll give you enough for four ships. That's all I've brought with me."

Captain Keenan frowned. That wasn't what he wrote on the note. Unfortunately, it was too late to back out. "Deal," he said grudgingly.

"My friends!" Magaliana cried in a desperate plea to save them. "My friends! You said you'd try to negotiate my friends!"

"Those two are more beneficial to me than to the Techno Mage." He especially wanted to keep the mechanic and Strong Arm now that he was getting less than he asked for.

Tears in her eyes, Magaliana jumped to her feet and swung at him, but in her weakened state, Keenan easily stopped her.

"You monster!" she spat in his face.

Irritated and beginning to lose his temper, Benedict shoved the Alchemist back to the ground as he wiped at his cheek. "*Dame* Wiegraf—"

"I would rather die than be separated from my friends!" she cut him off. "I've had enough of trusting you!" She scampered to her feet and darted straight for the forest. The pirates tried to stop her by shooting, but the Captain quickly stopped them.

"She is to be unharmed!"

"Your prisoner is escaping, Captain," the Techno Mage simply said, as calm as ever. Benedict growled and turned to his men, ordering the largest one after her. As the pirate began pursuit, Keenan spun back around to face the Techno Mage, who smirked in amusement. "You don't know what kind of treasure you're giving up, Captain. The daughter of a *Herr*. She is beautiful and intelligent. Much more intelligent than your goon."

Shrill trilling, yips, and whistles came from the natives in the forest. They were scarce at first, then grew louder and stronger. Keenan's hands formed into fists when gunshots fired.

The Mage stepped away from the large rock and approached the forest. He cast a glance over his shoulder toward the Captain and held up his index finger to indicate for him to wait one moment. When the Techno Mage disappeared beyond the trees, Keenan gritted his teeth as more gunshots fired, followed by the blood-curdling cry of one he could only assume was part of his crew. The pirate that had remained with him jerked forward to help, but the Captain threw his arm to the side to halt him.

Slowly, the sounds of the natives dwindled down to silence once more, and Magaliana ambled out of the forest with the Mage in tow. He instructed her to sit on the very rock that he had previously been sitting on. She obediently climbed the rugged surface and took a seat, never lifting her head to look at anyone. Benedict wondered if alchemy had gotten her in such a hypnotized state, and that perhaps this truly was the Techno Mage.

The man stopped in front of the fire, his attention back on the Captain. "And now you are two returning to the ship, as promised."

"And my payment?" asked Benedict, still studying Magaliana. He should have been angry at the whole situation, but now he was even more cautious. The quicker he got away from the man and this damnable island, the better.

"In the chest back here." He nodded toward the small boulder Magaliana sat upon.

The pirate stepped past his Captain; his pistol still aimed at the Mage as he warily went to verify. Holstering his gun, he grabbed the handle and dragged the heavy moss-covered strongbox back. The Techno Mage reached a gloved hand to his belt and unhooked a rusted key. With that maddening, gentle smile seemingly always on his lips, he tossed the key over the fire, and Keenan caught it with one swipe.

"Look inside. Count it if you have to."

The lid clicked as the key turned, and the shiny gems, jewelry, and coins reflected the stormy clouds above. The pirate dug in down to the bottom and pulled out a diamond necklace and a golden ring, inspecting them closely, then tossed them back into the chest and gave his Captain a nod.

Good. Everything in the chest was real. The Captain turned his attention to the Mage as the mossy strongbox closed again.

"A pleasure doing business with you." The Mage tipped his hat.

Benedict acknowledged him with a nod, then helped his henchman with the heavy chest. His eyes went to Magaliana before he turned, who looked ever so pitiful. "Do liven up, *Dame*," he called out to her. "As long as your friends cooperate, they'll be safe."

Magaliana didn't respond. She didn't even lift her head. They carefully placed the chest in the remaining boat, and both pirates had to push it offshore before jumping in. The Captain faced the coast, his eyes on Magaliana as he rowed. He was still irked about receiving less than he had asked for, but as he got further away, he was just glad to be distancing himself more from that hypnotizing man.

The Techno Mage turned to Magaliana and she finally lifted her head; then he turned his attention to the Captain with a grin. Keenan

frowned when the Mage mockingly waved goodbye.

CHAPTER 12

Magaliana stared at the Mage. What had he done to her?

She had run into the forest but hadn't gone far. There was no way that she was going to risk escaping the Captain only to fall victim to the 'locals', as he called them. She ducked down in a bush with ease given her petite frame, and watched Captain Keenan's goon run right by her, none the wiser. She stayed as still as a statue, so focused on calming the heart threatening to pound out of her chest that she was surprised to find the Techno Mage suddenly standing next to her hiding spot. Peeking up at him from behind thick leaves, she found his attention focused ahead, toward the sounds of the natives, which grew increasingly louder. Suddenly, his ice-blue eyes fell directly on her, and her heart skipped a beat; she hadn't made any noise, how did he find her?

He winked, and that was the last she remembered.

Blinking away the confusion, she followed his gaze out toward the ocean, where Captain Keenan safely boarded his ship. She felt a pinch of hatred, but it quickly turned to dread as the realization settled in that she was alone with the Techno Mage. She heard a shuffle and dropped her attention to see him kick at the sand at his feet, breaking the transmutation circle, which released its hold on the ravaging waters.

He was mad. He was insane. Her eyes flicked fearfully back to him, only to find that he was already looking at her. She recoiled in horror.

"Come," he said in that ever-gentle tone. "Let us get off this island and return to my ship."

She didn't budge. There was no way she was going anywhere with somebody who could control nature with glowing sigils, no matter how charismatic he seemed. And how was he even getting her off the island? Were they going to walk on water? There was no other ship around that they had seen from aboard the *Raider*.

The man pointed out in the distance, on the opposite shoreline from where Captain Keenan had moored. She saw nothing but the horizon in between the untamed waters and brooding clouds, but then something frothed, stirred, and swelled from beneath the violent waves. Rigid metal framework pulled up from the raging Pacific Ocean, revealing a small airship. Magaliana watched in amazement and disbelief as the zeppelin rose from the deep, defying all odds of explosions from the weight of the water crushing the hydrogen cells and gasbags inside its rubberized cotton skin.

A thick rope ladder dropped down from the aircraft, dancing wildly until the Mage snatched the bottom. He extended a gloved hand to Magaliana, but she swiftly shook her head.

"I will not hurt you, *Dame*, but I can promise that if you stay here, the natives will."

"I'll take my chances," she hissed.

The Techno Mage chuckled softly. "We can do this the easy way—with your cooperation—or the very easy way—with you hypnotized again."

"You hypnotized me?" she asked in disgust.

"It was simple alchemy to calm you down. I could teach you, but that would involve your cooperation."

She frowned at first—they clearly had completely different definitions for hypnotism—but then eyed him curiously. As much as she didn't want to go with him, she was interested in the option to learn his alchemy. And if he was so willing to teach her, she wondered if she could also glimpse how he managed to make his sigils glow.

Sliding off the rock, Magaliana cautiously placed her feet on the ropes. The Mage did the same as he snaked an arm around her waist, pulling her against him. She stiffened at his touch, but he gave her one of his charming smiles before he looked up. The ladder began to rise.

Two men helped them aboard the airship. Before the hatch closed, Magaliana caught a glimpse of the *Raider* taking off, and her heart sank. A panicked whimper escaped her, and she collapsed, her legs having given out from beneath her. The Mage knelt before her and gently moved some of her stray blonde dreadlocks away from her face. She quickly pulled away, frantically digging at the hatch, determined to open it.

"Ike and Art are on that ship!" she cried. "I need them!" She didn't want to be alone with the Techno Mage. She didn't want to be separated from them more than she already was. Tears streamed down her cheeks and her body trembled when she realized she was far too weakened, her attempts futile. Wailing, she crumpled onto the hatch.

The Techno Mage removed a glove and began tracing something onto the airship's floor while he hummed. His actions were slow and drawn out, his crooning ever so soothing. With every move, Magaliana's hysteria lessened until she fell silent. Her eyelids grew heavy, and she could have sworn she saw a glow appear on the floor before her eyes closed. She felt someone scoop her up before she finally succumbed to slumber.

Magaliana awoke with a start, her heart racing and her eyes quickly scanning the tiny, unfamiliar room before she carefully sat up on the bed. The bunk's blue curtains were open, allowing her to see the sliding door, slightly ajar. As quickly as her body would allow, she stood up on shaky legs, dragging her feet to the door and picking up the metal wings that rested on the tiny table in the process. She brought the intricately-crafted gift to her chest and shut her eyes when they threatened to well up. Then she frowned and opened the door.

Making her way toward where she deduced was the front of the ship, Magaliana peered into the cockpit. The Mage sat by the control panel, his uneven raven hair glistening as he leaned forward and flipped a few switches.

"How nice of you to join us, *Dame*," he said without turning around.

Magaliana took a step back in surprise. She didn't think she had made any noise.

"Please," he said as he spun in his seat to face her, "come in."

It took her a moment, but she swallowed hard and glared at her captor. "What did you do to me?"

"Nothing. Have a seat." He pointed to the empty chair next to him.

Magaliana wouldn't give in. "I demand that you release me, safely, at once."

He smirked. "This part of the Pacific Ocean is non-negotiable, *Dame*."

"I have a name, you know," she snapped.

An amused chuckle escaped his pierced lips. "Then what name shall I call the daughter of *Herr* Wiegraf?"

Magaliana continued to frown, her eyes locked on the man before her. Then she shut her eyes as she swayed from a dizzy spell. There was a rustle and suddenly she was lifted off her feet. Her eyes shot open and she glared as the Mage placed her in the empty seat before returning to his own.

"Get the *Dame* some water, please," he asked over an airwave receiver.

"Yes, Sir."

Magaliana's eyes traveled to the blue sky before them. Her mind raced, torn between thinking of her friends and wanting to know more about the Mage's alchemy. "What did you do to me?" she repeated sternly, her attention back to the man.

"I already told you," he replied as he pressed a few buttons, his attention ahead. "But if you must know, there was no alchemy involved. I sang you to sleep. Your exhaustion took care of the rest."

"I saw you activate a transmutation circle."

"Deactivate, actually."

Magaliana blinked in surprise. "What?"

He finally turned to her. "I deactivated the circle that I had originally cast to hide the airship underwater. Ah, thank you," he added as one of his men stepped inside the cockpit to give Magaliana a glass of water. She accepted it and softly set the wings in her lap but did not drink while she studied the Mage piloting the ship. She was so sure that he had used alchemy on her again, but now she questioned herself. The ship rising from the water was so amazing that it really couldn't be explained except with alchemy. She didn't remember there being a sigil on the ground when she was first pulled aboard, but then again, she wouldn't have noticed much in her panicked, frenzied state.

"Magaliana," she said.

"Pardon?"

"My name is Magaliana."

The Techno Mage gave her a soft smile. "*Dame* Magaliana it is."

"And what of your name?" she asked. "Or should I just call you my captor?"

"Joss," the man offered. "Techno Mage Jocephus Gideon, Captain of the mythical airship the *Faugregir*."

"The *Faugregir*?" She broke her gaze to look around the tiny airship. "This is the *Faugregir*? The mythical ship of legends?"

Jocephus chuckled warmly. "This, my dear, is nothing but a quick escape. A tiny transport airship. No. No, this is not my magnificent *Faugregir*."

"What are you going to do with me?" she asked, the fear returning.

"Absolutely nothing. I am taking you to the *Faugregir*, where you will stay until I claim compensation from *Herr* Wiegraf. You will also have full reign of the ship. Well..." he paused, "... to a certain extent, of course."

She eyed him suspiciously. "Why are you being so nice to me?"

"Why shouldn't I be? Why do I feel that you are equating me with a villain?"

Magaliana hesitated. He was right; nowhere was it ever mentioned that the mythical Techno Mage was a bad man. He was simply someone who flawlessly combined alchemy and technology. "Heroes don't make daughters of nobility their prisoners. Villains do."

"Villains don't give their prisoners full reign of their mythical ship, either," he casually replied, turning his attention back to the sky.

She stared at him for a long moment. She refused to believe that everything she knew about the mythical man—which wasn't much, she had to be honest with herself—was false. He did, after all, go against the beliefs of both the Upper and Lower Lands. He was pleasant, but at the same time, he was greedy—outright telling her that he would collect compensation.

She hugged the metal wings as her attention drifted to the sky before her. Her eyes welled up as her thoughts went to her friends, wondering if they were safe and well. She shut her eyes to keep the tears from falling, wishing to go back in time to when life was normal.

She realized that she had fallen asleep, curled up in the chair in the cockpit, only when she was stirred awake by somebody calling her name.

"*Dame* Magaliana. *Dame* Magaliana, wake up. I thought that you might like to see this."

Groggy, Magaliana looked around the tiny ship's controls, unsure of what she was supposed to do. The Techno Mage pointed ahead, out the giant window.

"Look." He grinned.

She couldn't see a thing as the airship glided through thick clouds. Suddenly, they emerged into the open, where a large object floated in the distance. The more she blinked and focused, the more it looked like a mountain covered in moss. She gasped in awe when she realized the moss was actually large canopies of trees and grass growing on the giant mountain. Flocks of colorful birds converged toward the foundation, and spectacularly pristine waterfalls tumbled down the rock face.

Magaliana grabbed the wings from her lap and stood as the airship got closer. Her eyes were wide and her jaw had long since hit the floor.

"Preparing for docking," the man said.

Magaliana sat back down but continued to stare, astonished, out the window. Enormous blades spun all over, helping the giant rock to navigate. Steam clouds puffed out from various pipes and colossal metal and stone golems stomped around its surface.

The ship continued on, and just when Magaliana thought they would crash in the side of the giant floating mountain, Jocephus landed the small airship onto a plot of flat land covered in the greenest grass she'd ever seen.

"We're here," he said. "Come on."

He took her hand and tugged at it playfully, leading her out onto the grass, which rustled in the warm breeze. She made her way to a railing at the edge of the flat land, her steps slow and shaky. Carefully wrapping one hand around the top of the barrier, she glanced down, where more trees grew from the rock and waterfalls cascaded onto the Lands Below like rain. The fluffy white clouds seemed a million miles away. There was no way the floating mountain was a ship... was it?

Her legs gave out as she was suddenly hit by her first ever case of vertigo, but the Techno Mage caught and steadied her, chuckling. "Welcome aboard the *Faugregir*, *Dame* Magaliana."

CHAPTER 13

Benedict returned to his ship safe and sound and retired to his quarters for the remainder of the morning after giving his crew new coordinates. He was still irked that the Techno Mage had only offered enough compensation for four ships instead of five, but he was glad to be as far away from him as possible, his own life intact. There was just something unsettling about the man...

He did feel a tinge of remorse when he thought back on how distressed the woman was when he didn't trade her friends along with her, but what he said was true: they were more useful to him than the Mage. Besides, the Techno Mage skimped on his part of the deal, so it was only fair that he kept the mechanics.

It was past noon when Keenan made his way to his prisoners, looking at both Arteus and Ikarim through the grate of the hold. "You, there! It's time to help repair the ships, starting with this one."

"I will do nothing," Arteus said matter-of-factly, "until I see Mags."

"Your friend has been traded to the Techno Mage and is no longer your concern." Both mechanics' eyes grew wide in shock. Keenan opened the grate and a broad-shouldered pirate pulled up next to him, golden teeth visible as he grinned, bullwhip in hand. "But I am a man of my word—somewhat—and will release you once the work is done."

"I'd rather die!" Arteus rushed up the stairs, enraged.

"Dying is the easy way out," Benedict sighed. "But torture..."

The large pirate expertly lashed at Arteus. He stumbled backward, glaring murderously at the flogger as a crimson stream dripped down his cheek.

"...Torture can last a while." The Captain glanced at Ikarim, still in the hold. "Are we going to have a problem, mechanic?"

Ikarim did not put up a smidgen of a fight, as Keenan expected. He raised his hands next to his head and made his way out of the hold peacefully.

"Fix my arms and I'll fix your face before I fix this ship!" Arteus spat.

"Art," Ikarim warned, glowering at the Captain. "There's no bargaining right now. Come on, let's get to work before they decide to kill us. The faster we fix their ships, the faster we can save Mags."

"Killing you all depends on the Strong Arm's temper," Captain Keenan pointed out. "Give them tools and have them start on some tasks."

The pirates shoved the mechanics forward, and Captain Keenan caught Arteus' hateful glare. The Strong Arm was pushing the buttons on his already foul mood, and he was hardly able to restrain himself from ripping the young man apart.

***

After a long afternoon of tasks upon tasks, the mechanics took a well-deserved break nibbling on charred fish and soggy rice in the hold. Ikarim's skin was sticky from sweat, and the humidity of the evening wasn't cooling him off any.

Frankly, the workload for the pirates wasn't any different than what he did at the shop. But there were fewer breaks than he was used to, and he could do without the sneering and jeering of his new associates.

"I hope she's all right..." Arteus eventually muttered.

"I hope so, too."

"She didn't deserve this. I should have done more to—"

"Don't." Ikarim stopped him short, shaking his head. "Don't beat yourself up over 'could haves' or 'would haves'. Focus on 'cans' and 'wills' instead. We can find her. We will find her."

Arteus parted his lips to speak but paused at a ruckus from above deck. Ikarim got to his feet with a raised brow and stepped over to the ladder, glancing past the grate to the pirates rushing about.

"Doom Crusader ships have arrived! Alert the Captain!"

There was a jumble of cheers, and Ikarim quickly lost interest. They would more than likely be ignored for the rest of the night, and that suited him just fine; it would give him more time to think through a plan. So far, nothing he had come up with could hold up without severe consequences. He returned to his friend's side, who remained silent, obviously brooding.

A figure appeared overhead, glancing down past the grate.

"You should both get some sleep. It will be an early morning and a long day ahead, I'm afraid," the Captain said, seeming much less grouchy than earlier in the afternoon.

Arteus glowered and opened his mouth to retort, but Ikarim stopped him with a hand to the shoulder as he normally did. "Thank you, Captain," he replied, turning to his friend as Keenan's form disappeared from view. "We'll get out of this. I promise."

CHAPTER 14

Magaliana had eagerly accepted a tour, and the Techno Mage led her down hall upon hall, and floor upon floor. The ship's exterior—cleverly disguised as a mountain—was magnificent. The inside, however, contained a whole new standard of beauty that she had never imagined possible. It reminded her of the village of Èze, which she had visited with her family on their way to Nice, France, but condensed on the inside rather than atop high cliffs.

"This is... amazing!" she said, barely able to contain her excitement as she followed Jocephus onto another floor. "I don't understand... How has nobody ever seen a ship this size before? How has it remained a myth for so long?"

"The *Faugregir* creates its own clouds to keep hidden. The ship adjusts course based on the direction and speed of the wind, so that it is always covered," he explained.

They had walked entire floors filled with steam rooms, living and sleeping quarters, and meal halls. There was even a level dedicated strictly to farming. She was thoroughly impressed, however, by the floor which contained a market; the aroma of spices permeated the air and calls from the different vendors trying to distract and direct her to their wares tickled her ears, almost overwhelming.

There was a strange high-pitched hum when they entered another long corridor. She had heard it down previous halls, but it suddenly seemed louder and drew more attention to itself. Magaliana winced. "What is that noise?"

"Hmm? Oh. Don't worry about that," he casually replied. "You will get used to it quickly, I promise."

She followed him up a few stairs to a lift; they seemed to be the preferred method of travel between floors inside the ship. They stepped onto the platform and the attendant closed and securely locked the gate, then pulled a lever on the control panel nearby. Gears and coils grinded and rumbled as the lift rose, and steam shot out of a nearby pipe. Magaliana swayed slightly and grabbed at the gate to steady her body.

"You're exhausted, aren't you?" Jocephus said in his ever-gentle voice.

She did not answer; she didn't want to reveal more about her situation than she already had. She rested her head against the gate, clinging to it to keep her weakened body up. She was suddenly very aware of her empty stomach.

Chirping sounds replaced starving growls, and Magaliana quickly pulled away to look outside.

The floor before her was even more amazing than the market. Greenery covered everything as far as her eyes could see. What little sunlight remained of the evening sky barely shone through the thick forest canopy, covered by a massive, clear dome. A flock of birds landed among some patches of colorful wildflowers and large, moss-covered statues. Magaliana gasped at the beauty.

"This is my golem cemetery. It's where the golems come to die."

Her attention shot back to Jocephus as she tried to determine if the man was serious or not. He did not meet her gaze, instead focusing on the room ahead. Their lift came to a stop, and a new attendant unlocked and opened the gate.

Magaliana was the first to step out. She looked down, immediately taking notice of how soft the ground felt beneath her feet. She slowly moved toward one of the towering statues. The mechanical construct was heavily rusted beneath the mossy surface. Cautiously resting a hand on the idol's leg as if it would somehow instantly disintegrate, her eyes slowly rose until they rested on the giant golem's face. She tilted her head slightly. "How do they work? How do they die?"

"Some are steam-powered and made entirely of metal, like this one," he said. "Some are metal and run off of alchemy infusions, like that one over there."

Magaliana turned her head to see that Jocephus pointed to another golem at the base of a tree. Her fingers slowly drew back from the moss and rust as she approached the golem in question. Her eyes fell to a pile of scraps, and she wondered if they had previously belonged to this automaton. What did Jocephus even use the golems for?

"Others," he drawled, "metal or stone, are made of a merging of both. Like those scraps once were."

"A merging of both?" She glanced away from the remnants.

"Metal or stone merged with alchemy. Fused. Very powerful, but just as prone to death as everything else."

"But you can't fuse alchemy and metal, that's impossible. It's a myth." Her mind went back to the sigil he drew—or deconstructed, rather—in his getaway ship.

"It isn't impossible, I've accomplished the task. Are you forgetting that I am the Techno Mage? The *Faugregir* is also a myth according to you, yet here you are..."

Still weak and overcome by so much, Magaliana swayed, lightheaded. Jocephus, suddenly at her side, lifted her into his arms and headed toward another lift. She wanted to squirm out of his grip but thought it best to conserve what little energy that she had.

The next level revealed a wide hallway with double sliding doors at the end. The Mage skillfully opened them and carried her into the large, regal living quarter, where he laid her on the canopy bed's comfy layers of blankets and pillows.

"This will be your room," he said. "You have free rein of the ship... To an extent."

"Where am I not allowed to go?"

"You'll be well aware of those limits. Believe me." His pierced lips softened into a smile as he turned to leave. "I trust you remember where the dining hall is if you're hungry?" He did not wait for an answer. "Rest well, *Dame* Magaliana."

Her eyes remained on the doors long after Jocephus shut them behind himself. She didn't know what to think. She was surprised she could still formulate coherent thoughts after the whirlwind that was Gesselmeyer's death, the *Raider*, the *Faugregir,* and the golem cemetery. Her attention finally moved away from the doors, ignoring the rest of the room, and fell to the metal wings in her hands.

She missed her friends. She was worried about them, but most of all she just wanted them to come to her rescue. Lithe fingers lightly ran over the feathers but paused as her mind traveled back to the golem scraps. Curiosity getting the best of her, she donned her wings and dragged her feet back to the lift.

She glanced up to the towering floor assistant, who simply watched her in silence. She found him entirely too serious and slightly intimidating. "Um..." she squeaked. "I'd like to return to the cemetery, please..."

He opened the gate and Magaliana stepped onto the platform. She soon found herself back within the beauty and tranquility of the lower floor. With difficulty, she removed both of her shoes and slid her feet onto the soft greenery before beelining for the metal giant that ran off of infusions at the base of the tree.

Kneeling in the grass, she examined the rusty, moss-covered structure, noticing that the wires were much smaller than the ones in Arteus' arms. It was a shame he had kept them a secret from her for so long; they were truly a work of art. But the golem's wires almost looked like actual veins, and she wondered how the infusion could even slosh around inside such a constricted area from something with such large volume.

An exhausted yawn escaped her, and the weight of her weakened state washed over her like a heavy wave. She didn't have the energy to return to the room, nor did she have the want to. She was content to be in a cemetery so peaceful and beautiful, rather than be locked up in yet another room. Removing her gift from her back, she curled up at the base of the golem, tracing her fingers along the edges of the feathers and cogs before she quickly fell into a dreamless slumber.

A knock startled Magaliana awake. Her senses buzzed uncomfortably for a moment before she heard it again. Her eyes shot open and she sat bolt upright.

The cemetery was dark, the silver glow of the crescent moon barely shining through the forest canopy. A third knocking made her realize that it was coming from somewhere around the golem, and she moved quickly away. Rustling footsteps approached her from behind, the warm, dim glow of the lantern illuminating the figure who held it. Her eyes locked on to the copper platter Jocephus balanced in his other hand. "The cooks informed me that you never grabbed anything to eat. I came to deliver this to your room, but you weren't there. I figured this is where I'd find you..."

The knocking came again, and Magaliana's attention darted back to the construct. The Mage smirked as he kneeled and set the lantern and platter down on the grass.

"The material is resting. Like an old house popping and creaking in the middle of the night, this one knocks. Probably some cogs or pressurized steam pipes loosening up. You should be half starved by now," he added. "Please. Eat something."

Magaliana slowly turned her attention back to the mixed array of fruit, salted meat, and a small loaf of bread. As much as she didn't want to admit it, her body retaliated against her, and her stomach growled embarrassingly loud. She snatched a handful of berries and shoved them into her mouth as if her life depended on it. And it did. She couldn't fight it anymore. She plucked grapes from their stalk and scarfed them down faster than she could process her own actions. She grabbed some of the meat next, and the Mage lightly chuckled.

"So, you were half-starved, then."

Magaliana ate and ate until she thought she would explode, but really, she hadn't ingested much at all. It was just more than she had consumed in a very long time.

"Come, let me take you back to your room." The Mage got to his feet, offering to help her up.

She shot him a pleading look. "If I could," she started timidly, "... could I remain here?"

Jocephus raised a brow. "You want to stay in the cemetery?"

"I don't consider it a cemetery at all, actually. It's very peaceful here. I like it."

The Techno Mage flashed her that bewitching smile and retracted his hands. "As you wish."

He bid her a good night and returned to the lift, leaving the food platter. Sinking back down into the grass, her mind roamed on all the information he had given her. Soon, her eyes grew heavy and she fell back into a much-needed sleep.

CHAPTER 15

A low note sounded from the boatswain's pipe, becoming high pitched for two seconds before it abruptly broke off, followed by a verbal call for breakfast. Ikarim sat on a log along the shore, plate of food in hand, but he did not eat. The ship had dropped anchor somewhere during the night, and it was the first time he had the opportunity to observe and figure out where they were.

Both mechanics had been woken before the crack of dawn, and Ikarim had already put in a few hours of work before breakfast. They'd split him up from Arteus, much to the Strong Arm's dismay, and Ikarim had to silently remind him with a hand to the shoulder and a shake of the head to keep his temper in check before they went their separate ways.

He scanned the scattered crew for his friend and instead spotted Keenan aboard the main deck of the *Raider*. A second figure walked up to him, and they discussed something before Captain Keenan pointed to someone in the distance. Ikarim followed the general direction and spotted Arteus. With a confused frown, his gaze shot back to both men, only to find the Captain alone once more, looking in Ikarim's vicinity, perhaps even directly at him.

His eyes never left the pirate as he wondered what the man wanted with his friend. Did he even point to Arteus?

"Not eating anything?" came a voice from behind him. Ikarim tore his attention away and gave his friend a half-hearted smile as he shook his head. Arteus sat next to him. "Probably better off. The gruel was lukewarm and way too watered down."

An amused smile made its way to his lips before he glanced back at the Captain, but he was gone. "What do they have you doing?"

"Manual labor," Arteus answered. "Pushing, pulling, lifting... They think I can do it all because I'm a Strong Arm. It's exhausting. It would be so much simpler if I had an infusion."

"But with an infusion, you would try to escape," Ikarim pointed out.

"Wouldn't you?" He flexed his cybernetic fingers.

"Not until we come up with a plan. Without one, it could get us killed. It could get Mags killed, for all we know."

The boatswain's call whistled again. Before they parted ways to return to their tasks, the pirate that had spoken with Keenan stopped them. "The Captain would like to see you," he said to Arteus.

The mechanics looked at one another, confused. Arteus shrugged and went to the *Raider*. Ikarim went to follow, but the pirate stopped him. "The Strong Arm only."

"Whatever the Captain has to say to Art, he can say with me present as well," Ikarim countered. "Besides, I need to be there to keep his temper in check."

"The Strong Arm only," the man repeated menacingly.

"But..."

"Get back to work, mechanic, or you'll be lashed."

More and more pirates surrounded him, and Ikarim backed down. He glanced at Arteus, whose face grew red at his friend's treatment.

"Art..." Ikarim cast him a warning look to not make any rash, hot-headed decisions. The lanky man did not acknowledge his silent plea with anything but a look in return before he turned and continued toward the *Raider*.

Ikarim frowned at the pirate that had delivered the message. Unable to change the situation, he headed back to his duties, but not before casting a quick glance over his shoulder to make sure Arteus was in check.

He returned aboard one of the many airships that had joined them the previous night, back to the hull where he was repairing one of the steam-powered suppliers. Picking up his wrench, he continued his repairs, listening in on an argument near one of the engines. One of the pirates called for a need of additional coils, while the other stated that it was too far along and needed to be replaced entirely. Ikarim glanced up from his work to the generator in question, tilting his head in contemplation before he joined them. It sounded like a simple fix, and he wondered if it truly was.

"May I?" he asked.

He had caught the two pirates off guard. One took a step back, but the other snarled. "What would you know?"

Ikarim rolled his eyes. "Let me have a look." He inspected the front of the generator, then the rear, opening its panel. A mess of wires, cogs, buttons, and switches awaited him. Getting down on all fours, he grabbed a screwdriver from a kit around his thigh and unscrewed a hinge. Another panel loosened, and Ikarim flinched as hot steam shot forth. He waited a beat before he looked.

"If you care to know..." he reached inside to flick at a spring, "it's the resistor coil and the adjacent collar. Might be prudent to replace the winding, too, but you can salvage the rest just by replacing those. If you do, the steam will be more concentrated to the pipes, leading to more power. The ship will be faster," he added, elbow-deep in the generator's interior.

"Then I'll leave you to it," the unpleasant pirate snarled.

To Ikarim's surprise, a small crowd had gathered around the generator, but slowly scattered, sneering and making rude remarks. He sighed and glanced to the supplier he was repairing, then back to the generator. It seemed like his to-do list was never-ending. At this rate, the Captain would probably keep him forever.

Some time passed, and Ikarim not only repaired the one generator, but a second as well. He had just gone back to working on the supplier when a familiar voice startled him. "Nice job... Ike, was it?"

His attention snapped to the Captain, before he quickly glanced around for his friend. His heart sank. "Where is Art?"

Captain Keenan slowly wiped at a wrinkle in his crisp shirt. "Don't worry, your friend is fine and has returned to work. I promise."

Suspicious, Ikarim kept his eyes on the Captain for a long moment before he returned to his repairs.

"So fast and thorough. Did the mad Scientist teach you your skills of trade?"

"He wasn't mad," Ikarim retorted.

"Who taught you?"

Irritated that the Captain was pressing to learn more about him, Ikarim pulled away from his work and frowned at the man. "My father taught me the bare basics," he finally relented. "The rest, I learned on my own." What the Captain didn't need to know was that by 'bare basics', it meant whatever his six-year-old brain could retain at the time.

"Your father, hm?"

"He was an engineer for Queen Victoria's Royal Navy."

"Was?" Benedict raised a brow.

Ikarim inhaled and exhaled deeply, still frowning. He didn't take pleasure in giving his captor so much information that could potentially be held against him, or worse—keep him captive. "He had an accident. Lost his arm. And his job. Now if you'll excuse me, I have work to do."

Ikarim returned to his repairs and forcibly ignored the Captain's presence until he heard footsteps walking away. He shut his eyes for a moment to clear his mind before he continued his work.

Lunchtime arrived and Ikarim decided he would eat this time, or risk collapsing on the job. It felt like he had worked an entire week within a single morning, and his muscles protested strongly. Arteus eventually joined him.

"What did the Captain need?" Ikarim asked.

"He wanted to look at my arms," Arteus admitted. "See how they worked."

Ikarim nearly choked on his food. His friend was still alive, which meant he did not attack Keenan as he had threatened so many times. "And you let him?"

The Strong Arm cast him an unamused look. "Of course not. But I didn't act out, if that's what you're getting at."

Ikarim cleared his throat in embarrassment but didn't have time to quip when a voice bellowed, "Ships approaching!"

As pirates scrambled all about and orders were shouted, Ikarim looked into the distance to try and spot the incoming ships' loyalty. "More of Keenan's fleet?"

"It's the Royal Guard!" a pirate shouted, followed by curses.

Arteus cast his friend a sidelong glance. "Hopefully our hero Cambridge has come to rescue us."

Amid the chaos, both young men were shoved, pushed, and dragged back aboard the ship, accused of being the ones who gave away their location. Arteus put up a decent fight, as expected, refusing to get back in the hold. Ikarim decided that, despite telling his friend not to do anything rash or hot-tempered, the coming of the Royal Guard was a perfect time to slow the pirates down.

His hand closed into a fist and he spun around swiftly, sucker punching one of the pirates right in the jaw. He immediately regretted his uncharacteristically violent decision when he received two blows in response, one in the stomach and one at his ribcage, which knocked him down with a cry of pain. Arteus called out his name, but Ikarim couldn't reply through the pummeling he took while he was down.

Suddenly, a gunshot echoed through the sky. A random pirate hit the deck, a pool of blood beneath his corpse. Captain Benedict's arm was still outstretched as smoke escaped the pistol from the shot. "That's enough! All of you! Get them in the blasted hold and get to your stations on the double!"

A chorus of "Yes, Sir!" sounded as they shoved Ikarim painfully into the hold and Arteus, for once, went peacefully.

"Ike! Are you...?" he started, alarmed.

"I'm fine, I'm fine..." Ikarim managed as he wiped blood from a cut on his lip. Breathing was a chore, and his already-sore muscles screamed, but he didn't seem to have anything broken, at least to his knowledge.

Cannons and gunshots fired on deck, and men cried out in victory and pain. The sound of two blades clashing meant that the Royal Guard had boarded and the Queen's soldiers fought their way onto the ship.

"Magaliana!" a voice cried from the chaos above.

Arteus turned to Ikarim. "That's Cambridge." He rushed up the stairs and gripped the grate, shaking it as hard as he could. "Cambridge! Sergeant Cambridge!"

"Magaliana?" The familiar figure glanced down into the hold. "Where is Magaliana?"

"Let us out!" Arteus called back in irritation, shaking the grate as hard as he could with his cybernetic arms. Ikarim gritted his teeth and limped to the base of the ladder while Cambridge quickly worked the lock. Suddenly, a click sounded, and Cambridge froze at the pistol aimed at his temple.

"I'm afraid that the *Dame* is no longer aboard my ship, Sergeant," said Captain Keenan.

Cambridge's eyes went wide and his hands slowly rose next to his head. Arteus shouted and, with one final push, shoved the grate from the hold's entrance. He rushed out, and Ikarim followed, the sudden adrenaline temporarily silencing the objection of his muscles.

A gun fired. Ikarim flinched and paused in his actions. Cambridge's body stiffened, but it was Benedict who winced as he took a step back and dropped his pistol in favor of grabbing his bleeding arm.

"That's enough," called a gruff voice. Ikarim recognized it as none other than Brigadier General Franklin Darley.

CHAPTER 16

Everyone seemed to be at a standstill awaiting the next action, including Ikarim. He didn't have a weapon, his arms weren't made of metal, and his battered body constantly reminded him he couldn't even hold his own in a brawl. Whatever move came next, he wanted as far away from the action and crossfire as possible.

"Benedict Keenan," the weathered General acknowledged, calm and calculating, his gun aimed at the Captain once more.

"Where is Magaliana?" asked Cambridge, his composure restored after realizing that he hadn't been shot after all. "Where is she!?"

As glad as Ikarim was that the Royal Guard came to his rescue, his dislike for Cambridge almost tripled. Not only did he seem to think that he was a perfect match for Magaliana and pushy in his methods, but he was demanding too, with his own pistol pointed at the pirate, not even giving him time to answer.

"I told you," Benedict smirked. "She is no longer aboard my ship."

"So help me God, if you don't tell me where she is, you'll find yourself with another bullet in your body."

"That's enough, Sergeant," ordered Darley, his eyes never leaving the Captain.

"With all due respect, Sir," Cambridge replied, "threats of violence seem to work best with pirates."

"Oh," Keenan started, his bloodied hand swiftly reaching for the sword on his belt. "Is that what that was?"

Benedict thrust out at Cambridge's hand and dodged both the General and Sergeant's shots. Ikarim shrank away to the ship's frame, out of the way. He needed a way to help, but everywhere he looked, there was chaos.

He did a double-take as another bandit aimed their gun at the General trying to immobilize Keenan. Ikarim called out to Darley in warning, and the shot whizzed past the weathered man as he spun around and shot the offender. The pirate hit the deck, but two more ran at Darley with their blades ready.

Arteus dove for Captain Keenan's dropped gun and used it to thin out the herd coming toward them. It was a great idea. Ikarim's gaze fell on the fallen marauder's weapon, but to reach it, he'd have to be right in the middle of the cross-fire. He wasn't too keen on acting without thoroughly thinking it through, but his current situation didn't allow for much wiggle room.

Captain Keenan slashed at Cambridge again, trying to get the gun out of the Sergeant's hand.

"Where is Magaliana?" Cambridge dodged the pirate leader and pulled out his own sword, dual-wielding his weapons.

"We don't know!" Ikarim called back. "We've been separated!" His eyes went back to the fallen gun, and his mind whirled on his decision. Should he? Shouldn't he? He quickly weighed the pros and cons; whatever decision he made, he needed to survive for Magaliana's sake. He couldn't die and leave her to whatever fate her new captor held.

Cambridge continued his never-ending dance with Keenan. "I'll kill you!"

"You can try," the pirate smirked. "I've fought worse scenarios than this... And won."

He struck and the Sergeant dodged. Benedict went to slash at Cambridge's waist, but feigned when the man spun to avoid the hit, hacking quickly in the other direction and slicing the gun out of his hand. Cambridge cried out in pain as the weapon tumbled away, landing near Ikarim. His eyes darted to it, and he took his chance. Gritting his teeth at both his pain and stupidity, he pounced.

Keenan lunged forward and kicked at the back of the Sergeant's left knee, dropping him. Cambridge went to swing his sword but met with the tip of a very sharp and bloodied blade aimed directly at his throat.

Ikarim rolled onto his back and went to pull the trigger, but a large explosion of cannon fire stopped him. Men went flying, along with pieces of the ship. The mechanic shielded himself as best he could from the debris. Everything hurt, and he wasn't sure if it was new pain or not. When the chaos settled, he kicked some of the planks off and his eyes darted about, disoriented. He found Captain Keenan on his back, hands by his head in surrender with Darley's sword and pistol aimed right at him. He shot Darley a daring look before two soldiers pulled him to his feet.

Keenan winced, then smirked. "Well done, General."

"Lock him up," Darley instructed, his dark eyes still on the Captain. "I want extra security watching him. We'll take him to England where he'll be tried and hanged."

Keenan forced a smile as they walked him off his own ship.

"Ike!" Ikarim turned his attention to Arteus, who rushed toward him. Ikarim's only reply was a nod that he was all right—despite the cuts and blood. He couldn't say the same for Cambridge, impaled from the explosion. Despite the irritation he felt toward the man, Ikarim did not wish this fate upon anyone. He also couldn't help but think that it could have been him instead.

He swallowed hard, then looked back to the General.

"Follow me," Darley said. "Stay close. We've won with that last explosion, but there's still a possibility of things getting ugly really quick." Ikarim hobbled past Cambridge's corpse and followed Arteus and the General from the damaged *Raider* to an anchored zeppelin. "Tell the soldiers inside that you are the captives from the raid. I'll join you in a moment."

Ikarim gladly complied and boarded the ship, only to come face to face with soldiers and their weapons drawn. He was thankful that he was in front of Arteus; he foresaw a whole different encounter were it the other way around.

"Wait!" He raised his hands defensively by his head. "We are the captives from Handsel Gesselmeyer's raid. Darley brought us here."

One soldier immediately dropped his weapon. "Weren't those orders to find Lady Wiegraf?"

"According to Cambridge, yes," Arteus frowned.

"We're... We're her friends," Ikarim added. "We've lived together for years."

The other soldiers holstered their guns. "Follow me," one of them said.

Despite his soreness, Ikarim moved first. The men led them to a small room where a medical officer immediately stepped up to Arteus and grabbed his face, examining the gash on his cheek. Ikarim could tell he wasn't too thrilled about being touched without permission, so he made sure to stay close in case his temperamental friend decided to act on his displeasure.

The doctor released Arteus' face and inspected his arms some before he darted for the door and disappeared. The mechanics exchanged confused glances, but they were short-lived when the doctor returned almost as quickly as he had disappeared. "On the bed, please," he said to Ikarim. "You, the table," he added to Arteus, heading for the cabinets filled with supplies.

Ikarim limped to the short bed covered in a thick white sheet. The medical officer placed a band on his head which contained a light and a multitude of magnifying glasses. He returned to Ikarim and shone the bright light into his eyes, forcefully inspecting them. Ikarim winced; he was fairly sure that not only could the doctor see his brain, but he was now going to be blind for the rest of his life. The man removed the device from his head and muttered to himself, and Ikarim blinked away the spotlight.

The medical officer tended to his bleeding lip and the various more severe cuts and scrapes on his body. The clear liquid he used smelled sweet, but it stung.

"Sir," came a voice from the doorway.

The medical officer only acknowledged the newcomer's presence with a nod as he continued to tend to Ikarim. "Take a look at our young friend here," he motioned toward Arteus.

The new soldier's eyes instantly lit up as his attention fell on the lanky man's cybernetics. He approached and Arteus frowned, pulling his arms away.

"Art..." Ikarim started, "it's alright."

He could tell Arteus was none too pleased, but eventually—after a stern look from the doctor—he shoved one of his arms toward the soldier to inspect.

Ikarim's bruises were treated next and though the dark green paste didn't sting like the antiseptic, the pungent aroma was far more unpleasant, with or without the hint of mint.

"What is the verdict, Private Chamberlain?" the doctor asked as he finished applying bandages around Ikarim's torso.

"These are explicitly well-crafted! Aside from tightening a few bolts and screws, there is really nothing much wrong with them..." Chamberlain trailed off as he inspected the damaged wires. "What do these do?"

Arteus' scowl proved that he loathed the idea of somebody inspecting his arms. "They're for infusions," Ikarim intervened.

Arteus shot him a glare, then sighed. "This is what it looks like, untouched." He lifted one of his pant legs, revealing the cybernetics beneath with blue liquid coursing through the wires.

"Ah! I understand now; you're a Strong Arm. And... Leg..." the soldier concluded as he returned to inspecting the damaged wires in Arteus' arms.

"Can you help him?" came a familiar voice from the door. The doctor and private both spun around to salute the General. Darley's dark eyes were on Chamberlain as he awaited an answer.

"I think I can find similar wires. Unfortunately, we don't have any infusions on board, Sir."

"Then make that your next project, Private."

"Yes, Sir."

Darley looked to Ikarim. "How about you? Will you live?" Ikarim gave a faint nod. "Good. You can both follow me."

CHAPTER 17

"When did you realize that Lady Wiegraf was no longer aboard the ship?"

"Keenan told us," Ikarim replied.

They had brought Darley up to speed on the events since Gesselmeyer's death. Even though the trio all mourned the loss of the Scientist together, Ikarim felt sorry for Arteus the most; the turn of events made him focus more on Magaliana than his own father. And though he knew that there was nothing his friend would like more than to concentrate on the woman he loved, the circumstances were much different.

The visible gloom that washed over his friend now that he had time to process everything absolutely broke his heart, but there was still that spark present—the one that would continue to fight for Magaliana no matter what. Ikarim could see it in his eyes, and though it was inspiring, it also worried him; it usually meant more rash decisions and actions.

"But we did set anchor," Ikarim pointed out. "And if you found us in Australia, we're guessing that she can't be too far." He had to admit that he was thankful that the large continent belonged to the British. They were lucky the General was in the area, as the Germans never would have been. Ikarim could only imagine still being Keenan's captive were that the case.

"We have ordered additional crew to search the Pacific, but without a precise location, it's hard to determine."

"We understand," Ikarim confirmed, slightly discouraged.

"The *Deutsches Kaiserreich* have communicated that they have a branch stationed near your home and shop to prevent future pillaging. In the meantime, any information you can think of that can be of any help, please, let me know. We are headed back to England to try Benedict Keenan and request further aid from Her Majesty Queen Victoria. We are working closely with the *Deutsches Kaiserreich*, and we'll have them inform Lord Wiegraf of the information you've provided."

"Thank you." Ikarim was grateful for everything that the military were doing, and he was especially appreciative that the General was so open to briefing them with so much information.

"In the meantime, please, make yourselves comfortable."

"Thank you," Arteus said, finally breaking his silence. "For the rescue, for our welfare, and for everything you are doing to ensure Mags' safe return."

Darley gave a nod and left the room. Arteus' gaze fell to the floor as sadness enveloped him once more. Ikarim rested a hand on his shoulder and gave a short-lived smile.

"We'll find her, Art. We'll find her safe and sound."

***

Magaliana slowly opened her eyes to the sound of birds chirping. Rays of sunshine pooled all around her as the sun tried to peek past the forest canopy. She was still in the cemetery, and it was just as peaceful and warm as before her slumber. It made her smile.

Her eyes found the platter the Techno Mage had left her the previous night. There was barely anything left as the culprits pecked happily at the remainder of the fruit. They were startled away by Magaliana's movement as she stretched, their wings flapping faster than truly needed.

The metal wings that Ikarim had fabricated rested near her head, and her smile faded as gloom set in. "Oh, Ike," she whispered as she

153

shut her teary eyes, hugging her gift tightly. "Art... Please come save me..."

She allowed the warm, salty tears to fall for a moment, but her grief quickly turned to fury. She was separated from her friends and sold to a mythical man. Suddenly feeling disturbingly filthy in Keenan's shirt, she decided that she would get cleaned up first and foremost. Getting to her feet, she donned her wings and made her way to the lift.

Her first stop was the quarters Jocephus had loaned her for the time being. She had paid little attention to it before and hoped such a regal suite would at least contain a bath. She slipped past the double doors and quietly shut them behind her.

Now that she was able to get a better look, it seemed that it might have once been somebody's permanent room. The rug, covers, and drapes were all a mix of dusty rose and white colors, and every wooden piece of furniture—from the bedposts, chiffonier, and even the vanity set—accentuated perfectly. She made her way to the vanity, where gorgeous pearl necklaces cascaded from the jewelry box and breathtaking agate cameo brooches were scattered on the surface. As she continued to look around, a frame caught her attention atop the chiffonier, and she couldn't help but pick it up to inspect it further.

The woman in the portrait was beautiful. She was well-posed, like a lady, with her dark hair pulled back in some intricate hairdo beneath a long-brimmed hat that shaded her face from the surrounding sunlight. Her lips were dark, Magaliana could only guess ruby red.

"Lady Juliet Beckford," came a voice from behind, startling her. "Daughter of the world-famous alchemist Wilfred Beckford."

Magaliana spun around to find Jocephus inches away, his attention on the framed photograph. He carefully took it from her, and she put up no fight as she tilted her head, observing him. She had a feeling he personally knew the woman in the portrait. "Was this her room?"

Jocephus mouthed a silent "oh, yes" as he nodded, his eyes still on Lady Juliet.

"Did you know her?"

"Yes, I do know her."

She blinked in surprise. Did that mean Lady Juliet was still alive? Now she was even more curious about the man's reaction. Did Juliet choose someone else over him? Did she leave him?

Magaliana slowly and cautiously pulled the frame away from the man lost in thought and set it back on the chiffonier where she had found it. When she turned back around, the Mage's eyes were shut.

"Joss?" She felt a tinge of compassion for him. Whatever had happened seemed to affect

155

him deeply, and though he claimed to simply be a man awaiting recompense, she briefly wondered if the reward money being offered by her father would aid the lady.

Jocephus opened his eyes, but it took a few seconds before his distant gaze returned to the present. He gently smiled. "I trust you slept well?"

"I did..." she answered, weary of the change of subject. "Rather peacefully, actually."

"Have you eaten, yet?"

"No, I'm... Not very hungry," she confessed. "I would like to wash up, however, if that is all right... Maybe get some new clothes?"

"Of course," he replied, the soft smile still on his lips. He swept an arm in the direction of a side room and Magaliana stepped inside, slowly and quietly shutting the door behind her.

The bathroom was just as luxurious. She ran a hand across the smooth porcelain tiles of the paneled walls as she made her way toward the marbled washstand, her eyes on the encased bath in the middle of the room.

She paused at a table where various floral soaps, herbs, salts, and scented oils were lined up behind a vase of wilted flowers. She picked up one of the colorful glass bottles labeled 'Otto of Roses'. She was impressed—and also hardly surprised—that Lady Juliet would own the costliest of all perfumes. She removed the rubber cap and instantly threw her head back; the scent of the hundred-leaved rose was beautiful, but excessively powerful.

Her eyes travelled to the thin, chemise dresses pristinely folded on the shelf above as she put the bottle back. It seemed that Lady Juliet had everything... except Jocephus. What happened?

She freshened up at the washstand and returned to the main room to find clothing laid out for her on the bed. She ran her fingers across the silky white shirt, her eyes falling to the iridescent hem ruffles of the bronze-colored skirt. She shook her head; even Lady Juliet's clothing was as regal as everything else. Magaliana dressed anyway, then sat at the commode and looked at her reflection in the mirror. Her dreadlocks were messy and her skin seemed to lack color, which she guessed was from lack of nourishment.

She tied her hair in her usual way and stood up to inspect herself once more. The ensemble was gorgeous, but seeing it on her body simply reminded her of all the private events her parents made her attend while introducing her to her suitors. Thankfully, the wings added their own charm and complimented nicely with the clothing. With newfound determination, she walked out of the room.

She searched for tools and bottles on every floor but found none. She was a woman on a mission: if she was to be kept upon the

Faugregir for any duration of time, she needed to keep herself busy, and the golems in the cemetery would give her plenty to do.

Eventually, she arrived on an unfamiliar floor. She cast the attendant a curious glance as she stepped off the lift, but he said and revealed nothing. The wide hallway was similar to the one that led to the room she stayed in, but the door at the end was much smaller and made of thick steel. Try as she might, she couldn't remember being shown this particular level during her tour.

The maddening hum was particularly obvious here, and Magaliana had to grit her teeth to ignore it. She gently placed a palm against the steel and could feel ever-so-faint vibrations. Trailing her hand down to the intricately carved doorknob, she tentatively turned the handle and pushed.

The door opened. She stepped into the room and carefully shut the door behind her, trying to be as quiet as possible; she had the feeling that she wasn't supposed to be there, but something had caught her eye.

Glowing green vines were tangled about the wall, ceiling, and floor of the room, which was much, much bigger than the steel door suggested. She inspected some of them and realized that they were tiny wires much like the ones contained inside the golems, full of green liquid. Unlike those, however, these vines appeared to move, almost as if they were alive. Unsure what to make of them, Magaliana found her way to the center of the room where she'd swear she hit the jackpot.

Thick, wooden tables were filled to the brim with blown glass bottles, containers, and plates of powders. Controlled fires burned in a few jars, and she shivered from excitement. This was her area of expertise. The equipment was more than she had owned in Gesselmeyer's shop, and definitely more diverse than what they owned in his house. Enraptured, she inspected every single object until she spotted a figure past the curios with black markings on his back and shoulders, sitting cross-legged in front of the tall window.

Startled, Magaliana took a step back, accidentally bumping her hip into the table and knocking off one of the bottles, which shattered as it hit the floor. She brought both hands up to her mouth, her eyes wide in a mixture of fear and apology.

The figure stirred from his meditation. "*Dame* Magaliana."

She froze. The person with markings over his body was none other than the Techno Mage, and he knew that she was standing behind him without even turning around.

"I'm so sorry!" She rushed around the table and began picking up some of the shards.

The last thing she wanted was to have the Mage angry with her. She couldn't risk her upcoming release, or even endangering herself. Jocephus eventually kneeled near her and carefully flipped her glass-filled hand, allowing the pieces to fall back to the ground. Confused, she met his gaze and swallowed harder than she really meant to. That gentle smile always playing on his lips was so hypnotic...

"I will have somebody clean this up."

Magaliana quickly glanced away in embarrassment, but her eyes didn't travel far; they shifted to the black markings that stretched over his arms and chest.

"Does it scare you?" he asked as he stood back to his full height. He opened his arms and slowly spun around, inviting her to completely view them. "Do they strike fear into your heart?"

Magaliana gradually got back to her feet, quietly inspecting the markings. She recognized the alchemical formulas and symbols, but there were also various words in many unknown languages, and even animals and objects. "Are they supposed to?" she stuttered, hesitant.

The Mage took a step toward Magaliana, and she backed away. He continued to approach her until she was pinned against the table. "You tell me," he said rather mischievously.

Magaliana's heart raced. She feared for her life, but she was also curious about the markings. She inspected them a little more, especially the formulas, hoping to grasp a concept or two, but none of it immediately made any sense. Her gaze met his once more as she ever-so-slightly shook her head. "N-no..."

Jocephus pulled away, returning to his meditation spot and slipping on his silky black shirt. "There you have it, you have nothing to fear. Now, what can I do for you?"

"I..." She had practically forgotten why she came to see him to begin with. "I would like tools and bottles, please."

Jocephus raised a brow. "Whatever for?"

"I want to fix the golems."

A chuckle escaped him. "If you're planning your escape—" he started, but Magaliana cut him off.

"I want to fix the golems in the cemetery. Please," she tried again.

Jocephus seemed pensive. In the very short time she had known him, Magaliana found it rare to see him with a serious expression instead of his usual gentle smile or playful smirk. "Nobody is capable of fixing them but me."

"Please," she begged. "You will not permit me to leave, and I don't know how long you'll keep me here. At least allow me a hobby to lose track of time... Please, Joss."

Jocephus watched her carefully a moment more. She wondered what went through his mind as he seemed to consider her words quite carefully. "Very well. I'll have tools brought to the cemetery for you. Grab what you need here," he gestured to the tables.

She exhaled with gratitude, her heart fluttering in anticipation. "Thank you."

She turned to the table and began picking up glass bottles, inspecting them carefully. Her attention was diverted, however, back to the vines by the door. She narrowed her eyes in intrigue. "May I ask a question?"

"Of course."

"What are those vines over there? The green ones. They're unlike anything I've seen..."

"That, my dear, is alchemy, but in a purer form."

She raised a brow and shook her head. A purer form of alchemy? She didn't understand how that was possible.

Jocephus approached the jars of controlled fire. "As an Alchemist, you are aware that alchemy is an equivalent exchange. You take elements and transform them into their opposite." He covered one of the flames with a lid, then removed it after a few seconds, allowing the smoke to escape. He picked up the jar and tilted it above an empty glass bottle, pouring out a clear liquid. Magaliana had been taught this growing up, though she was thoroughly impressed that the Techno Mage did it all without the aid of a pendulum. "You know that fire can turn to water and air, and that air can turn to water and earth.

You can get more complicated and say that oxygen turns to hydrogen, lead turns to gold... Or you can make it into a purer form."

Jocephus poured the water in a plate of sand on another table. Magaliana followed closely, curious and observant. He dipped his index finger into the mix and stirred until it was properly absorbed, then he used both hands to knead the wet sand. Soon it did not look like sand at all, but clay. Magaliana frowned, then glanced about for a pendulum. "How are you...?"

The Techno Mage only replied with an amused grin as he molded the clay to look like a miniature golem. Instantly, it hardened and turned to brass, then to bronze. Vines grew and wrapped themselves around the statuette, and she wrinkled her nose when green insects emerged, but she was so enthralled she couldn't turn away.

He sprinkled a fine crystallized powder onto the figurine, and Magaliana gasped as it began to move on its own. Jocephus held his hand out closer for her to see. It was an amazing spectacle, and she couldn't even comprehend how he was doing it.

Suddenly, he sandwiched the miniature golem and crushed it, revealing nothing but dust as he pulled his hand away. He poured the dust into the empty glass bottle, and the tiny particles instantly liquified once inside. Magaliana was speechless.

"The entire ship—the *Faugregir*—is built this way. Technology and alchemy merged together. Magic." He corked the bottle and offered it to her. She was reluctant to take it. Magic? More like sorcery... She was convinced that what he had just done was not alchemy. However, she had to admit it was truly fascinating.

Magaliana finally accepted the bottle and inspected the green substance that seemed to glow with a life force all its own. "May I keep this? To study?"

"Be my guest." He bowed.

Excited, Magaliana finished picking through the objects available to her while Jocephus placed them in a wooden pail. With new liquid to study and the promise of tools to keep her occupied, she thanked the Mage and made her way back to the cemetery.

CHAPTER 18

A large belt filled with tools awaited Magaliana when she reached the cemetery. She smiled, pleased that the Mage had kept his word and it had arrived so quickly, even before she did. Resting the pail and gear at the foot of the first towering golem, she pulled out the bottle of pure alchemy.

"How did you do this...?" she mused to herself.

She wracked her brain trying to figure out how Jocephus retained every single secret directive without the pendulum. It just wasn't possible; there were too many formulas, too many transfiguration circles and ingredients to retain it all. And if that were the case, then he was far more intelligent than imaginable, and she feared what he was truly capable of.

Setting the bottle down by the pail, Magaliana unbuttoned the sleeves of her silk blouse
and rolled them up, ready to get to work.

She toiled on well past lunch, only nibbling
on what the cooks brought her here and there,
but her lunch largely remained untouched.
Sheets of copper were laid out on the ground in
the same order in which she had removed them,
leaving the golem with one dismantled arm and
long, fine veins dangling from the shoulder.
Now she knew why Ikarim loved tinkering as
much as he did: it was pretty satisfying. Of
course, he would have had the arm taken apart
in a quarter of the time that it took her.

"Are you warm?" asked a familiar voice.

Magaliana jumped, startled. Having dressed
down to nothing more than her silk undershirt
and bloomers, she scrambled to reach for the
blouse and skirt that she had carefully placed by
the golem's foot.

"Joss!" she shrieked, hiding behind the giant
idol's leg and quickly dressing.

"Apologies, but you do not have to dress for
me," he said gently. "I brought dinner."

Magaliana's cheeks flushed pink in embarrassment. "I just... Didn't want to get the clothes
dirty," she squeaked. "They're too beautiful. Did
they belong to Lady Juliet?"

She peeked around the leg to find Jocephus
a few feet away with a tray full of food.

"Yes," he answered, his eyes on her. "They are hers. Would you prefer mechanic coveralls?" He placed the tray of food down and sat in the grass.

Once fully dressed, she cautiously stepped out from behind the golem and nodded. "If it would not cause you any trouble, then yes, I would."

Jocephus smiled that genuine and hypnotic smile. "No trouble, *Dame* Magaliana. However, may I offer a compliment? The dress suits you beautifully."

Magaliana frowned, averting her gaze to the tray of food. She was reminded of Cambridge's advances, but her flushed cheeks betrayed her into accepting the charismatic man's compliment.

Jocephus grabbed a piece of salted meat. "You should take more breaks from your work or you'll be ill from exhaustion."

"I'm enjoying what I am doing, so it can hardly be considered work," she said as she tentatively looked back to him.

He smiled. "Very well. Please, join me for dinner." Lowering herself into the grass across from the Mage, she reached for some bread and nibbled on it. "Is there anything else that you might need?"

Magaliana shook her head. Really, the only thing holding her back from further studying the golems was the fear of soiling the beautiful clothes.

They continued to eat in silence. Jocephus eventually took his leave after their dinner—the platter of food remaining with Magaliana after he made her promise she would eat more.

Eager to get back to work, she quickly dressed down to her undershirt and bloomers once more, then stepped over to the wooden pail. She had found the opening, a small fuel ring attached to the golem's back, where infusions could be fed into it. She did not want to use the green infusion that Jocephus made earlier, so she decided to make her own. Grabbing the platter of food, she emptied the remnants onto the grass without any regard to her promise, reached into the pail, and poured fine sand from a leather pouch onto the tray before gathering three long sticks. She stuck them into the ground around the platter for leverage, tied the tops together with string, and wrapped a quartz prism with the rest of it. She dangled the crystal from the makeshift pivot until the tip dented the smooth surface of the sand ever-so-lightly.

She placed two jars next to her system, then kneeled before her project with a satisfied nod. It was time to do what she did best.

Magaliana inhaled deeply, then flicked the crystal clockwise. She did so a few more times until the crystal formed a circle on the extremity of the sand-filled platter. She watched it care-fully, waiting for it to center itself and begin os-cillating.

With the ingredients and objects set out be-fore her, she got to work: A pinch of salt with one swing. A counterclockwise stir with the next swing. A fire created with the third swing, and add them all together per the symbol displayed in the sand. The flames of Magaliana's con-trolled fire turned purple, green, then blue. She covered the jar with its lid and waited a few sec-onds before removing it. A royal blue smoke es-caped as she poured the glowing sky-blue liquid into an empty bottle. Corking the infusion, she got to her feet and climbed the golem's other arm with ease. Sitting on the mechanical beast's shoulder, she wrapped her legs about the large head and leaned backward until her back was flush with the back of the golem.

She unscrewed the fuel ring and tried to see what was inside, frowning as her position made it difficult. Sitting back up, she rolled over and slid forward on her stomach. Her grip around the golem's head was definitely not as great as when she was upside down, but she just couldn't see. Her hands fiddled with the opening, and her entire body shook from the awkward position and lack of strength to keep herself up.

She gasped as her legs barely held on. She wrapped her toes and ankles around as tightly as she could, but her trembling grew even worse.

169

She tried to slide back up but found herself unable to. Gritting her teeth and mentally cussing out the silky material she wore, Magaliana quickly calculated the distance she would fall and concluded that if she was lucky, she would have enough time to roll without hitting her head. The thought brought no comfort. In a panic, she attempted to scramble up the golem's back, but continued slipping until she fell.

Tensing up and shutting her eyes as hard as she could, she twisted her body in mid-air as she expected the fall... Except she never hit the ground. She slowly peeked at her situation, then both eyes shot open in shock.

Jocephus had one hand extended forward, a glowing transmutation circle drawn into his palm. Heart racing, she realized she was standing upright, her feet floating inches away from the grass. She whimpered. How was he doing it? It couldn't possibly be with alchemy! He had to be some kind of sorcerer! As much as the thought terrified her, it also brought up conflicting thoughts of wonder and amazement.

The Mage slowly stepped forward, closing the distance between them until his face was inches away from hers. He placed his hand up against the golem's leg, causing the transmutation circle to disappear and Magaliana's feet to gently make contact with the grass. Pinned between the man and the construct, her whole body trembled with fear and adrenaline.

Jocephus exhaled in relief. "I could have gotten you a ladder, *Dame* Magaliana..." he whispered.

With her breath caught in her throat, she stared up at him, unable to move. Finally, Jocephus took a step back.

"I'm glad you didn't get hurt. I've brought you some coveralls." He offered her the neatly-folded clothes.

Magaliana's legs finally gave out from beneath her, and she fell to her knees.

"How...?!" she asked, incredulous. Tears of frustration welled up in her eyes.

"Alchemy," was the Mage's very gentle and simple reply.

Magaliana shook her head. "That's impossible!"

He gave her a faint, sympathetic smile before he set the coveralls down at his feet. "Let me fetch you a ladder."

She watched him walk away and wiped at her tears. She just couldn't understand. He kept saying that it was alchemy, but how was he doing everything without a pendulum? And even if he prepped for everything beforehand, how did he know to prep a transmutation circle that would prevent her from hitting the ground?

The memory replayed in her mind, and she let out a sob, trembling once more. It just couldn't be alchemy, because she had never

seen, heard of, or studied anything even re-
motely close to what he accomplished. It was
maddening.

Wiping at her tears again, Magaliana took a
few deep breaths before she donned the tan coveralls. They were slightly big, but not nearly as
loose-fitting as anything she borrowed from Arteus. Her gaze fell to the transmutation symbol
in the food platter, and she suddenly got an idea.
She reached for some charcoal and drew the for-
mula for controlled fire into the palm of her
hand.

Nothing happened.

She outstretched her palm as she had seen
Jocephus do, but still nothing; there was no fire,
and the circle definitely didn't glow. Unimpressed, she shoved the platter of sand aside and
carefully placed her hand beneath the pendulum
instead. She flicked the crystal clockwise and
waited for it to swing back and forth along her
palm.

When it had finished and still nothing happened, her heart sank and she lost all motivation
to continue.

She was curled up at the golem's foot when
Jocephus returned with a ladder. He laid the
ladder down in the grass, then kneeled with his
gaze upon her. Apathetic, she did not move or
speak, though she did manage to look away,

ashamed. The Mage was silent for a long moment before he finally spoke. "Please try not to get hurt, Magaliana."

Hearing her name spoken without her title sent shivers through her entire body, and her eyes fluttered shut at the sensation. She still didn't fully trust him—who could with everything that he did in the name of alchemy?!—but she had to admit that the charismatic man made anything sound good.

She only opened her eyes long enough to watch him walk away after whispering good night.

CHAPTER 19

Jocephus made his way to the center of the *Faugregir*. He was a man on a mission.

Stepping off the lift, he turned his attention to the attendant. The wiry assistant's feline-like pupils on this particular floor dilated and contracted in the Mage's presence, and when it opened its mouth to speak—with what almost appeared to be a half-eaten squid stuffed inside—a gurgled shriek came out. The tendrils wiggled and flayed, and Jocephus simply nodded to the hazed being. He didn't physically understand what was said, but he didn't need to, nor did he care.

Thick, intricately-designed brass double doors awaited at the end of the hall. Jocephus approached a lever and monitor, which glowed with a faint greenish hue the closer he got. Satisfied the magic was working, he dipped his hand through the display and pressed a large, flat button at the back.

The infusion bubbled inside the vines clinging to the ceiling, floor, and walls. Jocephus pulled the lever and the mechanisms at the core of the doors turned and churned. Finally, he reached into one of the pouches about his belt and pulled out a small copper cog. As he had done hundreds of times before, he expertly placed it inside an indentation in the door like a missing puzzle piece. He turned the gear like a dial, which produced a series of clicks until a large vibration occurred on the other side and the doors slowly opened.

Jocephus removed his silky black shirt as steam escaped the room and hung it off the lever before he stepped inside. His skin immediately beaded with sweat from the tropical heat as the doors, which provided the only short-lived breeze, shut behind him. The room was very stuffy and dim, most of the infusion-filled lanterns extinguished, and the high-pitched hum was at its loudest. As much as he was used to it and tended to ignore the noise, he was very aware of its presence every time he entered. Thick, wet, slimy tendrils moved and wiggled everywhere. Jocephus stepped past them toward a large dome at the center of the room, connected at the top with tubes, hissing from steam. In between each hiss, heavy sighs issued from inside the dome.

Jocephus lightly trailed his finger over the surface of a particularly thick, slimy tentacle as he approached the hemisphere, causing it to shudder. A high-pitched whine sounded about the room, and Jocephus grinned mischievously.

"Did you miss me, sweetheart?" he asked nobody in particular. The room replied with another whine.

He pressed a few buttons on a control panel, extending a steel bridge from the dome over a pool of green liquid—the same substance that was in the veins and vines all around—that surrounded it. Jocephus stepped onto the walkway and made his way to the second dashboard, where he flicked a few switches. The dome's door slid open, and a cloud of steam escaped. Nestled in a tangled thicket stood a naked woman.

"Oh, Juliet..." Jocephus whispered, his sense of yearning almost more than he could bear as he slowly looked her over in admiration. He knew every inch of her translucent body by heart; from her green, slimy locks of hair formerly so silky black and rose-scented, to the tangled explosion of extra appendages shooting out from her back, to the tiny tendrils that were once dainty fingers on the hands he loved to feel over his arm. The deep sighs she produced each time her chest fell from breathing was practically music to his ears compared to the high-pitched hum of the machines keeping Lady Juliet alive.

His boots splashed in the shallow puddle of alchemical liquid beneath the woman's bare feet, and he paused inches away. Cupping her cheek, he brushed his thumb across her closed eyelids. "It's about time to fetch our Portuguese Prince, don't you think?" The woman said nothing, but the room shuddered eagerly in response. "I will fetch your *Príncipe*, and you can feast to your heart's desire, my love."

There came a high-pitched whine to his words, and he smiled. He had learned to read her body language and sounds. Unlike the hazed attendant, he understood Lady Juliet perfectly.

"Yes, you would like that, wouldn't you?" His fingers trailed from her cheek to stroke her slimy hair. "Before I fetch him, however, I need to make a stop in Germany. You see... We have a *Dame* on board with us. She is the daughter of *Herr* Wiegraf. Now you might not like the idea too much, but if I were to wed her..." The room shuddered, displeased at his words. Jocephus wiped at the sweat on his face with his free hand before he quickly continued, "If I were to wed her, Juliet, it would be a powerful political move and grant us so much potential!" His fingers left her hair to caress her lips instead. "Just think! The daughter of a German *Herr* and English Lady. True, we still won't have as much power as the Queen over England, but imagine what we could do with Germany! Just imagine, my love..."

177

Jocephus pressed his lips against the woman's and kissed her gently. Her body shivered in delight, as did every vine in the room. Jocephus wiped the slime from his lips, then grinned.

"The *Herr* is offering a rather large reward for the *Dame*'s safe return. I guarantee that he is looking for her himself right now. So, if I were to go to Germany and visit Mother dearest, things could get interesting. In the meantime, I need to step up my game. The *Dame* doesn't fully trust me, but I've seen the look in her eyes when I perform alchemy. I know she's curious about it. She's an Alchemist, you know..." he trailed off. "Soon, my love, we will find a way to change you back."

The woman groaned in reply. He returned to petting her oily hair.

"Now, now, sweetheart..." he said, "of course I love you just the way that you are. But wouldn't you be happier being back to normal? Where you could run and jump and laugh and smile? I miss your smile, Juliet..." The last words were whispered, bittersweet, as his gaze fell to her lips. His heart ached for the past. The nostalgia grew heavier each day. He leaned in once more to kiss her. "I miss your smile," he whispered again.

With his free hand, he wiped his lips and the sweat that poured down his face as he flipped a few switches on the dashboard. He watched the naked figure slowly vanish as the dome's door slid shut and the steam built up once more. Then he returned to the first control panel, and the steel bridge retracted, protecting Lady Juliet from potential intruders and unwanted guests.

"I shall return, my love!" he exclaimed loudly as he walked away, trailing his finger on the same tentacle he had before.

As he pulled the thick doors open and stepped out of the hot and humid room, his skin practically heaved a sigh of relief. Running a hand through his soaked hair, he grabbed his silk shirt and made his way back to the lift where the hazed attendant handed him a towel. He dried himself off, put his silk shirt back on, and headed back to the cemetery. It was dark out, but he was certain Magaliana was still there.

He arrived to find her not where he had left her. Scanning the area, he spotted a bump near the fallen golem. He approached and found the young woman curled up, using the ruffled skirt as a pillow.

He needed to get her to trust him. And he had an inkling that the way to fully unlock her heart was to teach her some transmutations, maybe even walk her through some. She was a highly intelligent woman; he had noticed that when he saw her for the first time, interacting with the Captain. He'd have to be careful, because one wrong move could ruin everything... but he was quite sure that he could have her wrapped around his finger in a matter of days.

His eyes travelled around the forest for a moment. Why did she like the cemetery so? What was it about the golems that made her want to stay? It was such a strange request; he still didn't understand it.

The Mage's gaze fell back on the young woman sleeping soundly before he turned around and walked away.

CHAPTER 20

It was slightly before midday when the airship docked at a quaint little village in Upper Germany. The Mage was up before sunrise to reach his destination with as much nonchalance as possible. Adjusting his black gloves before disembarking, he turned to the pilot.

"Remember: Wait precisely one hour, then leave," he instructed. "It should take me twenty minutes to reach the mansion by horse carriage. From there, it all depends on the *Herr*'s wife. We know of the *Herr*'s current whereabouts, correct?"

"Yes, Sir," the pilot replied. "His location this morning was in Spain. We have an insider making sure that he remains there a bit longer."

"Good. It will be easier to deal with the Lady than the *Herr* at the moment." He quickly flipped through his folder, making certain that he had what was required. His intel had gathered private information on the Wiegrafs, which the Mage had spent a good portion of the morning studying. He was confident in his ability to pull off his plan, but it wouldn't hurt to read through the papers once more while on his trip to the mansion. "Remember, one hour. Then I want you to stay at a speed of twenty-five knots. That should give me ample time."

"Yes, Sir."

Jocephus disembarked and casually walked toward the stables, listening to the dialect carefully; one step out of line would make him suspicious. He was intentionally overdressed in his crisp, black uniform as he tilted his top hat in greeting to passersby. If there was to be any gossip to reach the *Herr* and the Lady, he needed it to be impressive and positive.

Upon his arrival, he was greeted by an old, balding man with missing teeth. Jocephus politely bowed and spoke expertly in German, "I wish for a four-horse carriage, please."

"Four-horse?" the man repeated as he glanced to a notepad where many things were scribbled down and stricken out. "That will cost two *Gulden*."

The Mage reached into a pouch and pulled out one hundred *Gulden* instead. He placed it on the counter, and the stable owner cast him a suspicious glance. Smiling that gentle smile as he always did, he kindly explained, "I am in a bit of a hurry, you see. You can keep the tip if you can have them ready in the next ten minutes."

The old man's eyes went wide and he rushed to the back door, yelling for the stable hands to have the best four-horse team ready within ten minutes, else they were all fired. He returned to Jocephus and grinned a toothless grin as he took the money and invited him on a tour. He humored the old man by feigning interest, and within ten minutes on the button, the stable hands had secured a four-horse team with a large carriage.

"Thank you." Jocephus bowed. "You shall have your horses returned to you within a few hours."

"No hurry!" the old man said, still grinning from the riches he just made.

Jocephus entered the carriage, and a thin man with a rather large brown mustache gave the reins a lift. The horses trotted along. "Where to?"

"To the home of *Herr* Günther Zum Wiegraf, please," Jocephus replied, opening his folder.

"Understood," the driver replied.

He studied the papers to the sound of clopping hooves. They contained all the information he required to gain the upper hand in any situation; from the *Herr's* schooling and military records, the Lady's family tree, and even the Wiegrafs' finances. Arriving before an enormous mansion within a timed eighteen minutes, he climbed out of the carriage, dug into his pocket, and pulled out ten *Gulden* for the driver who profusely thanked him. Petting the horses for a job well done, he headed toward the mansion's entrance. His eyes roamed about the white brick exterior with red trim as he used the heavy knocker to announce his presence. It was an interesting choice to go along with the blue roof, and he briefly questioned whether the family's income on his papers were correct before the door opened.

"How may I help you, Sir?" the butler drawled in German.

It was impressive that the man, nothing but skin and bones, could stand as tall as he did. He remembered reading that the attendant's family had served the Wiegrafs for centuries, and based on his wiry snow-white hair, he wondered if the man had served a full century himself.

"I would like an audience with Lady Ruth Wiegraf, please," Jocephus replied, also in German. "I have business to discuss with her."

"Follow me."

Unlike the outside of the building, he could easily match the family's finances to the interior's late-Baroque-style decor. He wasn't quite impressed with the exceptionally ornamental and theatrical architecture. The bright, attention-seeking sculpted molding, colorful frescoes, scrolling curves, and golden gilding just screamed that they didn't know what to do with their wealth. He respectfully removed his top hat and the butler placed it on a rack before escorting him to the parlor, which wasn't any better.

"Wait here, I will fetch my Lady," the butler said.

Jocephus nodded and approached frames of airships and portraits along the back wall. One depiction contained a young German *Herr* in decorated military attire, standing next to a beautiful woman in a long, flowing wedding dress. Both looked young and oh-so-serious. Neither one seemed happy with their politically-arranged marriage.

The next frame contained a family portrait, and Jocephus couldn't help but smile. There stood the *Herr* and his beautiful wife—both older, wiser, and content—with three children in front of them. There was a boy, no older than twelve by the look of it, evidently unimpressed with the fact that he had to stand still for the photograph. Next to him was a little girl with plaits in her hair, no older than six, appearing unsure with the entire situation. In the mother's lap was a baby with recognizable curiosity in her eyes: Magaliana.

"Can I help you?" came a woman's voice with a thick, German accent.

Jocephus tucked his folder beneath an arm as he turned to face Lady Ruth. The thin woman aged well in comparison to the portrait he was just studying. Aside from a slight mixture of gray in her loose blonde bun and very few new wrinkles, she looked almost exactly the same. And of course, he could clearly see the resemblance to Magaliana.

The Techno Mage smiled. "Ah! Mum!" he said in English.

"Who are you?" she asked in her native tongue, a guarded frown on her features.

"How impolite of me, my Lady. Allow me to introduce myself. The name is Jocephus Gideon, at your service." He bowed deeply.

"And what business do you have with me?"

"I have a proposal, Lady Ruth, that I think you'd like to hear. Do you suppose we can discuss this over tea?"

Lady Ruth observed him with uncertainty, her blue eyes hard as she ran her thin fingers through the lace of her sleeves. Eventually she nodded and called to her butler to prepare some tea.

She led him to a small table by the fireplace, and ever the gentleman, he pulled out one of the overstuffed chairs and slid the woman in slightly before taking a seat opposite of her. The butler appeared with tea soon after. At least the fine china used was in good taste, with roses and gold trim—just the way Juliet liked it.

Jocephus and Lady Ruth prepared their tea in silence. While he filled his teacup and added only a squeeze of lemon, he was inwardly amused that Lady Ruth placed three sugar cubes into her cup, filled it only halfway with the hot beverage, then filled the rest up with milk. How very weak of her British heritage.

Taking a few sips, the woman finally spoke. "Now, on to this business of yours, Master Gideon..."

"Ah, yes. Lady Ruth, I know that *Herr* Wiegraf is away, so I have come to you, asking for your and the *Herr*'s blessing for your daughter's hand in marriage."

Ruth almost looked insulted. "Is that your proposal?"

Jocephus shook his head and smiled gently. "No, Mum. The proposal comes later. I say we deal with one matter at a time, if you will."

"Master Gideon. I am certain that you are a wonderful man, but I have not heard of you. You have stated no title, military or otherwise. My husband is a very powerful man. He wants nothing less for our daughter—"

"And nothing less she shall have, Mum, if I may," he said, politely cutting her off. "I am an extraordinarily rich man, and very powerful, in my own right. I am seeking a political alliance as well. The way I see this, we can unite the United Kingdom and Germany, stronger than ever before."

"What power do you have, Master Gideon?" she asked, slightly pompous.

He didn't even flinch at her tone. He knew how to knock her down a peg, and so far everything was going according to plan. "The power of uniting technology and alchemy. The power of uniting the very thing that tore our lands apart."

Lady Ruth still seemed so very suspicious, so very unsure. He could tell the wheels in her head were turning. The war that separated the lands also separated the social classes: the alchemy users, who were mostly rich people, had no problem separating from the tech users, who constantly had to scrape by.

Jocephus continued to smile gently, but deep down inside he grinned like a maniac. It was time for the plan to move on. "Magaliana would be the perfect person to unite both, what with her knowledge of alchemy and the mechanical work she does at *Doktor* Gesselmeyer's shop..."

Her expression fell. That was it. She played right into his game. Continuing his theatrics, he quirked a brow as the woman brought a hand to her mouth, forcing tears back. She rebounded bravely and looked at Jocephus, shaking her head. "Have you not heard, Master Gideon? My daughter has been taken hostage."

"Has she?"

"Yes..." Lady Ruth frowned. "How can you not know about this? The entire Royal Guard and *Deutsches Kaiserreich* are searching for her. The news has been spread around the world."

"I think what I'm trying to say, Mum..." he began, taking a sip of his tea, then placing the cup back on the saucer on the table, "... is that I know where your daughter is."

Her face paled, and she dropped her teacup, which spilled all over her long, lilac dress and shattered on the floor. Her hands gripped the arms of her chair. Jocephus grinned internally as the woman drowned in a sea of disbelief. Perfectly on cue, he stood up and placed his folder onto the chair, gently resting one hand upon hers—which was ice-cold—to pull her out of her drowning state.

"Do you... Do you really know..." she stuttered.

"Yes." He smiled. "She is safe and sound."

Lady Ruth's distant gaze was suddenly sharp again. Her hand snatched away faster than a striking snake. "Are you the one who kidnapped my daughter?" she growled.

"I assure you that I am not, and that the pirate responsible is currently facing charges."

"Oh, my daughter!" she sobbed happily. "My poor, poor daughter!"

"Now this is my proposal, Mum," he said. "I will bring you to her, in exchange for your blessing for Magaliana's hand. I know that I still need the *Herr*'s blessing, but for now, in between you and I..."

He won. He had Lady Ruth wrapped around his finger. Her love for her daughter made her an easy target and easy prey.

"Yes!" she sobbed with joy. "Yes, yes, of course you have my blessing! Please! Take me to my daughter! Oh, my poor Magaliana...!"

Jocephus continued to smile as he extended his hands for Lady Ruth to take. "My airship awaits."

CHAPTER 21

The Mage's zeppelin sat near the mansion, ready to allow Lady Ruth onboard.

She had rushed to dress while the butler cleaned the shattered teacup. Jocephus continued to innocently study the photographs, occasionally making sure out of the corner of his eye that the folder he planted remained where it was for the *Herr* to find upon his return.

Lady Ruth returned wearing a long, burgundy dress. The stray strands of her hairdo were neatly tucked back in as she adjusted her lace collar, ready to leave, ready to see her dear daughter.

"Welcome to the *Ending*," he said once outside, gesturing toward the airship.

"The *Ending*? Quite a curious name... Almost as curious as how you got this ship when you arrived via horse and carriage."

Jocephus wanted to laugh, but ever the actor, he smiled his charismatic smile. The woman was giving one last-ditch effort to make him slip up and performed horribly at it. He wanted to tell her to leave the politics to the men, but he bit his tongue. He was too far in the game to screw up now. He had crossed all his Ts and dotted all his Is and needed to move forward with the plan at all costs. "I wanted to take in the beauty of the land firsthand. I told my pilot to fetch me once he had finished some errands."

Of course, the real reason for taking the carriage was to draw the least amount of suspicion. If his meeting with Lady Ruth failed—which he was confident it wouldn't—he was to return the same way that he arrived, keeping himself safe from bad or fearful gossip that could potentially expose the *Faugregir*.

The woman nodded, seemingly content with his answer. She took his offered arm to help her board the airship. "Why ever would you have given it such a name?"

Jocephus gave a soft chuckle. "An ending is required before every new beginning, wouldn't you say?" Boarding directly behind her, the mage instructed his crew to prepare for takeoff. "Let us bring Lady Ruth to her daughter."

One of the crew members led the woman to the passenger deck, while Jocephus had a quick word with the pilot.

"Remember," he warned. "Don't deviate from the plan."

"Yes, Sir."

"The slightest deviation, and we might not make it out of there alive."

"Understood."

Jocephus found Lady Ruth pacing next to the large windows. He took a seat on one of the benches alongside the windows and beckoned her to join him as the zeppelin took off.

"My daughter..." Lady Ruth started as she sat. "Please tell me that she was unharmed during the pirate raid."

"To the best of my knowledge. A little starved and exhausted, but that has been remedied."

"Oh, my poor daughter..."

"Everything is well now. She eats, she sleeps, and she spends her days fixing things," he added truthfully.

"Why hasn't she asked to come along with you?" she asked. "Why hasn't she wanted to let us know that she was all right?"

"Truthfully, she has wanted to see you. It was, regrettably, I who would not allow it. You see, I feared that the rage everybody felt toward her captor would fall ill in relation to me and that I would get the blame, despite being the one who rescued her."

"But if you really rescued her as you claim, we would have understood!"

"Lady Ruth," Jocephus said patiently, "with the entire Royal Guard and *Deutsches Kaiserreich* searching for your daughter, how likely would it be that I would not have been imprisoned? I am not military, nor am I a man that very many have heard of. I preferred to wait and talk sensibly to you first. Mothers know best, after all," he added sweetly, "and tend to be more nurturing and less... brash and overprotective as fathers, if I may."

"Oh, Master Gideon... You do not understand how happy you have made this old mother. When possible, I would like to inform my husband that our daughter is safe. He will deal with your reward."

"No reward necessary, Mum. Your blessing for your daughter's hand in marriage is reward enough for me."

"Master Gideon..." she started with a smile and tears of joy.

"Joss will do, Mum," he said gently. "Joss will do."

She stood to look out the large, angled windows, wringing her hands as any worried mother would. The airship came to a sea of clouds, then began to descend. Immediately, Lady Ruth became alarmed, as Jocephus expected; he wasn't concerned. He still had everything under control.

"Why are we descending into the Lands Below?" she asked, seemingly offended that somebody of her status need set foot in what was considered slums.

"This is where we were hiding. We needed to make sure the rest of the pirate crew did not find us."

"It's nothing but barren land!"

"Not true," he said, utilizing the intelligence from his paperwork. "There are tunnels all throughout the mountain range, as well as underground."

"I've... heard mention of this. You're right," she said with slight relief, yet still hesitant.

"Follow me, if you will." Jocephus led her to the hatch door and opened it, then tossed down the ladder, which dangled and danced below them as the zeppelin continued its slow descent. Lady Ruth looked horrified, but the Mage gave a comforting smile. "There is nowhere for my ship to land, so we must do this the difficult way. Don't worry," he added as he stepped onto the ladder first, descending until he was on the third rung, and held out a hand to help her. "I'll be with you the entire way."

The woman looked terrified. Ever patient in his perfect plan, Jocephus gently coaxed her. "Your daughter awaits, Mum. I want this reunion just as much as you do. *Dame* Magaliana deserves your comfort after everything that has happened."

Lady Ruth's eyes hardened with determination, though she trembled like a leaf when she accepted his hand. The ladder wiggled violently beneath them and she let out a loud screech, but the Mage comforted her as best he could, encouraging her to continue as he safely pinned her in between himself and the ladder.

"Match my steps," he instructed her.

Agonizingly slow and ever-so-cautious, they made their way down. Once at the bottom, Jocephus jumped off and pulled her down with him, steadying her so she did not fall. He spun her in the direction which they needed to walk. "This way."

The terrain was rough—Lady Ruth had quite the obvious hard time keeping up, all part of his flawless plan. Aiding her more often than not, he pointed ahead to a figure with dreadlocks just when the noble woman complained that she could not take another step.

"Magaliana!" Lady Ruth stumbled toward her daughter over the jagged landscape and tripped over the hem of her long dress, tearing it in the process. Falling, she scraped her hands and knees and wiped them carelessly as she stood back up. Jocephus figured that one of her knees bled where the burgundy fabric darkened. But she was so determined to reach the figure ahead, she continued on limping.

The airship had caught up to the Mage, per his instructions, and he stepped onto the ladder and was pulled up. Below him, the scavenger turned, and the noble woman halted in realization that the figure wasn't her daughter. She shrieked as the airship sped away.

A large explosion boomed beneath them. Despite his perfectly executed plan, Jocephus gritted his teeth, anxiously awaiting the report that they had evaded damage from the Carronade. He quickly looked out the window to the mauve mist surrounding the stricken area; it should have crushed Lady Ruth to the ground at her feet. He then glanced up at the hole in the overcast sky caused by the Carronade, which slowly closed as the clouds moved on.

Hearing footsteps approaching, Jocephus spun around. "Report."

"Everything is in order, Sir," said the captain. "Zero damage sustained."

"Excellent. Now back to the *Faugregir*. Once I disembark, head to Portugal to fetch the *Príncipe*."

"Aye, Sir."

Jocephus took a seat and shut his eyes. The first part of his plan had been executed almost flawlessly. Now he had but to wait to execute the next.

CHAPTER 22

Magaliana lost track of how many times she failed to imitate pure alchemy. She had watched Jocephus carefully but was clearly missing one or more steps because she just couldn't duplicate it. She even went so far as to break down each action individually, performing it again and again until it was satisfactory.

She had created the fire. That part was easy.

She had snuffed out the fire. That act was also a no-brainer, since she was an Alchemist. However, she could not get water from the smothered fire.

She adjusted her measures repeatedly and retraced through her mental notes, finally producing a few drops. Thrilled, she continued to tweak and improve her method until the water level was acceptable. The next task was trying to knead the sand into clay, and that was the step that had kept her frustrated most of the afternoon.

"My, you've come quite far already," said a familiar voice.

Startled, Magaliana spun around to see the Mage standing nearby with a platter of food. With a huff, she turned back around to her project, persistent on getting it to work. She did not care about the food; all she wanted was to succeed.

Jocephus chuckled as he set the plate down then slowly ran his fingers along her arms until he reached her hands, leading her through the alchemy. Magaliana got goosebumps from the initial contact. With difficulty, she shoved the fluttering sensation in her stomach aside in favor of watching his actions carefully.

The Mage had her create fire and snuff it out. She had done it so many times that it felt just as natural as he made it out to be. He aided her in pouring the water onto some sand, then forced her fingers to carefully knead it.

"Do you feel that?" he whispered in her ear. Shivers slid down her entire body and a shuddered breath escaped her. "You must knead it exactly right. There..."

Magaliana almost missed it while she wondered how this man affected her so. He was very charismatic, but sometimes she wondered if he was hypnotizing her.

There was an ever-so-slight difference in the sand, and she forced her mind to focus away from the mysterious Mage to the subject at hand. It did not look any different than wet sand normally did, but she definitely felt it. The more Jocephus led her hands to knead it, the more she felt the clay, and eventually saw it transform.

It was always so amazing to witness. She still couldn't believe that the Mage did all of this without a pendulum. Her heart racing in excitement, Magaliana slightly turned her head to try and look at him, but he stopped her. "Pay attention, Magaliana."

Her attention shot back to the clay. It began to harden and shine as it turned brassy, then hardened to bronze. Jocephus had her hold it in her left palm, then placed her right hand on top of the hardened glob.

"Are you ready?" he whispered in her ear, sending shivers down her body anew.

Before she could answer, he firmly pressed her hand into the bronze, and her mind spiraled back to focus. She met with some resistance—the clay was solid, after all—and she opened her mouth to protest but paused. The bronze crumbled as he led her to crush it. Her palms were eventually pressed together, sandwiched in between his. His right fingers gently dug in between hers and he pulled her top hand away, revealing a small pile of fine dust in her left palm. She inspected it closely before Jocephus closed her fingers around the dust and moved her hand over top of the jar where the fire had once been.

"Open your hand," he instructed.

Magaliana did as she was told, and Jocephus turned her hand sideways to spill the contents of her palm into the receptacle. She gasped at the sensation as she watched the fine powder-like substance instantly turn into a green liquid once it fell from her hand and touched the glass of the jar.

Jocephus had completely walked her through a transfiguration.

She tried to wrap her head around what they had just done, frustrated that she hadn't taken any physical notes. Those thoughts dissipated, however, when the Techno Mage gently trailed his fingers over her arms as he stepped away. Her eyelids fluttered shut at the gooseflesh.

"You'll get there on your own," he said. "I have faith in your abilities."

Magaliana's eyes shot open and she spun to face him. "Teach me more," she begged. "Please, teach me more."

She desperately wanted to learn this pure alchemy. Mostly, she wanted to prove to herself that alchemy really could be performed without a pendulum. Her curiosity was insatiable, especially when she couldn't figure it out on her own.

"Not just yet." Jocephus picked up the platter of food and headed back toward her. "I want to see how far you can get on your own. I want to see your limits."

Magaliana growled at his words. Fine. If he wouldn't teach her more, she'd have to figure it out on her own. She turned her back to him and attempted the transfiguration spell again.

"Please eat," she heard him say.

"I'm not hungry."

"Eat," he said, more sternly than his usual gentleness, "or I will not teach you anything."

Magaliana's heart skipped a beat and she spun back around to face the man who now sat in the grass, wondering if he was serious or not. The profoundly serious expression that replaced his usual charismatic smile made her reconsider her choice.

Defeated, she sighed as she joined him. She couldn't risk not having him teach her. She couldn't afford to not know the secrets of pure alchemy now that her curiosity was piqued.

When she bit into a piece of melon, the Techno Mage finally smiled. "You need food and water to survive," he said, in between bites of food. "It also keeps your mind sharp. Without a sharp mind, you can't focus, and you will not succeed in making pure alchemy. Just something to consider."

His words made sense. She needed to be careful and take her meal breaks. Perhaps that was why she hadn't been able to succeed in recreating the transfiguration lately. She really hadn't eaten much.

He tried some casual small talk while Magaliana nibbled on a tiny amount of food—enough to satisfy him—but she didn't pay much attention as her thoughts were purely focused on replaying the transmutation in her head. Sometimes it seemed simple, but when she went over it again, it suddenly seemed impossible.

She was so lost in thought that eventually she simply got to her feet and returned to trying to reproduce the spell. Eventually, she looked over her shoulder, a technical question burning on her lips, but Jocephus was no longer there. She wasn't sure if one minute had passed, or one hour. Shaking her head to rid the fog invading her mind, she turned her attention back to her work.

The sun eventually set, and Magaliana's progress was regressing. She had managed only once to knead the sand into clay, but she could not get it to harden and turn to bronze. When she tried again, she couldn't even get the sand to turn to clay. The longer she tried, the more even the simpler tasks such as creating water from the fire vapors seemed entirely too advanced for her.

She stood in the moonlight that pooled past the canopy, tired and frustrated. Growling, she pulled at the dreads in her hair and spun in place, exasperated. She quickly paused when she saw Jocephus before her with another plate of food. "I'm surprised that you are still awake at this hour, Magaliana. Normally, you would be asleep at the foot of one of the golems."

"I can't... I can't do it," she sighed, dropping her hands to her sides and her chin to her chest in defeat.

The Mage put the food down, took her hands, and softly spun her around to guide her once more. They had only reached the clay stage when Magaliana pulled her hands away from his.

She tried hard to focus on every single tiny movement that the man did, but her brain just couldn't handle it anymore. In fact, she often found herself thinking of how smooth his hands felt against hers instead. Pulling away from the Mage, she huffed and placed her palms against her temples.

"You should get some rest," he said compassionately, despite everything. "You're exhausted."

"Teach me!" she cried, spinning back around to face him. "Explain it to me with words, so that I can understand!"

"Words aren't needed. You need only feel," he replied, picking up the plate of food. "You need food and some sleep, then you can try this again tomorrow with a fresh view."

He gave her a tranquil smile as he offered the plate, but Magaliana slapped it out of his hands in frustration. She didn't want food or sleep; she wanted to master the transmutation!

At a barely-detectable twitch of annoyance in the Mage's features, her heart dropped, and the realization sank in of what she had just done. Tears welled up in her eyes and she parted her lips to apologize, but Jocephus whispered good night first and walked away.

Lips quivering, Magaliana waited until he disappeared on the lift before she fell to her knees and sobbed. Had her exhaustion and frustration finally gotten to Jocephus? Had she blown her chances of him teaching her more? She curled up in the grass by the dropped food and hugged herself as she cried.

"Ike..." she whispered. "Art..."

Eventually, she fell asleep.

CHAPTER 23

"*Príncipe* Francisco Braganza-Saxe-Co-burg," greeted the Techno Mage, arms open and welcoming in front of the large thick doors to Juliet. "T'is a pleasure to meet you."

The Portuguese man looked worse for wear; scales covered his entire naked body like a fish out of water. The Mage always enjoyed seeing how the haze affected everyone differently. He found it very interesting.

"I demand to be released at once!" the prince growled in a thick accent.

"*Príncipe*, we've no time for this at the moment," Jocephus said as he removed his silk shirt. "Besides—just look at yourself. You are a monster. Best remain here, where nobody can see you."

The monarch stared at the markings covering his captor's body, horrified. Spinning around to run away, he stumbled and fell instead.

The Mage hung his silky shirt off the lever as he always did, ignoring the attempt at escaping. "*Príncipe*, today is your lucky day! I saved your miserable little life!" he said with a grin. "But I'm not done with you yet. You will serve a greater purpose. Come."

The Prince scampered to his feet with difficulty, only to be grabbed by the unearthly attendant. Casting the man an unsympathetic look, Jocephus opened the door to the tropical room as the assistant shoved Francisco inside.

The thick doors closed behind them, and the Prince spun back, pounding on the thick steel with all his might.

"Let me out!" he cried in his native tongue.

"There is nowhere to go, so it would be best if you followed me."

"Where are you taking me?"

"To see your Queen," he replied simply.

When the Prince began pounding on the doors once more, Jocephus continued toward the dome.

"It's impolite to keep her waiting, you know..." he drawled over his shoulder.

The Prince made a sound of disgust, and Jocephus smirked. He knew Juliet's wiggling tentacles disturbed the hazed man—this wasn't the first time this happened, nor would it be the last—and more than likely that spooked him enough to join the Mage for protection.

Jocephus activated the door to the dome and once the steam exited the glass, the Prince gasped.

Lady Juliet's brows were furrowed in agony, her lips were curled, and her breath short. It always pained Jocephus to see her in such a state of hunger, but it was short-lived.

"What is this?" demanded Francisco. "What monstrosity is this?!"

"Monstrosity? Please, *Príncipe*, you are in the presence of the future Queen, and your creator. She is a Goddess."

Juliet opened her mouth, and a sweet-sounding dulcet tone escaped her. Unlike her shrieks, groans, whines, and moans, the melodic sound was soothing, drawing Francisco to her like a moth to light. Hypnotized, he ambled onto the platform, captivated by the siren's call. Jocephus proudly watched, a grin on his lips.

The tentacles in the dome untangled and reached out, coiling around the Prince like a snake until all that remained visible was his head. Lowered down between her legs until his nose was flush with her labia, he was then slowly pushed inside. Juliet's body stretched like rubber as she gradually swallowed him whole. Little by little, her tendrils released him so that she could fit more inside of her. She squirmed and shivered and shuddered, tiny moans escaping her as she continued her siren's call.

Once the Prince was fully inside of her, Juliet shut her mouth, ending the melody. The Prince, curled up inside of her enormously stretched stomach, snapped out of his trance. Through her translucent skin, Jocephus watched him try to kick and punch his way out, panicked.

Tilting her head back, Juliet swallowed. At that action, the monarch was instantly crushed. Her semitransparent belly was suddenly painted red as blood gushed forth from between her legs and landed in the mana puddle at her feet.

"Do you feel better, my love?" Jocephus stepped toward the woman, caressing her cheek with his hand.

Kneeling, he ran his fingers through the blood-soaked mana, swirling it together. It was her own little life circle; the blood of the hazed mixed with the pure alchemy created a stronger haze whenever the Carronade fired. Jocephus always wished to dissect the hazed and study them, but not only was it dangerous for him, he would also be depriving his beloved of her meal.

He stood back up and lifted her chin with his bloodied fingers, placing a kiss upon her lips before he walked away and locked everything behind him. The next step in his agenda was breakfast with the Alchemist.

CHAPTER 24

"Magaliana..."

She stirred in her sleep when Ikarim spoke her name. It was so unlike him to use her given name fully instead of simply calling her Mags.

"Magaliana, I brought breakfast."

Her eyes shot open and she sat up instantly, disoriented. Where were Ikarim and Arteus? Where was Gesselmeyer? Who was the man kneeling in front of her?

The gentle smile on his lips brought her senses back to reality. She exhaled deeply and rubbed at her eyes.

"Were you working all night?" he asked as he set the platter down.

"No, I fell asleep not long after you left."

Jocephus chuckled lightly. "I told you that you were exhausted..."

"You did." She watched him take a few bites from his bread and vegetables, and frowned as she recalled the events from the previous night. "Joss, I..." she started, but fell short.

"Hmm?"

"I want to apologize for my actions last night. Please... Please don't reconsider teaching me..."

The Techno Mage wiped his hands as he finished his bite. There was no apparent anger or annoyance anywhere on his features. "Frankly, Magaliana..." he began, his ice blue eyes finally meeting hers, "... I had forgotten about it."

"I..."

"I believe that I must also apologize," he interrupted. "You see, I am really just some stranger who refused to satiate your curiosity and incredible desire to succeed."

"Joss..." Magaliana sighed. She did not expect him to apologize. She did not think he needed to.

"I just have a specific way of teaching, you see. I need to see what you can do at your best... and at your worst. And for that, I apologize in advance. Allow me to teach you something simple as my proof of apology. Come closer."

Magaliana tilted her head in consideration, then crawled around the platters until she was next to him. Jocephus extended his hand to take one of hers. Hesitant, she cautiously allowed him, and he turned her hand over.

"The ability to perform alchemy and transmute items not only depends on how well the alchemist is able to follow instructions, but also how well they know their history."

With his index finger, Jocephus slowly traced a large circle into her palm. "Alchemy, a type of chemistry, comes from the Arabian word '*al-kimia*', which refers to the preparation of elixirs by the Egyptians."

He gently traced a triangle inside the circle's circumference. "The Arabic part '*kimia*', in turn, comes from the Ancient Egyptian Coptic word '*khem*', which referred to the dark mystery of the primordial First Matter... but also the fertile black soil of the Nile."

Inside the edges of the triangle, Jocephus traced a square. "It is believed that this symbol..." he traced a circle inside of the previous shape, "...plus a man... and a woman..." he added as he traced the masculine and feminine symbols next to one another inside the smaller circle, "...was all that was needed to create the Philosopher's Stone."

The Techno Mage brought Magaliana's palm up to his lips, and gently blew on it. Magaliana, captivated by the history lesson, got goosebumps from the sensation. The invisible transmutation circle inside of her hand began to glow a golden color. She gasped in awe when what appeared to be a fine dust materialized from Jocephus' breath. Soon, she had a palm full of sand.

He pulled his face away and reached for her other hand, cupping it down atop of the granules. He then tapped the top of her hand three times. It felt as if the sand grew heavier with each touch. Pulling her top hand away, the Mage revealed that her palm held a solid rock instead.

Magaliana's eyes widened in astonishment. Was this really the Philosopher's Stone in her hand? Was it truly that simple? She felt that she had to forget everything she knew about alchemy to make sense of it all.

"Clearly, concocting a Philosopher's Stone requires a great deal more complicated moves than this, so this isn't it," Jocephus said matter-of-factly. As he spoke, the rock crumbled and turned to dirt. Magaliana gasped and quickly cupped her free hand next to the other one to prevent it all from spilling.

Jocephus rose and created alchemical fire, which he extinguished and turned to water. Returning, he poured it over the earth in her hands, and it immediately germinated. Shoots peeked up from the soil and reached for the sunlight in the cemetery. Eyes wide in amazement, Magaliana let out an excited squeak as small buds appeared and blossomed into beautiful flowers.

Grabbing the flowers by the stems, the Mage cut them from the roots and handed Magaliana the bouquet with a smile. She released the earth as she accepted them, shut her eyes, and inhaled the fragrant aromas.

"Apology accepted?" Jocephus asked.

Magaliana giggled. The Techno Mage really wasn't a bad man at all; he was smart and accomplished with his alchemy.

"Yes," she said as she opened her eyes. "I accept your apology."

Magaliana bent over the bottom half of the golem that afternoon, in so deep that she had to occasionally swing her legs for balance to keep from sliding inside the towering being. Her arms were barely long enough to reach the bolt with the wrench. A few unladylike words escaped her as she tried to loosen a particularly rusted joint, which would allow her to continue taking apart the idol to see how it worked.

A knock on the brass startled her. She screamed, dropped her tool, and cussed again. Extending her legs, she swung them downward which gave her the strength and momentum to pull her upper body out of the golem, balancing perfectly on the lower part of her midriff. She heard a faint chuckle from behind and turned her attention to Jocephus with a glare.

"The knocking was meant to draw your attention so that you would not be startled by my voice. It appears my plan backfired. Here, allow me to help you down."

Still scowling, Magaliana eyed him for a moment before she slowly climbed down the ladder and grabbed the Mage's offered hand. He helped her down onto the grass and pulled her into him to help her regain her balance.

Jocephus reached for her chin and gently lifted it to better inspect her. Magaliana raised a brow, confused, even though her face grew hot.

He smirked. "You have dirt and oil on your face. It suits you."

Magaliana finally cracked a smile. She was normally always complimented by her suitors when she wore dresses; even Jocephus had admired her when she wore Lady Juliet's clothing. But the Mage approved of her even when she was filthy, and it elated her. It was refreshing to have somebody accept her for being herself, and not simply because she was a noble.

"Are you attempting to court me, *Herr* Gideon?" she asked coyly.

"If I was," he replied in German, which made her heart flutter, "would you allow me to?"

Her cheeks were suddenly warm, and she became hyper aware that he was still holding her. Tongue-tied, she could only meet his tender gaze.

"I brought you gifts," he added in his native tongue. He gently released her and stepped toward a pile of leather-bound notebooks sitting on a nearby stump, picked up the top one, and flipped through it quickly before he handed it to her. "My personal notes."

Magaliana took the notebook and gasped as she quickly scanned the three first pages. "Your alchemy notes!" She scanned a few more, then flipped back to the first page in order to study it more intently. "Oh, Joss..."

"You can borrow them. Study them."

Magaliana looked up and noticed his adoring gaze. She blushed faintly and parted her lips to speak, but paused, turning her attention toward the lift to find the cook with plates of food.

"Ah! Good man," Jocephus said. When she turned her attention back to him, he sheepishly mouthed that his hands were full as he pointed toward the leather books. Magaliana smirked.

They ate lunch and discussed alchemy, but every time Magaliana asked Jocephus to run her through the pure alchemy transmutation again, he refused.

"Why not?" she frowned.

"I told you: I need to see what you can do at your best and worst. Look over my notes. Study them. Practice them, then try and recreate the transmutation from memory. I want to see how much further you can get on your own."

She was disappointed, but also excited to dive into the Mage's notes. She desperately wanted to know how everything was done without the aid of a pendulum and wondered what other secrets had been kept from her during her schooling.

Magaliana was deep into the first notebook when Jocephus had returned for tea later in the afternoon.

"How goes the studies?" he asked.

"It's all so fascinating!" she admitted. "It's surprisingly in depth compared to anything I've ever read or been taught on the subject!"

Jocephus poured the tea as Magaliana placed the notebook down. They discussed what she had already gone over, and eventually she grabbed the journal again to go back over the notes she had already read.

She blinked in shock as it disappeared from her hands. With a frown, she reached for the notebook, but Jocephus pulled it just out of reach with a playful smirk.

"Joss, please!" she giggled. "Give it back."

She stretched and stretched, eventually getting to her knees, but he continued to hold it just inches away from her reach. Trying once more, her eyes went wide when she lost her balance, falling into him. A chuckle escaped him as he fell into the grass, then began to read aloud from his notes. Blushing as she rolled off and laid on the ground next to him, Magaliana listened attentively.

After dinner, Jocephus finally agreed—somewhat—to teach Magaliana. She traced the transmutation circle in her palm just as he did earlier in the morning.

"When you blow, it has to be just right," he said. "Recall the sensation. Recreate it. Don't do it too hard or too softly, or you'll get something else entirely."

Magaliana leaned into her palm and took an intake of breath. She shut her eyes and tried to recall exactly at what intensity he did it. When she was ready, she opened her eyes and blew softly.

Nothing happened. The transmutation circle didn't even start to glow. She tried again, a little harder. Still nothing. With a frown, she took a deep intake, but Jocephus gently placed his free hand over her mouth.

"Recall the sensation," he reminded her. "I didn't blow that hard."

She released her breath through her nose and shut her eyes. When he moved his hand away, she opened them again. "This is so much more difficult than using salt or sand and a pendulum," she huffed.

"I agree, but it's worth it. And when you can succeed at this, you'll be able to accomplish so much. *We*..." he emphasized, "... can accomplish so much. Try again."

She raised a brow, confused as to what he meant, but eventually she shut her eyes, trying to remember the sensation once more. She recalled that it was gentle enough to give her goosebumps. She honed in on that sensation, her heart palpitating as she thought back to the Mage doing it again.

That was it—it was now or never. She kept her eyes closed and held onto the memory, the sensation, and blew. Her breath escaped her in a faint shudder, and she felt the heat in her cheeks from the blush. She opened her eyes to check on her progress only to find that, once again, nothing occurred.

"What does this mean?" she asked.

"It means that you need to study more." He handed her one of the notebooks. "And that practice makes perfect."

Jocephus stood up, but Magaliana remained on her knees in defeat, placing the notebook at her side. Tears stung her eyes and threatened to fall. She just couldn't understand the pure alchemy. She allowed a shuddered breath to escape her instead of a sob.

Suddenly, Jocephus pulled her to her feet. Surprised, she noticed his sympathetic expression; before she could say anything, he spun her around, took her hands in his, and helped her recreate the pure alchemy once more.

CHAPTER 25

It had been three days. Stubborn, Magaliana came along further and further in her studies. She did, on occasion, manage to fully replicate a few of the transfigurations from the notebooks—without a pendulum!—in front of Jocephus; however, there were other times that she failed when she tried again.

The Mage visited her often. They sat together for every meal, mostly holding lengthy discussions about alchemy, and Jocephus read to her from various notebooks during their afternoon tea. Magaliana could feel herself becoming drawn ever closer to him. He seemed so attentive and caring, and even encouraged her to get dirty and dig for the answers to her questions. Before leaving, he would always help her replicate some transfigurations up to a certain point.

That night, they laid on the grass—Magaliana's head opposite the Techno Mage's—and looked up past the tree canopy. They discussed the stars in relation to alchemy, then both fell silent. Jocephus was the first to break it after a long while. "Why don't you ever leave the cemetery? You are not confined to this floor, alone..."

"I like it here. This is the only place that I don't feel imprisoned."

She knew that her sentiment was biased as she had very rarely ventured anywhere else, but her initial purpose was to keep busy... And keep busy she did.

The Mage eventually got up.

"Must you leave so soon?" she asked with a pout.

Jocephus gave her a dejected smile and bent down, extending his hands out to help her up. He did not release her, even after she regained her footing. Her heart sank at his troubled look, and she wondered if she was the cause. "Joss? What's wrong?"

"I am torn. Originally, I was to return you to *Herr* Wiegraf, but..."

She frowned. She didn't like where the conversation was going. When she began to pull away, he suddenly stopped her.

"Magaliana." He took both of her hands in his, getting down on one knee. "I know that we have not known one another for very long, but every moment that I've spent in your presence these last few days have been nothing short of extraordinary. Enchantress, you have cast your transmutation circle about my heart, for you are all I think about night and day. The first time I touched your hands, I couldn't imagine not being able to hold them. And your smile... A single smile from you puts one thousand in my heart. I have barely scratched the surface in learning about you, but I want so much more. I wish to know you intimately... inside and out. Magaliana..."

She swallowed hard, knowing what his next words would be. She trembled in anticipation.

"Will you fulfill my wishes and deepest desires by becoming my wife?"

"Oh, Joss..." she whispered. The conversation didn't go where she thought it would. In fact, this was so unexpected that she could barely formulate a proper contemplation. She thought that he was going to change his mind about turning her in, that she was going to be a prisoner forever. Now she understood why he was torn.

As much as she wished that everything returned to normal, that she would be reunited with her friends, she realized that she was also content with her new normal. Learning pure alchemy made her happy. Trying to revive the golems made her happy. She even looked forward to the Mage's visits. Rejecting her suitors was only to spite her family because she did not want to be forced into marriage.

Jocephus was not forcing her. He was not a suitor sent by her father. Magaliana realized that she had fallen hard. Tears stung her eyes, but they were not from sadness.

"Yes! Yes, I will be your wife."

Jocephus swiftly stood back up, gently cupping her face with both hands. He leaned his forehead against hers as he touched her lips with his thumbs. "Your words have made me so incredibly happy."

***

Magaliana actually ventured out and away from the golem cemetery the next day, exploring more of the *Faugregir*.

She wandered to the kitchens and surprised the cooks, found her way to Juliet's chambers and had a long, well-needed bath, ventured outside and simply admired the scenery of the floating isle of an airship, and also explored more of the other floors, eventually finding the forbidden one.

An attendant stood guard in front of the lift. Magaliana approached, but unlike the other assistants who gladly allowed her onto the platform, the large, square-jawed man did not budge. Tentative, Magaliana politely asked if she could get to the next floor, but her request was met with silence.

When she tried to squeak her way past him, the attendant quickly snatched her arm. She gasped in surprise at the man's speed, given his muscular size, and glared when he shoved her back, barely managing to keep her balance. Rubbing her sore arm, she defensively raised her hands and walked away.

"What's on the floor that I can't explore?" she asked the meditating Mage the moment she arrived in his quarters.

Jocephus glanced over his shoulder with a smile. "It fills me with joy to finally see you out of the cemetery."

"Joss..."

Turning his attention back in front of himself, he was silent. With a frown, she started to speak again, but Jocephus finally replied. "It is what keeps the isle afloat."

"Is it alchemy?"

Another long pause. "Something like that."

"Will you allow me to see it, someday?"

"... Someday."

"Will you let me leave?"

Jocephus finally spun around from his position on the floor to look long and hard at her. She had fully captured his attention. "Have you reconsidered my proposal already?"

Magaliana quickly shook her head. "No, it's just that... I need to return to *Doktor* Gesselmeyer's home to get my belongings. I also need to shop for a wedding dress." Jocephus stood up and slowly approached, but Magaliana continued. "I need to inform my extended family of our engagement, I need..." Tears welled in her eyes, and her voice broke. "I need to know if Ike and Art are alright. They could still be with Captain Keenan, or worse! They could—"

The Mage interrupted her by placing an index finger onto her lips. He smiled that gentle smile she loved so much. "Your friends are well; they have been rescued by the Royal Guard."

Magaliana sobbed with joy and he wrapped his arms around her in comfort. He wiped at her tears when she calmed down.

"Alas, for the rest of your requests, the two rules that I set in place when you first arrived are still active: You have free reign of the *Faugregir* except for one floor... And that you can have anything and everything except freedom from the *Faugregir*, unless I take you someplace with me."

Taken aback, she blinked, confused. Why was she still being held prisoner? "Why?"

"I am a figment of most people's imagination, Magaliana, as is my ship. I prefer to keep it that way."

Tears welled up in her eyes again. Her heart felt like it was being crushed in a vise. Jocephus' expression changed to confusion, then tenderness as he tried to wipe the tears away from her eyes. "Why are you crying, my dove?"

"I just fear that your words mean I will never again see Ike and Art. They are my best friends. I will perhaps never hear from them or my family ever again, either."

"Are you reconsidering?" he asked, pained.

She did not answer. It was her turn to be torn. Could she really abandon everyone for a man that she had technically been sold to only days prior?

"Magaliana..." the Mage started.

"Joss, please!" she begged as another sob threatened to escape her. "If I cannot leave and am to abandon everything and everyone, then please, at the very least, allow Ike, Art, and my parents to come to the wedding!"

Jocephus' eyes hardened. Magaliana whimpered. She had just made the hardest decision in his favor; would he still refuse her?

"Please, Joss..." she begged, unable to keep her voice from cracking. "Please allow me my friends and parents. It can be my wedding gift. I will ask for nothing more."

He turned away from her and began to pace, deep in contemplation. Magaliana joined her hands together and brought them to her mouth in silent prayer. Her legs felt like jelly, and she was even afraid to breathe, lest it change his mind.

Returning to her, he seemed hesitant, but then smiled. "Of course. My wedding gift to you, my dove."

Magaliana cried, relieved. The Mage wrapped his arms around her until she calmed down, wiping at her tearstained cheeks.

"You have made me a happy woman," she said.

"And I will never stop doing such. I have one condition, however..."

Magaliana didn't know how much more of this she could take. Casting him a concerned look, she dared to ask.

"That we not wed on the *Faugregir* in order to preserve its secrecy." He took her hand in his, a gentle gesture of comfort. Raising it to his lips, he kissed her knuckles ever-so-softly. "I can arrange another airship. One of my most grand, next to the *Faugregir*. Would this be satisfactory?"

Magaliana nodded and smiled, the anxiety leaving her like a heavy wave of relief.

The Mage slowly released her hands and stepped away from her. "Write your letters, and I will send them out post haste."

"Thank you," Magaliana whispered.

"I must warn you," Jocephus added, pausing at the door. "There shall be no mention of the *Faugregir* whatsoever."

"Of course."

He opened the door and vanished, leaving Magaliana alone in his quarters.

CHAPTER 26

Ikarim stepped out of Gesselmeyer's empty shop. Everything had been sold—from the tiniest screw to the plot of floating land that the shop was on. His eyes fell on Arteus, who watched a large airship drift off with the remaining items.

Darley dropped them off at the mansion the morning after their rescue, and Ikarim spent the whole day in his room silently replaying the events since Gesselmeyer's death in his mind. He wondered how he was supposed to return to normal without the Scientist who raised him and the Alchemist he had grown to love.

Both mechanics barely spoke as the days went on. What little exchange they had involved brief discussions about what to do with the shop. Eventually, Arteus decided to sell it. It was a hard decision for his friend, but Ikarim was proud of him: Instead of wallowing further in his depression, he had actively done something. Ikarim knew that it had, for the most part, kept his mind off everything.

Stopping next to the Strong Arm, he noticed a sorrowful look on the thin man's features.

"Here," Arteus said as he held out a large bag of coins.

"What's this?"

"Five hundred *Gulden*, all yours."

"What?!" Ikarim choked. "Why are you giving that to me?"

"I've absolutely no use for it."

"Art, you've lost your mind. Keep it."

"Ike, please, take it," Arteus implored, his expression more pathetic with each passing minute.

Ikarim sighed and placed a hand on his friend's shoulder, giving him a reassuring smile. "Let's go home and talk about it over dinner. I think that we both need to get our minds off things, for a while."

Ikarim helped the cook make a rather simple beef stew for dinner, and despite agreeing to talk about the money for the sales, both men instead ate in silence. Arteus played somberly on the grand piano with countless careless mistakes, making Ikarim cringe as he quickly finished up with the dishes. His friend was usually a wonderful pianist; he loved listening to him expertly play, even though he himself couldn't carry a tune to save his life. At that moment, however, it seemed that his friend was too distracted and couldn't carry one, either.

Newspaper in hand, Ikarim made a speedy beeline to the library in an attempt to somewhat drown out the musical blunders. The paper was littered with text-dense chunks of ads for underwear and outerwear, furnishings, perfumes, *laufmaschine*, and analytical engines—he was hard-pressed to find any actual news articles. The ones that he did find, however, were just as disheartening as the muffled piano playing.

One article mentioned that the Carronade fired in Germany, which was excessively rare so soon after the previous time. Ikarim wondered if any members of royalty were caught in Ground Zero as the Prince of Portugal once was.

Another column mentioned a hefty reward set by *Herr* Wiegraf for the safe return of both his daughter and his wife. With a frown, Ikarim parted his lips to call out to Arteus, but he reconsidered—Arteus didn't need cause to be more depressed than he already was. He continued reading in case it offered any details as to how Lady Ruth disappeared, but the article offered nothing but an unfortunate reality that they were no closer to finding her or Magaliana.

As he scanned the pages for another report amidst the sea of advertisements, something caught his attention: the mention of the sky pirate Captain Benedict Keenan having escaped his trial. Ikarim's heart sank and he called out to Arteus as he rushed out of the library, skidding to a halt at the doorframe.

"... said that the Captain of the Doom Crusaders was nowhere to be found, moments before his trial was set to have started," he muttered as he read the article. "Art!"

"... had previously been apprehended off the coast of Fiji. The adopted sons of Gesselmeyer were rescued from that apprehension and are still considered safe. If anyone knows of the sky pirate's whereabouts, contact the military immediately," he finished aloud. His gaze travelled from the newspaper to his friend, who stood before him now.

"Do you think he'll be back for us?" Arteus asked.

Ikarim really didn't want to admit it to himself, much less his friend. "I doubt it..." He swallowed hard, knowing that he wasn't very convincing. Clearing his throat, he tried again. "He's too smart to get caught a second time."

Arteus stared at him, and Ikarim had a feeling he was either searching for the lie, or trying to convince himself of it, too. "I hope you're right." Ikarim dropped his gaze back to his paper to continue reading, but paused when Arteus added, "Why won't you accept the money, Ike?"

He said nothing at first. Why was the Strong Arm bringing this up now, of all possible times?

"I don't need it," he replied without looking up.

"You could add it to your funds..."

"I have plenty."

"You could travel the world," Arteus tried. "Fulfill your deepest desires."

Ikarim inhaled and exhaled deeply as he met his friend's serious gaze. "Save it, Art. Save it for yourself. Who knows what you will need to buy now that..." he stopped himself. He didn't want to mention Gesselmeyer's death.

"Why are you always so calm?" Arteus glowered.

Ikarim blinked in confusion. "Pardon me?"

"You're always so calm. It's as if you don't care."

"I do care, Art..." Ikarim frowned.

"Then show it! *Vater* passed away, we've been held hostage, we don't know if Mags is alive or not, and you're just... you're just..."

"Art," he started, choosing his words carefully, "I do care. But I need time to think things through. I need to be a rock and keep you out of your moods—"

"What moods?" Arteus hissed.

"You wallow in your depression. And you're quick to anger. I always have to keep you here, centered, pulling you back from the extremities."

"Oh ho, so you are a saint, are you?"

"I never said that..." Ikarim sighed.

"Do you think that you are better than me because you don't have cybernetic extremities?"

Ikarim shut his eyes and pinched the bridge of his nose. Why did he have to take everything so negatively? "You're also quick to jump to conclusions..." He looked to his friend once more. "You're veering way off the original topic. Let's calm down and try to be rational about this—"

Arteus got in Ikarim's face. "Make me."

"Wh—what?" he shrank back.

The thin man put up his dukes. "You want me to calm down, make me calm down."

Ikarim took a step back, hands up defensively. "Art, I'm not fighting you."

"Oh? Do you finally care? Are you finally feeling something? Like fear?"

Ikarim rolled his eyes. "I'm not afraid, Art, I just know that I can't win a physical fight with a Strong Arm. So please... Put your fists down, and let's talk like adults."

Arteus' eyes went wild in anger. "I'm not a child!"

Ikarim saw the swing coming and quickly dodged. The cybernetic fist flew inches away from his face, but it was the next blow that Ikarim hadn't expected; the Strong Arm's other mitt hit him right in his bruised side.

He cried out in pain as his whole world went dark. He fell to his hands and knees, teeth clenched against the pain. It was only seconds, but it felt like hours before he could breathe again. From his position on the floor, he turned his head and looked up at Arteus. The Strong Arm's eyes were wide in fear. He took a few steps back, then spun around and rushed down the hall, eventually slamming a door.

With a shuddered breath, Ikarim allowed himself to fall onto the floor in pain.

CHAPTER 27

Magaliana had gathered all the necessary tools and ingredients after sending out her letters and doing some small preparations for her wedding. She was determined to succeed at recreating pure alchemy. She had practiced hard and studied even harder, and Jocephus had even walked her through portions of the transmutation so many times she lost count. She wanted to finally do this on her own.

Creating the fire with ease, she snuffed it out and emptied the water onto a plate of sand. She dipped her index finger into the mix and stirred, then began to knead. The sand turned to clay, the clay turned to brass, and the brass turned to bronze. Cupping the bronze in between her hands, she paused.

She wondered if she would ever get the transmutation right. She had failed time and time again, what made this time any different?

She began to doubt herself, but she shook her head to set her thoughts straight.

She was content. Sure, she had been sold to the Techno Mage, but she had quickly grown to like him, and eventually love him. He understood her passion. She couldn't even discuss alchemy with Ikarim and Arteus the way that she could with Jocephus. A smile made its way to her lips as she thought about her husband-to-be, and butterflies fluttered in her stomach.

She had renewed determination. She could do it. She needed to do it.

Pressing her hands together, she crushed the bronze into a fine dust. Her heart raced as she pulled her top hand away, grabbing a nearby bottle. When she poured the sand and it turned into a green liquid, Magaliana squealed with excitement. Grabbing the bottle of pure alchemy that Jocephus made, she compared them side by side, turning slightly in order to get better light. Her eyes then focused past the bottles to the meticulously-deconstructed golem in the cemetery.

Her mind raced. Could she revive it?

She made her way over to the construct. With her tools nearby, she began to put the golem back together, piece by piece.

Hours went by before she heard her name being spoken. She quickly spun around, startled, and gave the Mage a determined glare.

"I figured that you would be here. I came to check on you as you have missed lunch, but...

What are you doing, my dove? Why have you once again locked yourself up in the cemetery?"

"Joss!" Magaliana rushed into his arms. "The golems. Please teach me how to revive them."

Jocephus chuckled lightly. "I've told you, only I can revive them."

"What do I need in order to be able to revive them like you?"

He smiled that soft smile she loved so much as he cupped her cheeks. "You are filled with so much wonder and curiosity. I have always admired your eagerness to learn, Magaliana."

He placed a kiss upon her brow, but Magaliana was growing impatient. She had a feeling that she knew exactly what he was going to say, and she wanted to show him what she had accomplished. "Joss..." she started, trying to get him back on track.

He inhaled and exhaled deeply before he met her gaze once more. "Well, for starters, you need to be able to perform pure alchemy."

It was Magaliana's turn to smile, though hers was more an excited grin. She shoved her hands into the pockets of her overalls and retrieved the two bottles.

"I can, and I did!" she said proudly. "Please, Joss... Please teach me."

Jocephus' smile faltered some, and this worried her. "My dove... Though I'm the only one who can do it... I don't do it. Hence the cemetery."

Magaliana's hands dropped and her smile vanished, defeated. Saddened, she lowered her head. Why wouldn't he allow her to try? Was it difficult? Was it impossible? Feeling the Mage's tender touch on her chin, he lifted her face to look at him. His lips were pressed together to form a straight line. "I'll look through my other notes and see what I can find for you."

His hand trailed from her chin to stroke her cheek. She smiled, relieved, and leaned into his touch. She was glad he was so understanding of her curiosity and determination. "Thank you."

"Anything for you, my dove," he said as he lowered his hands to take hers, leading her to the lift. "Let us get something to eat first."

Nodding, she followed him. Once on the platform, she cast a glance at the dismantled golem. This new task was going to be more difficult as it involved more than just alchemy. But she couldn't wait to prove herself more than capable.

CHAPTER 28

It took Magaliana three days to put the go-lem back together. She had thankfully been meticulous in the way that she decon-structed it; cleaning the construct took up more time than reassembling it.

Sliding down the giant shoulder, she ad-mired her own work once she was back on the ground. "We'll get you moving again in no time," she told it, almost fondly.

She fetched a lone notebook Jocephus had brought her after all the others. Flipping through the pages to one in particular, she skimmed over the notes before reaching into a bucket of items nearby, pulling out a large sy-ringe. Shoving it into her pocket with the bottles of green liquid, she set the notebook down at the golem's feet, then ventured around the con-struct to its back. Climbing the ladder, she reached the control panel.

She had already visually inspected all the vein-like wires to make sure they were free of holes and well-connected during the recon-struction, but she inspected the ones in the panel again to be sure. Reaching for the syringe and one of the bottles, she drew the green liquid into the glass barrel, then shoved the needle into a minuscule hole in the panel. She pressed the plunger and emptied the syringe of the fluid, then arched her back to observe the golem's head.

Nothing happened.

With a frown, she tilted her head, wondering if she had done something wrong. She circled the construct, making sure that there was no liq-uid leaking out before she filled the syringe with the second bottle and fed it into the control panel. Still nothing. Magaliana reached in, run-ning her fingers over the veins and wiggling them slightly to get the liquid to flow through them. Nothing.

"You are a hungry fella, aren't you?" she said to the golem as she climbed down the ladder.

She struggled to transmute five more bottles and finally started to see the green liquid through the veins. But unlike the bright liquid from the glass bottles, it seemed murky and dull.

"Your wires are pretty dusty, but don't you worry. Once it starts coursing through you, they'll clean out, and you'll be good as new."

Magaliana was exhausted after she transmuted seven more bottles. Wiping her brow, she gritted her teeth and urged herself to keep going. She was so close...

The liquid had spread through the vein-like wires to fill the construct, and she screwed the panel cover back on before she climbed down the ladder and made her way back to the single notebook that laid in the grass. Picking it up, she skimmed through the notes one final time, then dropped the journal at her feet, stretched her arms above her head, and clasped her fingers together. She stretched as much as she could, rising to her toes and resting back into the grass, extending her arms and palms forward, rolling her shoulders a few times and wiggling her extremities. Finally, she clapped her hands together and rubbed them furiously. It was now or never.

She drew a transmutation circle in the palm of her hand. It was a bit more complicated than the previous ones, but she knew she could do it. After all, she could now create pure alchemy.

Once she was done with the symbols in her palm, she traced similar ones on the bottom of the golem's body. Both transmutation circles glowed bright white for a moment, and it took everything that her exhausted mind had to stay focused and not jump for joy.

A startled flock of birds took flight, and Magaliana thought the golem had moved ever-so- slightly before the symbols faded to nothing.

She stared at it, tilting her head. The golem did not move. She waved her left arm, then her right. Still nothing. Huffing, she brought her hands to her hips, deep in thought. Grabbing the notebook, she read the notes three times. She had done everything right... So why was it not working?

She climbed the ladder back to the control panel. Fiddling around elbow-deep, she pulled her arm back out and inspected the vein-like wires. "I can't tell if the liquid is coursing yet or not. Your wires are too small and dirty. But your fire did not ignite, so I'm going to have to do it for you. Hang on."

The young woman climbed down the ladder and walked over to an oil lamp. Igniting it, she grabbed a small stick and returned to the golem. Lighting the stick with the fire from the lamp, Magaliana reached back into the golem to ignite the fire manually. With it lit, she waited, hopeful, but still nothing happened.

"There's no steam..." she glanced around, deep in thought, until her eyes rested on the oil lamp in her other hand. She had an idea.

Magaliana took the lantern apart and carefully lifted the warm glass globe to get a better look at it. Her gaze travelled to the interior of the golem, and with some difficulty, she maneuvered the object into the construct in an attempt to cover the flame, but the globe was too big. She pulled it back out and climbed down the ladder, making her way to her supplies.

She found a string and wrapped it around the globe multiple times. Tying it, she pulled the tied string down and off the globe.

Gathering her platter with some sand and her pendulum, she went old-school with her alchemy to create the next two ingredients that she needed. She felt more comfortable doing it that way. With a swing of her pendulum, she followed the secret directions and recreated her transmutations.

Magaliana left the string soaking in the new liquid as she left the cemetery to gather some cold water. Upon her return, she fished out the soaked string and placed it back on the globe. She easily created fire in a jar to the side, then lifted the glass over it. The string caught fire and she spun the globe quickly, watching the string burn. Once the flames died, she immediately submerged the globe in the frigid basin for water.

The globe broke in two where the string was, and Magaliana inspected it closely. The edge wasn't perfect. She wished Ikarim was around to help with that sort of thing, but for the time being, the jagged edges would do.

Returning to the control panel, she carefully maneuvered the piece of the globe to fit atop of the flame and pipe at the core.

Steam quickly filled the core as Magaliana pulled her hands back. She practically slid down the ladder to see what the golem looked like as steam escaped every nook and cranny. Her smile of anticipation became an excited grin when the eyes lit up.

This time the golem did move. The squealing from the gears starting up after so long and the whistling and hissing from the steam were almost deafening from such a large construct, but Magaliana did not cover her ears. When the cacophony died down, the golem looked at her and began to turn around.

"Halt!" Magaliana cried, pushing her arm forward and palm outward.

The transmutation circle on her hand and on the golem glowed blue, then green. The golem stopped. Magaliana blinked, both in shock and exuberance. It worked. It actually worked.

"Return to me," she ordered, her heart racing, threatening to beat right out of her ribcage. "Please."

The golem turned back toward Magaliana and kneeled before her.

She cautiously stepped forward and slowly placed her hand on the golem's knee. The glowing symbols vanished.

"I did it..." she whispered. "I did it!" She had to tell Jocephus. She had to show him that his notes had helped her. She had to show him that all thanks to him, she was able to revive the golems in the cemetery.

Magaliana spun around to rush toward the lift, only to find Jocephus already nearby, his ice blue eyes focused on the golem.

"Joss!" she shouted. "I did it!"

He didn't show the excitement that she hoped that he would. In fact, his expression was unreadable, his eyes never leaving the revived construct.

"Joss?" she said tentatively as she approached him. "Is everything alright?"

Jocephus suddenly spun around and rushed toward the lift.

"Joss!?" Magaliana blinked, confused. She reached out for him, but he was too quick. "Joss, wait!"

She started to rush after the Mage, but the golem began to move, so she turned back around and held out her hand for it to stop. The construct finished standing back to its full height, then stopped moving.

Magaliana glanced over her shoulder. Jocephus was gone. Had she made him angry?

CHAPTER 29

"We've succeeded!"

Jocephus had rushed back to Lady Juliet to tell her the news. He stood before her translucent body in the humid room, practically out of breath.

"*Dame* Wiegraf has not only recreated pure alchemy, but she has revived one of the golems. She is progressing so much faster than I had anticipated..." he began to pace the platform, his mind racing on possibilities that were once out of reach. "United, with the *Dame*, I will be unstoppable."

The being before him whined and her lips twisted in pain. Jocephus returned to her, gently cupping one of her slimy cheeks in his hand and stroking it with his thumb.

"Do not protest, my love. I will finally be able to create a cure for you. I just need to convince her to combine our alchemy, which I shall do post haste..." he leaned in and placed a soft kiss to her lips. The creature moaned in response, before another whine escaped her. He pulled away and wiped the goo from his lips with the back of his free hand. "I think it's about time that we go and fetch Lady Ruth for you, hmm? This means that we will have to push the wedding forward. You will have to be a little more patient."

Juliet's whine was a little louder than before. Jocephus smiled softly. "Now, now. Don't be jealous, my love." He moved his hand up and petted the tendrils at the top of her head. "I'm doing this for you, remember?"

Pulling away, he closed everything up and exited the excessively-humid room, sighing as his skin met the regulated air outside of the door. Taking the towel from the hazed attendant, Jocephus wiped the sweat from his body, then locked the thick door's mechanisms behind him. Slipping his shirt back on, he stepped onto the lift.

As he went to step off on the next level, he paused, blinking in surprise at the sight of Magaliana's tearstained face.

"I knew this is where you would be," she said as she held back a sob. "He wouldn't let me on the lift, so I waited for you."

Jocephus glanced at the large attendant, making a mental note to give the man a bonus for a job well done, before running the towel through his hair.

"Joss, I... I didn't mean to make you angry, I..." she started.

Handing the attendant his towel, Jocephus smiled gently at the woman and pulled her into him, wrapping his arms around her. "What makes you think that I am angry with you, my dove?"

"There was no emotion in your face. You didn't say a word and just rushed away."

Jocephus looked into her eyes and gently wiped her tears. "I am not angry, Magaliana. On the contrary, I am... extremely impressed by your progress and success."

"Then why did you rush out of the cemetery?" No matter how many times he wiped her tears away, they just kept on coming.

"What you did was so amazing that it gave me an idea, and I had to come check on the core. That's all."

"What idea?" she asked, curiosity slowing her tears.

Jocephus released the young woman and crossed his arms over his chest as he feigned deep contemplation. "I wonder..."

Magaliana took the bait. "Wonder what?"

"What if we combined our alchemy? I wonder if it can help save the core."

Magaliana's eyes went wide and she covered her mouth. "Is it dying?"

"It's... not at its full potential," he admitted.

"Let me help," Magaliana gripped his silky shirt. "Let me see the core so that I can figure out how to help—"

"Absolutely not," he cut her off. "It's far too dangerous."

Magaliana pleaded with her eyes, but Jocephus did not give in as he usually pretended to do.

"You will be able to see it in due time." Uncrossing his arms, he unlatched Magaliana's hands from his shirt. "Come. Let's return to your revived golem. Let me properly inspect it."

Back at the cemetery, Magaliana showed him that she could control the construct by having it walk around as she asked. Jocephus watched with feigned interest, but his mind was on the final part of his plan. It was time to execute. "I am so impressed at how far you have come, Magaliana."

She smiled at him, her excitement apparent. "It's all thanks to your notes."

Jocephus took her hands in his. "It's not my notes. This is all you. No other alchemist has even come close to replicating pure alchemy. To do it in just a few days is truly an extraordinary feat, and to successfully create pure transmutations... to do this," he added, nodding his head in the direction of the revived golem, "is an astronomical triumph."

Magaliana's cheeks turned red from his praise. "But your notes helped. Without them, I don't know how far I could have possibly gotten."

Jocephus cupped her cheeks with both hands. "You give yourself far too little credit, my dove. This came from being pushed to your limits. Your talent, your willingness to learn, and your perseverance through repeated failures... This is all you." He leaned in close. "This could change the world."

Magaliana's blush grew a deeper shade. "How..." she started, a quiver in her voice, "... how do we unite our alchemy?"

"I don't know. We'll figure it out together," he whispered. "But maybe..." Jocephus cautiously brought his lips to hers.

He had won. She was all his: mind, soul... and body.

CHAPTER 30

Ikarim stood in front of the closed door to Gesselmeyer's room with a plate of cold meats, cheese, and porridge in his hands. He contemplated hard whether he should knock or simply barge in.

Testing the handle, he found that it wasn't locked. Inhaling and exhaling deeply, he turned the handle and slowly pushed the door open.

"Art?" Ikarim glanced about in the dark room. "Art, I brought you some breakfast..."

"Go away," a faint voice spoke.

Ikarim didn't go away. He opened the door wider and stepped inside, wrinkling his nose at the stale air. Setting the plate down on the thick wooden desk by the door, he walked to the window and pushed the curtains aside, bathing the room in sunlight. He opened the window to get some airflow, then turned toward Arteus, slouched in a chair in a sorry state. The lanky man squinted uncomfortably at the sunlight, then glared. "I said go away."

"Art, you haven't eaten in days. Please eat. And sit up. That can't be good for your posture."

"Why do you care..." Arteus turned his head away, ashamed.

Ikarim pursed his lips. He hated when the Strong Arm was in his downward spirals; he had to pull him back out before Arteus caused more damage to himself than anything. "Because you are my best friend, Art. You're like a brother to me. And with *Doktor* Gesselmeyer gone and Mags missing... You're the only person I have left."

"So you are just going to pretend nothing happened, then?" Arteus glanced back at him.

Ikarim watched his friend for a moment. His bruised side protested painfully, but he ignored it. He stepped toward the plate of food. "No, I'm not ignoring it; you definitely punched me," he acknowledged, and Arteus looked away once more. "It seems that you have repented plenty, however. What more needs to be done?"

He wasn't expecting an apology from the hotheaded man, nor did he want one. He knew that his friend was plenty sorry for what he had done.

He held out the plate in offering as he approached. Arteus didn't move at first, but after a few long seconds he finally grabbed the plate. "Why do you forgive so easily?"

Ikarim opened his mouth to reply but was interrupted by a loud pounding at the front door. Both men glanced toward the hall. Ikarim knew that the *Deutsches Kaiserreich* were patrolling the area for their safety, so he wondered if it was one of them. But why would they come knocking?

More urgent pounding followed, so Ikarim stepped out of Gesselmeyer's room and headed for the door. What if they found news on Magaliana? His heart raced as he opened the door, but instead of the Imperium, a messenger stood on the other side with an envelope in hand.

"Arteus *und* Ikarim Gesselmeyer?" the man asked.

Ikarim nodded. Though he was glad that it wasn't an urgent matter from the military, he cast the stranger a cautious look. The man did not say another word and simply handed Ikarim the envelope, bowed his head, turned around, and returned to a small dirigible.

Shutting the door, Ikarim inspected the object in his hand. He didn't recognize the seal, and there was no name anywhere. He was still nervous, though. What if there was information on Magaliana's whereabouts?

"Who was it?" Arteus asked at the top of the staircase.

"A messenger with a letter." Ikarim broke the seal and glanced at the note for a signature. His heart skipped a beat when he saw Magaliana's name. He suddenly felt dizzy.

Arteus stumbled down the stairs and snatched the letter straight out of his friend's hands to read it.

"What...?" Ikarim asked, unable to gather his thoughts to formulate a proper sentence.

Arteus raised a shaking finger, telling him to wait for a minute. Going around the Strong Arm, Ikarim tried to read over his shoulder, but before he could get past the first word, Arteus gasped and dropped the letter. It fluttered to the ground.

"What's going on? What does it say?" Ikarim demanded, almost desperate, as he picked the note up off the floor.

"She's..." was all Arteus could manage.

"She's what?!" Ikarim pushed, thinking the worst. "Come on, spit it out!" He tried to skim through the letter to find out what had Arteus so shocked. He was unable to comprehend what he read. He wished and hoped and begged the universe that it wasn't a death notice.

"She's... getting married."

Ikarim did a double-take as he met Arteus' gaze. His heart sank. "Willingly?" His eyes fell back to the note in his hands, and he swallowed a rather large lump. If he felt this way about the woman he loved marrying another man, he could only imagine how Arteus felt. "Jocephus

Gideon..." he mused, reading over the letter. "Do we know anything about him?"

"Not to my knowledge," Arteus replied. "What if he's the Techno Mage? What if she's being forced to marry him? What if she didn't even write this engagement announcement?"

"Calm down, Art." But Ikarim had to admit that the same questions had also crossed his mind. He had to be the voice of reason though, for the both of them. He had to think through this logically.

Before he could say anything, another knock occurred. Ikarim opened the door, only to be handed another envelope by a different messenger. He quickly opened it before Arteus could get to it and shut his eyes with a gloomy sigh. It was Arteus' turn to demand to know the contents.

He waved the wedding invitation, heavy-hearted. "It's in three days."

"What's in three days?" Arteus frowned. "Not the wedding...?"

Ikarim didn't have it in him to answer as his friend grabbed the invitation and sank into the stairs to read it over.

They had three days. It was a very unusual timeframe, especially with the fact that Magaliana barely had enough time to even get to know this man that was to be her husband. As her best friends, they didn't even get a chance to meet this Jocephus person and judge if he was right for her or not.

"If he is the Techno Mage, why would he invite us?" Ikarim mused out loud.

"Because it's a trap?" Arteus challenged.

Ikarim eyed his friend for a moment. It was a valid point.

"Trap or not, we have to be there for her," Ikarim said, as much as it pained him.

A tormented sigh escaped the Strong Arm. Ikarim knew that it was just as difficult for Arteus to accept as it was for him. Watching his friend's pained eyes drop to his feet, Ikarim approached and placed a comforting hand on Arteus' shoulder. He had no words.

Ikarim eventually released his friend's shoulder and turned around to walk away but paused in thought. "We need to know if *Herr* Wiegraf is aware," he said, glancing back over his shoulder. "If this is a trap, we need a plan and as much help as we can get."

"I'll get the dirigible." Arteus dragged his feet out the door.

Ikarim glanced down at the engagement letter in his hands. "We're coming for you, Mags."

CHAPTER 31

Despite the warm and inviting colors in the extravagant office of the gaudy Wiegraf mansion, a cold and uncomfortable silence was heavy in the room while *Herr* Wiegraf looked them over. Ikarim was especially nervous, knowing Arteus' short temper might hinder their discussions.

"I still fail to understand why my beloved daughter decided to live with a *verrückter* and his strays..."

"My *Vater* was not a madman!" Arteus spat. "And we are not strays!"

"Pathetic little puppies adopted by a crazy man. Strays."

Ikarim knew that Arteus would retort—and he almost did—so he called out the lanky man's name in warning. Glaring at *Herr* Wiegraf, the Strong Arm swiftly stood up. "This was a bad idea. Now I know why she ran away: you're an insufferable, stuffy old man."

"I'd watch your next words carefully in my home," the German Lord warned coldly.

"No need, we're leaving." Arteus stepped away from his overstuffed chair. "Let's go, Ike."

"With your tails between your legs, like the strays you are," *Herr* Wiegraf drawled. "You are not men. My beloved daughter does not deserve your attention."

Arteus spun back around and swung a clenched fist at the German Lord. Ikarim barely had time to react, but he managed to jump up from his seat, launching himself at his friend, making him stumble to the side and miss.

"Art, stop!" Ikarim hissed. "We need his help..."

"Leave immediately. You are no longer welcome here," the *Herr* spat.

"Please!" Ikarim raised his voice as he stood in between both men with his arms out. He turned his attention to the German Lord. "Can you put your dislike for one another aside? The both of you," he added to Arteus. "We need to do this for Mags." He looked at the Lord once more. "Please?"

Herr Wiegraf glared at both of them but said nothing. Ikarim took this as a good sign, and slowly dropped his arms to his sides.

"What do you know about Jocephus Gideon?" he asked.

Herr Wiegraf continued to glare for a few seconds before he sat back into his chair. "Aside from the fact that he is marrying my daughter without my permission in three days..." he replied venomously, "nothing."

So he did get the invitation. That put them somewhat on the same page. Ikarim returned to his own seat and pleaded with Arteus to do the same.

"Do you think that this is a trap?" Arteus asked.

Magaliana's father was silent for a long moment, pondering the question. Ikarim even spotted his expression soften ever so slightly to one of concern. Eventually, he sighed. "I don't know what to think."

"What should we do?" Ikarim asked.

"You can do what you wish, I do not care." His tone hardened once more.

"*Herr* Wiegraf... We're trying to help," he said, exasperated. "I know that you have a lot on your mind, what with Mags and Lady Ruth..." Arteus' attention darted toward Ikarim at this, but he ignored it in favor of pleading his case. "Please... Let us help."

The German Lord watched him long and hard before he finally replied. "I can plan to counter a trap, but I cannot include you."

Arteus glared and parted his lips to speak, but Ikarim stopped him with a hand on his shoulder. "Understood." He rose. "But please let us know if we can help in any way."

"You may not like it," Arteus started as coolly as he could, given the circumstances, "but we care for your daughter, and want her safe just as you do."

"We promise that once Mags is known to be safe, we'll help you in the search for Lady Ruth in whatever way we can," Ikarim added.

The Lord did not agree to Ikarim's promise, but neither did he disagree, which was a good sign in the mechanic's eyes.

They followed the butler out of the mansion, and as soon as the door shut, Arteus snapped his attention to Ikarim and whispered. "What happened to Lady Ruth?"

Ikarim began walking toward their dirigible, beckoning his friend to keep up. "She disappeared. A suspected kidnapping."

"Do you think it's the Techno Mage?"

Ikarim gave Arteus a skeptical look before he climbed aboard. "We'll hopefully find out at Mags' wedding."

CHAPTER 32

M agaliana sat alone in a room aboard the *Endurance*—the Techno Mage's grandest airship next to the *Faugregir*—gently brushing the alchemy-changed silky tresses cascading down her back. She barely recognized the woman in the long, embroidered silk wedding gown staring back at her through the reflection. She had been an Alchemist—in oversized overalls with dreadlocks in her hair—for Gesselmeyer for a few years. Even her time as a *Dame* in the German Upper Lands were nothing compared to this.

A knock on the door made her stomach sink a little.

"*Dame* Magaliana?" came a woman's voice from the other side. "*Dame*, the wedding commences. They are waiting on you."

"Are my friends there?" she asked, picking up the mechanical wings on the table next to her. "Ike and Art?"

"They are, *Dame*."

Magaliana almost cried right then and there. She had been so worried that they wouldn't have received the invitation in time, what with Jocephus convincing her to move the wedding forward. Fanning a hand in front of her face to dry the tears that stung her eyes, she gave a shuddered exhale. "And my parents?"

"I did not see your parents, *Dame*. I'm sorry."

The door slid slightly ajar and a scrawny woman with straw-colored hair peeked in, casting Magaliana a concerned look. An older, portly woman pushed it open wider and came barging inside, taking the wings from the Alchemist and helping her to put them on.

"Are you certain that you did not see my parents?" Magaliana asked.

The younger waiting maid rushed in to help the older servant. "I'm sorry, *Dame*. I might have overlooked them. I do know about your friends, however, as they specifically asked for you..."

Her thoughts were all over the place. Were her parents angry with her? Did they not forgive her for rejecting all her suitors? Did something bad happen to them? Did they receive the invitation in time? She suddenly felt sick to her stomach. Could she go through with the wedding? Should she?

The thought of the Mage's loving smile as she walked toward the altar pushed down the ill sensation and brought the butterfly flutters back. Magaliana couldn't help but smile when she found herself looking forward to the kiss, recalling the euphoric sensation from their last one.

With her wings and veil secured, Magaliana gave a deep inhale and exhale, her thoughts on her friends to chase away the warm flush of her cheeks. She gave both maids an anxious smile as she adorned her dainty white gloves. "Lead the way."

Following the portly woman out of the room, she carefully climbed the stairs to the deck of the vessel where the gathering took place. It was a tiny, intimate setting, with low, deep-seated chairs that faced an arch covered in white ranunculus flowers. The faces were unrecognizable to her, which made her feel quite lonely and vulnerable. She glanced over the people twice in a quick attempt to spot her parents or her friends before she joined her husband-to-be at the altar.

She did not see them. Biting her lip to prevent herself from crying, she began her slow, solitary walk down the center, her attention focused on Jocephus as a robotic band of cyborgs in the corner began to play on their brass instruments.

She was almost to the front when she spotted Ikarim out of the corner of her eye. He smiled softly. Arteus sat next to him, but his forced smile appeared pained. Of course, he was depressed about her being with someone else.

Ikarim stood up as she leaped into his arms so suddenly that she threatened to knock him over. She hugged him tight while Arteus ran his hand down her veiled hair, tears in his eyes.

"I'm so happy to see you," Arteus said. "I feared that I never would again."

"Sir…" came a voice as Magaliana parted her lips to reply. She looked up as two burly men approached the trio. Fear and confusion found their way to her heart, but the Mage raised a hand up to stop them.

"Leave them," he ordered. "My betrothed has not seen her friends in a very long time."

Magaliana smiled at her husband-to-be, mouthing a thank you to him. She loved how understanding he was.

"Magaliana," came a strict voice from behind her. She released Ikarim and spun around to see her father. So, they did get the invitation. She ran to him with tears in her eyes, and he held her tightly. "Magaliana, be prepared for the attack," he warned in German.

"What?" she pulled away, confused.

"We shall attack soon and get you off this damnable ship and safely back home."

"No!" she gasped, taking a step back. "No!" she continued in English. "Joss has been nothing but kind to me. He saved me from the pirates!"

"No, my daughter," *Herr* Wiegraf said. "The pirate spoke before his escape. He led us to the Techno Mage and to you. Jocephus Gideon is a bad man."

"I admire your research," Jocephus said, clapping as he approached. "Now, if you don't mind, I would like to move on with the wedding."

"Over my dead body," *Herr* Wiegraf growled, pulling his pistol and aiming at the Techno Mage. Magaliana was stunned by her father's actions, but even more so when Ikarim and Arteus did the same.

"Tsk. Shameful." Jocephus pulled out a pistol as well, and Magaliana shrieked as dozens of sleek, steel airships from both the Imperium and the Royal Guard rose from the clouds, surrounding them.

"Please stop!" she shouted, but nobody listened.

Herr Wiegraf's eyes hardened as Jocephus simply smirked, clearly unaffected by the trap. When an array of various airships from the *Faugregir*—all different shapes, sizes, and designs similar to those of the rogues—made their appearance known and the wedding guests rose from their seats with their own weapons drawn, Magaliana realized that this was all an expected trap and counter-attack.

"Why do I feel that you have something to do with my missing wife?" asked *Herr* Wiegraf.

The Alchemist was rooted on the spot at her father's comment. That's right... She hadn't yet seen her mother. Despite her father's words, her gaze shot to the guests, searching for her mother.

"She went down to the Lands Below to try and find you, Magaliana," the Mage said, eyes and weapon still on her father.

"Joss!" Magaliana gasped.

"I'm afraid the haze hit. There was nothing I could do to save her from it."

"No!" she cried. "No! Why didn't you tell me?!"

"I couldn't bear to see you devastated. It breaks my heart..."

Magaliana's legs gave out, but Ikarim caught her and helped lower her to the deck. Grief hit her like a ton of bricks; she didn't exactly part ways with her family in a warm and loving manner. Tears rolled down her cheeks before a shot fired, and she screamed, unsure where the shot came from. *Herr* Wiegraf's pistol and droplets of blood fell to the ground.

More shots fired, from on deck and in the air. Magaliana crawled away from the fighting as both Ikarim and Arteus shielded her. With his uninjured hand, the *Herr* pulled his sword out of its sheath and lunged toward Jocephus. The Techno Mage gave a high-pitched whistle and raised a hand toward one of his men, who skillfully tossed him a sword. Catching it by the hilt, he parried the *Herr* with ease, and they locked in an intense sword fight.

"Stop!" she screamed, but her pleas fell on deaf ears. Getting to her feet, she went to try and stop her father from attacking her groom, but cannon fire impact knocked her back down again, the ship shaking violently.

"Enough... Enough!" she cried out, standing back up.

"I have a wedding gift for you, my bride!" Jocephus called over the sound of gunshots, cannon fire, and steel against steel. "I brought your hazed mother here to witness our alliance!"

Her mother was still alive? Before Magaliana could properly react to the Mage's words, another explosion drove almost everyone to their knees. When Magaliana glanced back up, Jocephus' people dragged a woman, deformed and disfigured, out into the open with a pistol against both of her temples. She shrieked at the sight of the monster.

"What say you, Sir?" Jocephus called out to *Herr* Wiegraf. "Is she not beautiful standing here at her daughter's wedding?"

Both Magaliana and *Herr* Wiegraf froze at the horror that had become Lady Ruth. It almost appeared her skin was melting off her bones in the heat. Enraged, Magaliana's father growled and lunged at Jocephus, who jumped back and aimed his pistol at Ruth's forehead.

Magaliana gasped again. Why was he doing this?

"I really didn't want to invite you, but I knew that my bride would not accept to be wed unless you were. So, I went and found myself some leverage. Unfortunately, things are getting a little hectic, so it's my time to retreat."

The Mage pulled the trigger, and Ruth collapsed to the ground in a pool of green liquid. Magaliana shrieked, then wailed at the loss of her mother and the betrayal from the only man she actually loved more than a brother or friend.

When Jocephus aimed his gun at the *Herr*, she darted forward to try and stop him. "Joss, no!" she sobbed.

"Mags, come back!" Ikarim cried as he rushed to catch her.

Magaliana grabbed Jocephus' outstretched arm to try and divert his aim. The shot fired and narrowly missed the *Herr*, who lunged at the Mage. Irritated, Jocephus flung Magaliana off his arm with such force that she hit the edge of the ship and fell backward, overboard. Her eyes went wide and she screamed a bloodcurdling scream, Ikarim's terrified face and outstretched arm the last thing she saw before she slipped into the clouds.

Her breath catching in her throat, tears fell from her eyes as she disappeared forever.

***

"NO!" Jocephus cried angrily once he realized what he had done. In the heat of the moment, he mistook Magaliana for some boarded military members trying to save the German Lord, and all he wanted was for them to release him when he flung the Alchemist off.

Jocephus went to go after her but stopped, turning his attention back to *Herr* Wiegraf with a spiteful glare.

"You cost me my whole life," *Herr* Wiegraf growled, swinging his blade.

"You cost me my WIFE!" Jocephus dodged out of the way and parried before taking the quick opportunity to pull the trigger and shoot the German Lord point blank through the heart. His satisfaction was short-lived as the airship rocked again from another cannonball.

At a loud hallooing sound, Jocephus glanced about and realized more ships had come to join the party... Except the airships weren't his or the military's; they belonged to the rogues.

"Retreat!" Jocephus called out, annoyed.

Grabbing the ladder from another one of his airships, he loudly cussed at the fact that his perfect plan was ruined by none other than himself. To top it off, he was now losing the *Endurance*.

CHAPTER 33

"Mags!" Ikarim whimpered, his arm still reaching for her even though he could no longer see her.

Everything was happening so fast he barely registered the anguished cry coming from Arteus. He saw his friend out of the corner of his eye and quickly pushed away from the edge to grab onto his arm, fearing he would jump off the ship after Magaliana.

"Art..." Ikarim started, then shrugged his shoulders, startled, when a gunshot sounded a little too closely to them. "Art, come on... we need to get to safety..."

"She's gone, Ike..." he wailed.

"I know." His vision blurred with tears. He hated himself for not being quick enough to save her. It was all his fault that she fell overboard.

But he had to be the voice of reason in the current situation. He could hate himself later. "Art, if we don't move, we will be gone as well..."

"First *Vater*, now Mags," Arteus sobbed. "I have nothing left to live for..."

"Art!" Ikarim shoved his friend out of the way, then let out a small cry as a searing, burning sensation grew outward from a spot on his arm. Hissing, he grabbed at the bloodied wound he had incurred while protecting his mourning friend.

"Ike!" Arteus sounded panicked, but Ikarim shook his head with a wince.

"I'm fine..." he said before his eyes went wide, looking past Arteus' shoulder.

Two men rushed toward them, swords cutting through the air in their direction. Arteus turned around and grabbed one of the blades, crushing it effortlessly with his cybernetic hand. The surprised attacker swung a fist at Arteus, landing a punch instead onto his metal shoulder as Arteus partially turned to deal with the second man. Grabbing him by the throat, he shoved him into the one with the broken knuckles. They collapsed, one gasping for air from his crushed trachea while the other cried out in agony over his hand.

Arteus turned to Ikarim. "Are you alright?"

Ikarim nodded with a wince. He never thought that he would end up getting shot, but now that he had, he wondered how some people—like *Herr* Wiegraf earlier—could just keep going as if nothing happened. The aggravating, searing pain was almost all he could think about. "I thought you had nothing left to live for?"

"Well, now I'm angry." Arteus kicked one of the men in the ribs. "I remembered that I still have one person left to live for," he added, "and some idiot went and shot him."

Ikarim gave his friend a faint smirk.

The battle didn't last much longer before what was left of the Techno Mage's goons retreated, and the rogues—realizing they were out-powered by the continuous approaches of the German and British military—withdrew from the party as well. Arteus rushed to the corpse of *Herr* Wiegraf while Ikarim, still holding his injured arm, dashed toward Lady Ruth. Dropping to his knees to check for a pulse, he paused when he heard a click. Slowly looking up, his gaze met with a pistol by a member of the *Deutsches Kaiserreich*. Arteus was in the same situation.

"Step away from *Herr* Wiegraf," the soldier ordered. Arteus slowly raised his hands and moved them toward his head.

"We are friends of *Dame* Magaliana," Ikarim tried.

"We are the adoptive sons of *Doktor* Handsel Gesselmeyer," Arteus added. "We are not the enemy."

"They're with me," came a familiar voice in English. Ikarim turned his attention to see Brigadier General Darley standing nearby, his own weapon trained on the German soldier by Arteus.

The soldiers took one last hard look at both Ikarim and Arteus before they finally pulled their weapons away and holstered them. Arteus dropped his arms, and Ikarim sighed with relief. While the soldiers busied themselves with the German Lord and his wife, Ikarim turned his attention to his friend as they got to their feet. Arteus' focus was on the edge where Magaliana had fallen overboard. Ikarim glanced back at the General.

"She fell over the edge," he called out as he jogged up to Darley.

The older man frowned. "Who did?"

"Mags."

The General's eyes hardened. "Where?"

"About a few knots south," Arteus said as he joined the two.

While Darley instructed one of the soldiers from the Royal Guard to form a search party and head to the Lands Below, Ikarim found his vision blurry with tears again. There was no way she could have survived that fall. For that matter, there was no way she could be intact, either. He thought that his legs were going to give out when a gentle, yet stern pat on his good shoulder snapped him from his thoughts.

"Let's get that gunshot wound healed up," the General offered.

CHAPTER 34

Disinfected and bandaged up, Ikarim sat in a chair outside of a meeting room which he and Arteus were, unfortunately, not invited to.

Arteus was silent. At times, when Ikarim looked at him, he seemed sad. Depressed. Other times, he looked angry. Ikarim could tell that the wheels in his head were spinning, and he was almost afraid of the outcome. Eventually, his lips parted to speak to his friend, but he remained silent when the doors to the conference room finally opened and a few soldiers rushed out.

"I want that man dead!" Arteus said through gritted teeth, and Ikarim jumped, startled, as Darley stepped out of the room. "I want the Techno Mage dead and Mags found!"

"Patience, Son of Gesselmeyer. We are doing the best we can..."

"It's not enough!"

"Art..." Ikarim warned when the General frowned.

"Fine," the Strong Arm said as he stood up. "I'll go find Mags, and then I'll kill that *Hurensohn* myself!"

"Sit down," Darley ordered. "This is in the hands of the *Deutsches Kaiserreich*, the Royal Guard, and every other military empire."

"Then I want to join the military."

"Art..." Ikarim started. He didn't like where his friend was going with this one bit. He was normally able to convince him against his thoughts from his blinding rage, but he wondered if this was going to be the first time he wouldn't succeed.

"Absolutely not," Darley retorted. "Joining the military for revenge is forbidden."

"I can do it by myself, or I can help you. Either way, I'm getting my revenge."

Darley's eyes hardened. "No military empire wants to enlist people who are only there for themselves and not their country. Enlisting for revenge is nothing but a distraction and could compromise the unit. When you enlist, you join a team and do not go on your own missions. Once you're in, you're there to do as you're told. You have no say."

"You can't change my mind."

"The defiant don't last."

Ikarim looked back and forth from his friend to the General. Neither said a word, and he didn't particularly like Arteus' silence, because it meant that the gears were still turning, and he had even less of a chance at convincing him against his hotheaded decision.

After a long pause, the General continued. "If you are serious about this, boy, then sit *down*."

Arteus glared at the military man for a moment before he replied "Yes, Sir," and sat.

"Art, you can't be serious," Ikarim finally said.

"Of course I'm serious. I've lost my *Vater*, I've lost Mags... I need to find her body, Ike. I need to find her and give her a proper funeral. And then I need to find the Techno Mage and kill him."

"Killing the Techno Mage is out of the question," the General stated.

"Then I will hurt him really bad before he is brought to justice," Arteus countered. "Are you joining me or not, Ike?"

Ikarim sighed. That was it, there was no convincing him otherwise. His mind was made up, and his revenge was only fuel to the fire. If the flames weren't tended to by joining the military, then something much worse would be the outcome down the road. "Of course I'm joining you. I've got to keep you out of trouble. But what if I don't pass Basic Training? I'm not nearly... I don't have..." he didn't even know where to go with this.

"Even if your friend were to join you, he'll need four weeks to heal from his wound and two weeks of physical therapy," the General chimed in. "Can you wait that long?"

Arteus frowned, deep in thought, his eyes falling to the ground. Then he nodded and looked back up. "Yes, Sir, I can."

Darley looked at Ikarim, and he eventually nodded as well, though with much less confidence. "Yes, Sir," he replied, barely above a whisper.

"Then Basic Training begins in six weeks. In the meantime, go fill out your paperwork, get some bloodwork done, and make yourselves useful with some chores aboard the vessel."

"Yes, Sir," the mechanics replied in unison.

Arteus stood up and walked past Ikarim without a second glance as he headed down the airship's hall. Ikarim watched him walk away for a moment before he looked back at the General, who's eyes were on him.

Wanting to escape the awkward silence, Ikarim sighed, wincing in pain when he got to his feet and paused at the doorway, looking over his shoulder to Darley.

"Please put in a good word for him..." he said quietly. "He may be short-tempered, but he means well."

"'Meaning well' has no place in the military, Mister Gesselmeyer. Short tempers especially don't last long."

"The anger will fade. The grief will be there for a while. But the love he has for his *Vater* and for Mags? I'd like to think that counts for something."

Out of the corner of his eye, his gaze made contact with Darley's for but a second before he continued from the room.

CHAPTER 35

Ikarim's wound had healed well. He had only finished his physical therapy for one week before they thrust him into the hardships of Basic Training.

He had no problem with the course building up his confidence and instilling discipline and obedience. That was the easy part. He found that the fundamental military skills were interesting, to say the least. But building up the physical fitness aspect? He had an extremely hard time.

They ran ten laps, did jumping jacks, and were in the middle of push-ups. Ikarim's arms trembled so much he could barely lift himself up. Glancing down the line every now and again, he saw how easily the physical activity came to the one with the cybernetic limbs. He hated it. With each exertion, he wondered why he had agreed to join Arteus. At the rate he was going, he would get kicked out of Basic Training and would no longer be able to keep an eye on his friend.

He suddenly felt a boot in the middle of his back.

"Just what do you think you're doing, Gesselmeyer?" The drill instructor demanded.

"Push-ups, Sergeant," Ikarim replied through gritted teeth.

"Is that so?" The trainer applied weight to Ikarim's back, who grunted in both pain and effort. It was no longer just his arms that trembled, but his whole body. "I thought you were doing push-ups, Soldier?"

Ikarim bent his elbows and tried really hard not to let his chest touch the ground, but he just couldn't handle it any longer. His arms gave in and his whole body collapsed.

"Pathetic." The drill instructor removed his foot. Ikarim rolled over onto his back as he winced in pain. "You're done for the day, Soldier. Go pick up your chore sheet and get to work."

"Yes, Sergeant," Ikarim wheezed.

"The rest of you can thank Gesselmeyer for added drills. Get up off the ground and do five laps of lunges."

There came grumbles before the entire camp called out "Yes, Staff!" and rose from the ground. They gave Ikarim dirty looks as they took one step and bent into a lunge, then another step, and so on. Getting to his feet, Ikarim cast a glance at Arteus, who did not meet Ikarim's gaze as he advanced through lunges.

It seemed to be the same thing day after day: Ikarim just could not keep up. He was ridiculed by the drill Sergeant, gained a few extra chores because of it, and dragged his feet at the end of the night, exhausted, when he returned to the room he shared with Arteus at the Garrison.

They rarely spoke to one another. In fact, Arteus was always cleaning his kit by the light of the lantern whenever Ikarim arrived. Ikarim was always so drained that he'd simply pass out and awaken the next morning from Reveille to find that Arteus had cleaned his kit as well. The few words spoken in between them usually occurred during the hour of clean up before parade.

"Looks like you're putting on muscle weight," Arteus said.

"I don't feel like it. It's hardly enough compared to everyone else—"

"Don't compare yourself to everyone else."

"Easy for you to say. You're not the one being picked on all day, every day."

"Oh, but I am."

Ikarim paused in making his bed and slowly stood back up to full height. He turned to face his oldest friend and looked him in the eyes in exasperation.

"Every time Sergeant Mills says the name Gesselmeyer, I take it personally," Arteus explained. "Because it's my name, too. It's *Vater*'s name. And it kills me that I can't just... just tear off my cybernetics to help you pass. Because you know that if I could, I would."

"I know," Ikarim sighed. "Thank you, Art. Really. It means a lot to me."

"I know that you want to give up."

"I do," Ikarim acknowledged, returning to his cleaning.

"Please don't. Because I need you by my side when we find Mags' body. And I'll definitely need you to stop me from killing the Techno Mage when I next see him."

Ikarim gave a forced laugh. "Oh, I doubt I'd be able to do that. I'm the weakest one of the group, remember?"

"How about this?" Arteus extended his cybernetic hand out in front of Ikarim, who looked at it with confusion. Where was his friend going with this? "You say the word, and I'll stop."

Ikarim blinked and looked back into his friend's eyes. "You're kidding, right?"

"No. You tell me to stop... And I'll stop. I promise. And I'll shake on it."

Ikarim's gaze fell back to the outstretched hand before him. Out of all the ridiculous things that he had done through the years, this was definitely one of the top. He grasped his friend's wrist, however, and Arteus' cybernetic hand closed around his, both men shaking on it.

Ikarim continued to struggle for a few more days and finally, after a lot of hard work, he was able to keep up with his crew. He was still physically the weakest link, but he was able to do more and thus was picked on less.

After a few weeks, their training became more advanced. They learned the basics of movement in the field, night operations, route marching, weapons handling, marksmanship, and digging trenches.

Arteus and Ikarim spent more time together in their downtime. They did their chores, then read every British and German newspaper they could get their hands on in case somebody found Magaliana's body, but there was never any mention. They tried to get info from the Brigadier General, but he never responded to their inquiries. When Ikarim asked his professor, he was told it was above his pay level.

Both men finally graduated Basic Training and immediately began their specialized training. As a mechanic and good with tinkering and repairs, Ikarim moved on to be a Weapons Technician, while Arteus was best for the Front Line as a Strong Arm. Unfortunately, this meant that they would no longer be roommates once shipped to different depots.

"Keep in touch," Arteus said as he gripped Ikarim's wrist.

"Same goes for you," Ikarim replied.

"Keep an ear out for any news regarding Mags. Let me know immediately when you do."

"You know I will." Ikarim released his friend's wrist and turned around to walk away but glanced over his shoulder. "Don't get killed on the front lines."

"Make sure that my weapons don't fail, and I won't!" Arteus called back out to him.

Ikarim chuckled and shook his head as he walked away.

CHAPTER 36

Over the period of two months, Ikarim was shipped out to France, Belgium, and back to Germany. Though it was far less physically demanding than Basic Training, it was mentally draining. All he wanted to do as soon as he returned to his quarters was sleep. He made sure, however, to get a hold of German and British newspapers wherever he went so he could keep an eye out for any news on Magaliana's body. He often fell asleep to news of rogues destroying and pirates pillaging. There was never a peep about Magaliana.

Back in Germany, he set up camp in a quiet corner by the medics and was helping with a few of the weapons that needed repair when a man rushed in waving a weapon. A few alarmed cries went up around the area.

"Where is your tech?!" he demanded.

Ikarim, already on alert from the figure having barged in, recognized the voice, and his heart skipped a beat. He set down the gun he was repairing and spun around to see a few fingers pointed in his direction, and some familiar cybernetic arms. "Art!"

"Ike, quick!" Arteus rushed toward his friend and shoved a massive munition into his arms. Ikarim blinked and almost dropped it, caught off-guard by the weight of the massively-thick stove pipe. "How soon can you fix it? We're winning on the front line, but not without this magnificent beast!"

"I..." Ikarim tried to restart his train of thought. "I don't know. I don't even know what this is, let alone what is wrong with it..."

"It's a gun, and it's jammed."

Ikarim gave him a look. "Obviously. Unjamming shouldn't take long, but I've not dealt with a weapon like this before. I wouldn't know where to start to find the problem."

"How long?!"

"I..." Ikarim stuttered. "Come back in a half hour?"

"Not good enough." Arteus grabbed Ikarim by the arm and scooped up a bunch of tools with his other hand. "You're coming with me."

Ikarim tried to pull back, but with his friend's cybernetics, it was impossible. Arteus forced him out of the tent and into the pouring rain. With the heavy weapon clutched against his chest and his mind a whirl, they splashed through puddles toward the front line, where he would be closer to the gunshots and to death.

The closer they got, the more Arteus hid Ikarim behind anything that would block incoming gunfire. The Strong Arm fired a few rounds with the other weapons about, and when the coast was clear, dragged Ikarim to the next safety zone, then the next, then the next, until they finally rejoined the unit at the front.

"Progress?" Arteus asked his unit.

"Get that gun back in working order!" somebody called. "We're losing again, we've already had to pull back twice!"

"Get to work, Ike!" Arteus dropped all the tools at Ikarim's feet.

"What the hell is this?" he asked as he pointed the weapon at the ground, while quickly looking for the source of the jam, which would typically be the trigger. "And where the hell is the trigger?!"

"Try the crank!" Arteus said. "And this beast is a *panzerbüchse*. An armored rifle hybrid made of—" he paused as a bullet ricocheted near him, ducked down, then peeked out and shot a few rounds.

"I don't even think I want to know," Ikarim groaned as he pulled the bar. The pedal-like lever near the projectile usually ignited the propellant when pulled. However, it seemed to be working just fine, which meant that the problem was elsewhere. Dropping down to his knees, Ikarim used some of the tools to quickly but carefully take apart the weapon. "Why the hybrid?"

"I was bored."

"Wait, you made this?!"

"Ike, I promise to tell you everything once we get out of this alive, but our chances are getting slimmer by the second. Please hurry."

Opening a compartment, Ikarim first raised a brow in confusion, then frowned. It was covered in soot, and there was a solid charcoal-like substance jamming the rig. Ikarim looked around for a rag but could not find any. How was he supposed to clean it?

Glancing about, he grabbed the hilt of Arteus' sword and pulled it out. A few of the soldiers from the unit paused and watched him closely, but the Strong Arm never even gave his best friend's actions a second thought. Placing his arm on the ground, he swiftly stabbed his sleeve and yanked his arm away, causing the material to tear. Ikarim pulled the sword out of the ground, dropped it next to Arteus, then pulled hard at the torn material to get it to release from the rest. He wiped at the soot on the inside of the large weapon, then grabbed one of the smaller tools and chipped the charcoal away from the device, cleaning it as quickly as he could, and put it back together. The whole thing took fifteen minutes, but to Ikarim, it felt like hours.

He called out to Arteus, who had moved up a few spots. "Art!" Give it a try!"

Arteus came rushing back and hid behind the mound, narrowly avoiding getting shot. He snatched the weapon from his friend and ran to the mound next to them, where he stuffed the front part of the tube full of charcoal.

"Art! What are you doing??" Ikarim hissed.

Arteus did not answer, moving quickly. He added cotton, then some pellets which looked to be made of lead. Peeking out from behind the mound, Arteus fully stood up.

"CLEAR!" he bellowed as his unit scattered, giving him a wide berth. "Fire Jet!" He tucked the weapon beneath his arm. Aiming it at a forty-five degree angle, he pulled the lever.

Nothing happened.

"Ike!" he growled angrily.

"Well, that's why it's jamming," Ikarim snapped back in exasperation. "Why the hell are you stuffing it with—"

Arteus had pulled the crank a few more times and it finally fired. The backblast was quite impressive, going back at least six feet, which explained why the unit had scattered. But the rain with which the enemy was hit was ingenious, even Ikarim had to admit. Flaming pellets and charcoal melted everything it touched.

It appeared the pellets were infused with al-chemy, which exploded once they made contact, making them even more deadly. He also figured that anyone handling that kind of weapon was either greatly courageous... Or carelessly venge-ful. He couldn't decide which side Arteus leaned on more.

There were cries and screams of agony as Ar-teus and the unit took the opportunity to move forward. "Come on, Ike!"

Ikarim quickly picked up the tools and fol-lowed Arteus. He remained silent as his friend continued to stuff everything into the hybrid and shoot.

Eventually, he turned to his friend. "You should stay here."

Ikarim didn't need to be told twice. Lowering himself down to the ground, he sat with his back against the mound as Arteus disappeared. His heart raced and his mind spun. How was he still in one piece on the front line? It was a scene worse than any battle involving pirates and the Techno Mage. Listening intently, he pulled out his revolver, preparing himself for the worst.

Had anyone else been left behind like him? Would anyone come back for him? Was Arteus alright? Ikarim silently mouthed a cuss as he glanced about, trying to find a solution to his predicament. He remained behind for a while, and felt utterly alone and concerned for the unit, but mostly for Arteus.

Eventually, he heard a victory cheer. Some-body won. Ikarim hoped that it was the good guys. He dared not move, however, not even to peek over the edge.

Footsteps approached, splashing through the rain. Ikarim cocked his gun and waited. They were coming for him. As the person swung around the mound, Ikarim took aim.

"Woah! Hey! It's me!" Arteus grabbed the barrel of the gun, pulling it away.

Ikarim exhaled in relief after realizing that he had been holding his breath. He took his gun back, removed the hammer from its cocked po-sition, and placed it back in its holster. "I take it we won?"

"For now. They've retreated, and most of the unit is following. I've been ordered to make more of these beasts." He grinned, kissing the massive weapon.

"Why were you stuffing it with lead?" Ikarim scolded as he followed Arteus back to camp. "That's the reason it was jamming!"

"The charcoal is for ignition and the lead helps fuel the infusion."

"Those infusion-filled pellets were a clever idea," Ikarim admitted.

Arteus grinned proudly.

Ikarim eventually returned to the health tent in one piece and got back to the weapons that he had been forced to abandon. After his chores that night, he made his way over to the Strong

Arm sitting by a fire. The rain had finally let up, though everything was still sopping wet. Arteus sat, frazzled, surrounded by a mess of weapon parts and a small broadcaster perched nearby.

"What are you getting yourself into?" Ikarim smirked as he bent over to observe a few parts scattered about.

"I don't remember how I made the first one," Arteus admitted.

"I'll help you."

The friends worked together. Thankfully, despite the adrenaline rush, Ikarim remembered how he had taken the hybrid apart and put it back together. Arteus was instantly in a better mood when he realized this. "I'll be honest, Ike, I thought of you while I made it."

"Now there's a scary thought..." Ikarim smirked.

"I'm serious! I kept thinking that you'd have it done and in working condition in no time. You'd probably add a few gadgets to it here and there for more power, more stability..."

"Less backfire?"

"See? I don't have a creative mind. I'm just brute strength."

"Brute strength wouldn't have created this, Art. A mechanic and musician would have."

"A grand piano won't get me very far on the front line..."

In the end, the new weapon turned out better than the first one. Ikarim had made it more powerful and stable, just as the Strong Arm knew he would, and he couldn't help but lessen the backfire as well, because that was an accident waiting to happen.

"Don't fill it with charcoal this time." Ikarim warned. "I added a section that will pull out the soot so it won't get gummed up, too, when you add the pellets."

"Thanks," Arteus said. "How have you been? I never got to ask you..."

"I've simply been."

"I've been the same, actually," Arteus sighed. "Any news on Mags?"

Ikarim shook his head, and Arteus dropped his gaze. "They'll find her."

"What if they already have and they just aren't telling us?" Arteus said. "It's been months..."

Ikarim pondered his words silently. It could very well be.

Arteus shut off the broadcaster and laid down as the white noise disappeared. "Thanks for joining me on the line, Ike."

Ikarim smiled and laid down as well. "Thanks for still being alive."

CHAPTER 37

Ikarim felt Arteus loom over his shoulder sometime before lunch the next day but didn't acknowledge his presence as he was rather intent on the small, fragile details of his current job.

"I've always been amazed at your work, Ike," Arteus eventually said. "Even in *Vater*'s shop. You were so good at repairing things and creating things..."

"Thank you," he replied, wiping the dirt from his brow. "How is the new weapon working for you?"

"We didn't get to use it, Denmark retreated pretty far overnight. We're packing up camp and heading out."

"Heading where?" he asked with a raised brow, wondering if his unit would follow.

"To the barracks, Gesselmeyer," his superior officer said as he passed through. "You've done enough camping for the time being. I suppose a bed would do us all some good. Prussia is joining northern Germany in this *Schleswig* War, so pack up, we're headed to Frankfurt."

Ikarim and Arteus looked to one another in silence before Ikarim eventually nodded for the both of them to get a move on. Sleeping in a bed, as uncomfortable as barracks cots were, sounded infinitely better than their current camping situation.

Ikarim was exhausted once they reached their first stop at a base camp, settling for the night. Thankful that their units had combined for the time being, he dragged his feet, every muscle protesting, to his friend's location. He found Arteus messing with the broadcaster with a displeased look on his face.

"I can't get a signal," he muttered.

"Here," Ikarim held his hand out. "Let me see it."

The Strong Arm handed over the device and Ikarim sat down next to the fire, fiddling with the settings for at least fifteen minutes before he looked to his friend with a sigh. Arteus' expression dropped.

"What are you trying to accomplish with this broadcaster?" he asked.

"I've been listening in, trying to hear anything about finding Mags' body."

Ikarim nodded. He understood where his friend was coming from, as he had pretty much done the same with any newspaper he could get his hands on. Reaching for a small roll about his waist, he fished for a tool and continued to tinker with the machine for most of the night. He attempted to get a stronger signal, or even any signal at all, at that point. He felt that they were literally in the middle of nowhere with nothing for the broadcaster to grab.

Every great now and again his gaze travelled to Arteus, who had eventually fallen asleep. There were a few times Ikarim was ready to give up for the night as well, but when he looked at Arteus, he had renewed determination to try again. He knew his friend was strictly running off revenge, and, honestly, who could blame him? He was hurt over the fact that Magaliana was marrying another man. Ikarim was upset as well, but he was more willing to come to terms with it than the Strong Arm was.

But Magaliana's death? Ikarim was good at keeping his grief to himself—unlike Arteus—but deep down inside, he wanted to inflict even a fraction of that pain on the man responsible. And he knew Arteus wished to inflict triple that amount.

Ikarim laid on his back with the device at his head. He turned the knob excessively slow, trying not to miss anything, but all he got for hours was white noise.

Finally, just as he was drifting off, he heard something.

His eyes shot open and his heart was beating so fast he could barely hear the white noise from the radio. He strained his ears to catch what had startled him, but he just couldn't make out anything. Did he imagine it? Then he heard it again. Ikarim quickly rolled over onto his stomach and touched the knob, fine-tuning it to better hear what was being said. He moved the knob just a tiny amount more, and he was able to make out a word very clearly.

"sechsundvierzig."

Ikarim glanced around to see if any of the other soldiers heard the voice over the broadcaster, but they seemed to still be sleeping soundly. Another number came over the broadcast.

"Sieben. Sieben. Fünf. Sieben. Norden."

Coordinates. Ikarim grabbed a tiny screwdriver from his pouch and scratched down the numbers into the ground by the broadcaster. More white noise made him wonder if he had lost the signal. Waiting a few seconds, he reached for the knob again, but before he could touch it the voice was there once more. "Twenty-three," it continued in German.

Ikarim scratched that number down as well.

"Five. Two. One. Zero. Degree East."

Sitting up, he glanced about to find something to copy the numbers onto, only to find Arteus sitting bolt upright, his eyes on the broadcaster.

Ikarim quickly grabbed a rag and a very sharp tool, poking holes into the cloth in the shape of numbers. Occasionally, he held it out to the fire to be sure that the numbers transferred correctly. The voice suddenly came up once more over the broadcaster.

"The Techno Mage awaits."

Ikarim's heart skipped a beat. Had he really just overheard the location of the Techno Mage? He looked to the device then to Arteus, who stared at him with wide eyes.

"Where do those coordinates lead?" Arteus whispered as he crawled closer to his friend.

"I don't know," Ikarim admitted, his mind reeling as he looked over the numbers. "East from here, definitely."

"We need to get there before the person that message was intended for," Arteus said, matter-of-factly.

"Art, we can't just leave..."

"Yes, we can."

"We'll get in trouble."

"I don't care."

"Art..." Ikarim sighed.

"Look," Arteus leaned in close, his whisper more urgent but barely audible for any other to hear. "Do you want to find him, or not? Do you want to get revenge for Mags and her family, or not? Because I'm going. And I understand if you want to stay here, but I'm not going to wait any longer. This is the perfect opportunity, and I'm taking it. What's your choice?"

Ikarim stared at his friend long and hard. He wanted revenge for Mags and her family, but if things went wrong, not only would they miss out on the opportunity; they would be charged with fines and possibly even thrown in jail.

"What's your choice, Ike?!" Arteus hissed as quietly as he could.

Ikarim nodded. He was with Arteus for the long haul, and definitely needed to keep him out of trouble.

Both men got up as quietly as they could, bringing only necessities—especially their re-volvers—with them. They snuck around the camp and the guard until they could safely hide in bushes.

"What do we do now?" whispered Arteus.

Ikarim looked at his friend. "Why are you asking me? You are the one who got us into this mess to begin with…"

"Because you are good at thinking things through while I am good at acting out."

"Clearly," Ikarim growled. Turning his atten-tion back to the camp, the gears in his head turned for a possible idea. He then looked back to Arteus. "We need a way out. A ship."

"An unguarded ship will be hard to come by around base," Arteus pointed out.

"But an unguarded ship around a small town—not so much. Follow me."

Ikarim and Arteus quietly snuck away from camp. Once they were far enough for the lookout to miss them, Ikarim made a run for it and Arteus followed. Despite his earlier exhaustion, Ikarim was thankful for his military training as he was able to run a longer distance and keep up pace without tiring out too quickly. He continued on, determined.

"Ike, where are we going?" Arteus asked.

"The tracks. We are going to hitch a locomotive ride."

"Pure genius!" Arteus said. "But how do you know there's a track in this direction?"

"I remember hearing a steam engine on our way to camp."

Eventually, Ikarim slowed his run to a jog. He kept up the momentum for a while longer, but finally slowed his pace to a steady walk. He was out of breath, and his legs wanted to give out from beneath him, but he forced himself to continue.

"How much longer?" Arteus asked.

"I don't know," he admitted. "I didn't pay attention to the distance of the sound."

"Are you sure we're headed in the right direction?"

"Art..." Truthfully, Ikarim was beginning to think he really didn't have any idea where he was going. It was pitch black out, so he couldn't see the distance to which they ran. What if they had passed it up? What if they were running alongside it the entire time? No... No, he just had to trust himself. They had to be close.

"Sorry. I just... I want to get my hands on the Techno Mage," Arteus admitted. "I want to wring his neck. Make him beg for breath and take his life away like he took Mags from us."

"I know," Ikarim said. "There's nothing I would appreciate more than watching him suffer, but you have to trust me on this."

"We need to get there before the intended audience."

"Art, you're not helping. Ah!" He pointed ahead. "I knew it."

There were indeed locomotive tracks before them. There was also, however, one problem and he could practically count down to the second the moment Arteus would also take notice and bring it up.

"Ike, there's no locomotive."

Ikarim finally stopped in his tracks, turning to face the tracks in one direction, then in the other. Quickly glancing over his shoulder to their camp in the distance swallowed by darkness, he looked back down the track. "This way."

"How do you know we're going in the right direction?"

"The sky is brighter this way," he said as he pointed in the direction that he decided they were to move. "It's either the sunrise or some-place extra illuminated. If it's the sunrise, then it's east and we're on the right path. If it's some-place illuminated, that means there's either a lo-comotive nearby, or—"

"A ship," Arteus interrupted, catching on.

"Exactly. Let's go."

Both men stayed along the tracks in silence. The further they went, the more the dread in the pit of Ikarim's stomach churned. They were def-initely in trouble for deserting the military. He doubted that Magaliana would have approved of them going through this, but he knew that there was no stopping Arteus so far into the game at this point.

Eventually, Ikarim paused.

"What's wrong?" Arteus asked.

His eyes were intent as he turned his head to look over the tracks behind them. Taking a step to the side, he pulled Arteus with him.

"A locomotive?"

Ikarim nodded, though whether the Strong Arm was able to see it in the dark or not was an-other matter entirely. "We don't seem to be near any major stop yet, so it'll be going full speed."

Both men waited. Once they could see the faint light in the distance, Ikarim took a few more steps back.

"Ike, where are you going?"

"It's too fast. We'll never make it aboard."

"Oh, no," Arteus growled. "I've waited long enough for this moment. We're taking it." He ran in the direction of the oncoming train.

"Art!" Ikarim hissed. "Where are you going?"

"Just keep running! And be sure to hold on tight when I get there!"

Ikarim stared at Arteus in disbelief. He wasn't serious, was he? They'd never make it alive! Cursing at himself for going along with this insane idea, he did as his friend instructed and ran ahead.

The locomotive whooshed past him. Just as he had suspected, it was moving too fast to safely jump aboard.

"Ike!" Arteus called from behind him.

Ikarim continued running at full speed, peeking over his shoulder occasionally to see where Arteus was. Finally, he saw a glint of the man's cybernetics out of the corner of his eye.

"Grab on!" Arteus called out.

Ikarim reached his arm out toward his friend but missed. He gritted his teeth and tried again. Their fingers barely connected.

"Ike! Hurry!"

"I'm trying!" Ikarim gave one last push, reaching out once more for his friend's out-stretched arm. Arteus was barely able to grab onto his wrist, yanking him forward. Ikarim's eyes went wide when his feet no longer touched the ground.

That was it. He was done for. He wouldn't make it.

Arteus struggled to hold on as his free hand grabbed his friend's shoulder. Ikarim panicked even more as he realized the Strong Arm broke the number one safety rule to staying alive while on a moving train—keep three limbs attached to the train at all times. Arteus had two hands on Ikarim as he tried to pull him up, and only hung on by his feet.

Finally, Arteus pulled Ikarim up and into himself. The Strong Arm stumbled backward but soon both men stopped moving. Ikarim was still frozen in fear as he looked out at the fast-moving ground. Finally, he turned his attention to his friend.

"That was..." Arteus started, trying to catch his breath.

"Let's not try that again," Ikarim said.

Art nodded and closed his eyes as he rested against the cart. "What now?"

Ikarim peeked out toward the front before turning his attention back to his friend. "We need to be very quiet and keep an eye out for somebody trying to kick us off. I know they are aware that we tried. I was running ahead of the locomotive, after all. And if nobody comes while the train is moving, they will definitely be on the lookout for us once we stop at the next station."

CHAPTER 38

Ikarim was thankful the remainder of the ride to the station was uneventful, but once the locomotive began to slow down, he scanned about, on the lookout for any potential person coming to look for them.

When the steam engine came to a stop, look for them they did.

"I saw one, but I'm sure they're not alone," said an approaching voice.

A wave of fear washed over Ikarim as his eyes widened in panic. Arteus rushed them both off the cart to the opposite side of the train, where he pulled Ikarim into a bush with him, hiding among the leaves. Three men approached, lanterns in hand, searching for potential stowaways. Ikarim watched them for a moment before his eyes went elsewhere, searching for a ship of any type that they could potentially borrow without intent of returning.

Unfortunately, they hadn't quite reached a small town like he hoped, but rather a tiny depot area that seemed like a fill-up station. Ikarim's attention shifted back to the three men as they grew closer to the bush, still searching for the train hoppers. He held his breath, hoping his loudly-thumping heart wouldn't give away his location.

Thankfully, the three men continued their search to the end of the train before turning back.

"Maybe the train was moving too fast..." said one.

"That won't be a pretty mess to clean up," another added as they made their way back to the front.

When they were far enough from audible reach, Ikarim finally released his breath. He allowed his heart to slow down back to somewhat normality before he finally whispered to Arteus, "There is no ship for us to take here. We need to continue on to the closest town."

Neither one moved until the train released steam and a loud clank sounded, which was their signal that it would be on the move within the next few moments. Ikarim gestured for Arteus to follow with a nudge of his head before darting out of the hiding spot toward the locomotive. The Strong Arm was quick to follow. Grabbing a hold of the coupling, Ikarim hoisted himself up in between cars and held on tight as the train began to move. His feet firmly planted and one arm wrapped around the ladder, his eyes were growing heavy in the monotonous chugging of the locomotive. He wished that he could just shut his eyes but knew that he couldn't risk losing grip and falling off.

Neither mechanic said a word. Frankly, Ikarim was too exhausted to know what to say, or even how to deal with Arteus' split-second decisions. He just hoped that the next few steps in their crazy plan went as smoothly as possible.

Eventually the train slowed. Daybreak had arrived, and the sun peeked on the horizon. Ikarim glanced about, his mind in a fatigued haze. He had to think of something as the locomotive continued to slow.

"Maybe we should jump off now and walk the rest of the way," he suggested, groggy.

"Good idea."

Ikarim leaped off first and almost lost his footing but Arteus caught him, gripping him by the arm and holding him steady.

"Are you sure you're fit to continue on?" Arteus asked, concerned.

Ikarim only nodded as they darted away from the train. The sudden adrenaline rush was just what his mind needed to wake up. At least they were too far away to be completely noticed.

They walked in silence until they reached the small village, where early-rising vendors were up and about getting ready for the day. Ikarim knew their respective units would have found out about their desertion by now and hoped that word had not yet reached their current location. Nevertheless, until they were out of their army fatigues and could blend in proper, they stuck to the shadows to remain mostly unseen.

Ikarim eventually exchanged their fatigues for various other articles with numerous beggars—while also giving them a few German coins—to cover their trail as much as possible.

"Art," he pointed, drawing the man's attention to a small docked dirigible.

"Let's go for it," Arteus acknowledged.

"Wait!" Ikarim held out his arm, then ducked down, pulling his friend with him as people approached the ship, parcels in hand. Ikarim groaned. There was no way they could take the airship now.

"Oh..." Arteus grabbed Ikarim by the shoulders to spin him around. A ship was anchored outside of a small junkyard. With its bulky, steel-paneled rear-engine module and giant wing-mounted turbine drums, the transport airship would definitely be able to go so much faster than the dirigible.

"We don't know what's wrong with it," Ikarim pointed out. It was by a dumping ground, after all.

"Absolutely nothing is wrong with it," Arteus said.

"How do you figure?"

"It's too clean."

Ikarim stared at his friend for a long moment, judging whether he was serious or not. Finally, the Strong Arm tore his eyes away from the ship to meet his friend's gaze, nodding toward the airship. Ikarim inhaled and exhaled deeply. He wasn't sure how much more trouble he could possibly get into before everything was said and done, but he wagered that this little stunt that they were about to pull was nothing in comparison to what else he could potentially do. Mentally preparing himself, he cautiously snuck his way toward it, followed by Arteus.

They counted five people boarding the ship with supplies, then watched them disembark empty-handed. Quick to notice the pattern in which they were moving, Ikarim ran aboard once all five men reentered the building, while Arteus stayed behind to keep an eye out.

What luck! The ignition was an easy one to start, and the key was conveniently left in plain sight. Grabbing it, he shoved it into the ignition and the motor roared to life. From the cockpit, he could see the five individuals barging out of the building to see what was going on. Arteus shot one in the leg, only aiming to wound and slow down.

"Art!"

The Strong Arm ran aboard and flung the docking board to the side so that nobody could come in with them.

"Can you take off?" Arteus asked as he rushed into the flight deck area.

"Weigh anchor, and I'll have us up in no time," he replied, pulling a few levers.

"I'm on it!"

"We also need coal! I'm not sure how much steam we have," he called as Arteus barreled down the corridor.

"It's on the list!"

Ikarim smirked as Arteus disappeared, pulling the wheel toward himself. The ship rose and advanced once the anchor was up. A few more buttons and careful maneuvering around the buildings, and they were off.

"Tasks complete," Arteus said upon his return.

"Take the wheel," Ikarim instructed him. "I need to figure out where we are going." Shuffling out of the seat, he dug around for a map and carefully measured the coordinates from the stabbed rag.

"It's a forest in Romania," he confirmed, turning back to his friend.

"Let's hope we're not too late."

They continued in silence. When it was safe, they took turns at the wheel while the other napped. Ikarim hadn't intended on adding theft to his list of accomplishments next to military deserter, but there was no turning back now. He was in too deep.

CHAPTER 39

"Art," Ikarim said urgently. They had been travelling for a few hours, and it was late afternoon when he spotted some ships in the distance with help from a spyglass.

"Who brought in the hired guns?" Arteus asked, his attention on the scene ahead.

It was a curious sight, but one Ikarim figured might have been the norm for the mercenaries: A lone ship surrounded by an array of various rogue vessels—a few sleek and aerodynamic, some with tall ship bodies attached to large balloons, a handful of zeppelin types, a sprinkle of repurposed bulky transport ships. The encircled wooden brig was definitely a sight to behold, with its unusual fin-like sails spread out like the wings of a dragon, and a terrifying representative figurehead of the maw of the mythical beast set at the prow.

313

"I bet you the Techno Mage is aboard that one." Ikarim glanced toward the map. "That looks to be the right coordinates."

Arteus made an attempt to crack his knuckles but due to the cybernetics, nothing happened. "He's mine." Vengeance dripped in his voice.

"This junker could fit right in," Ikarim confirmed.

They approached, only to find the mass of airships at war with one another, shooting their cannons and guns. Ikarim furrowed his brows; matters just got infinitely more complicated. He couldn't tell who the enemy was. With a hiss of disapproval, he surveyed the scene in an attempt to find the Techno Mage.

"There!" he said. "He's on the dragon ship."

Turning the wheel, they changed course, beelining for the Mage. Arteus stepped away to the hatch, grabbing the rolled-up mass of ropes that was the ladder.

"Toss it down!" Ikarim instructed as he rushed to his friend from the cockpit. "This ship is a lost cause, but we'll have enough time to climb down if we start now."

The hatch opened, tousling his hair as Arteus flung the ladder out. Ikarim watched the ropes and wood dance in the air before he paused, something catching his attention further down. Squinting, he focused on the forest in the Lands Below, covered in a thick haze. "What is that...?"

He had never actually seen the aftermath of an area after being fired on by the Carronade. Could this be it?

"Ike!" Arteus urged.

Focusing on the matter at hand, Ikarim descended, with Arteus mere seconds behind. Jumping off and onto the deck of the dragon ship, he barely had time to react when he was immediately forced to dodge a sharp blade by tumbling to the side. Arteus jumped onto the attacker, giving Ikarim a much-deserved moment to regain his bearings.

More rogues approached—or were they the Techno Mage's goons? He couldn't figure out who was an ally or an enemy, and it seemed that amid their chaos, they couldn't, either. Not wanting to kill the wrong team, Ikarim pulled out his revolver and aimed to strictly subdue and slow down, shooting the few who appeared immediately threatening to his or Arteus' life.

Glancing about for Jocephus, he whistled sharply to get the Strong Arm's attention when he finally spotted the Mage. Unfortunately, the fighting crowd and crossfire was overwhelming. Growling at the number of obstacles separating them from their target, Ikarim knew the only way to succeed was to unfortunately thin out the herd.

Both mechanics fought long and hard. The battle was only slightly easier for Ikarim thanks to his military training, but the amount of flashbacks to his time as Captain Keenan's captive were each more uncomfortable than the last. He kept his wits about him, however, and a watchful eye—when he could—on the location of the Techno Mage.

Eventually, it seemed like one of the teams won. Ikarim wasn't sure which side, nor did he particularly care to find out when he looked over to see the Techno Mage against the edge of the hull with a blade to his throat and his hands near his head in surrender. At the sword's hilt stood a fierce woman, her shoulder-length rust-colored hair whipping in the wind. A man with scruffy blond hair and a thick tuft on his chin stood by in a nonchalant pose, though he watched the woman intently.

Ikarim darted for the Techno Mage but a band of rogues stopped him at gunpoint. Arteus grabbed one of the guns and crushed it with ease, but bullets from the others peppered him until the infusions bled from his arms, temporarily paralyzing him.

They forcefully shoved him to the ground and pinned him in place. Ikarim surrendered peacefully, wincing from the force the mercenaries applied to keep him in place. But that hardly mattered. What caught his attention was the woman speaking to the Techno Mage.

"Take off your clothes," she ordered in English, her thick German accent apparent from behind her leather altitude mask. The Mage only blinked in surprise. "Take off your clothes!" she screamed. Jocephus obeyed.

"Greta…" the scruffy man gently warned.

"Why are you doing this?" asked Jocephus as he removed his clothes. "Am I to be your love slave?"

"No. I just don't want anybody to think of you as a fallen angel once you jump."

Ikarim's heart skipped a beat and an image of Magaliana in her wedding dress and metal wings falling into nothingness flashed through his mind. He shot a quick glance to Arteus to see if his friend had overheard as he did. They had never heard or read of anyone ever finding Magaliana's body. Was she still alive? Focusing on her, this woman did appear to have the same short height and petite frame. Could she be Magaliana?

"A fallen angel!" Jocephus' smirk and raised brows revealed that he came to the same conclusion as Ikarim.

"Jump," she ordered.

"Greta, that's enough," the man nearby said.

"Jump," she repeated, the anger returning to her tone.

Jocephus turned and grabbed the nearest rigging, climbing the thick gunwale of the ship. Ikarim noticed the strange markings covering his body, which made him slightly uncomfortable, and the only conclusion he could come up

317

with was that it was witchcraft.

The Techno Mage turned back to face the woman. "You don't want to do this," he started.

"Jump!" In the blink of an eye, she lunged forward, stabbing the Techno Mage in the shoulder.

"Greta!"

Jocephus stumbled backward, slipping off the edge. Flinging her blade back, it embedded itself into the wood of the deck as, in one swift action, Greta grabbed her pistol and pointed it below.

"Maggie!" scolded the scruffy man as he grabbed her shoulder and pulled her back, finally getting her attention. Ikarim froze at the name.

"Mags?" Arteus gasped from his pinned position on his stomach.

Greta spun around with such a spiteful glare to the man who had stopped her, then scoffed and stormed off when he didn't back down, but not before directing her gaze to Ikarim. The hard stare was foreign, making him instantly reassess if the woman truly was Magaliana or not. For a split second, however, her gaze softened, allowing him to recognize her beautiful green eyes and see the real her; hurt and scared.

"Mags, wait!" Arteus called out, but she did not turn around.

The scruffy man sauntered toward the captives, his unimpressed focus on the Strong Arm. "Who are you?" he asked in German.

"Arteus Gesselmeyer. *Doktor* Gesselmeyer's adopted son," he answered. "We're friends with Mags, please let us go!"

The man's eyes went from one mechanic to the other. "And that would make you Ikarim?" he said, switching to English.

The weapons tech cast him a suspicious look. "It depends who asks..."

"Come, now," he smirked. "Don't you recognize your own brother?"

Ikarim's eyes went wide. "Eliakim?"

"The one and only," he grinned, signaling to his men to release Arteus. "Follow me," Eliakim pointed to Arteus' leaking cybernetics. "We'll head back to my ship and have Greta fix your arms."

"You mean Mags?" Art countered with a glare.

"I mean what I said. She has not been this... Mags... you mention for quite a long time, now. She is Greta Kretschmer."

Ikarim cast his friend a warning glance before he followed his brother. Arteus, reluctantly, wasn't too far behind.

CHAPTER 40

The *Fang* was a quaint and crowded wooden barque with an immense, rigid balloon secured overhead. Massive masts were built at the top of the transverse rings as well as to the sides, where sails were attached and billowing in the breeze. Broad vanes propelled the ship forward from a central spot at the rear of the hull, while the tail fins directed the craft. The crow's nest, instead of being situated at the highest point of the main mast, was beneath the keel as the lowest point.

Ikarim followed his brother in silence to the medical room, where the scruffy man grabbed a few infusions. He hadn't seen his brother in so long, but he was conflicted about how he should truly feel—the man was a rogue, after all. While the pirates were their own level of despicable and the true criminals of the world, rogues were mercenaries, hired by whoever had the highest bid: Drug Lords, royalty, even the military. Eliakim was Captain of his own fleet, to top it off. Could he be trusted?

"I want Mags to make my concoction!" Arteus snapped. "And I thought you said that you were going to have her fix my arms?"

"Greta is..." he started, glancing out down the hall, "... currently indisposed, so you'll have to settle for me. And this is hers." He nudged his head toward the infusions as he reached for a rolled-up satchel of fine tools. "The 'Greta Special', as we call it.

"What do you mean by 'indisposed'?" Arteus growled.

"When the door to my quarters is closed, it usually means she wants to be left alone." Ikarim and Arteus looked to one another with worry, but Eliakim shrugged it off. "She does what she does then returns to my quarters, never to be seen for the rest of the night. Nothing to be concerned about."

Eliakim worked delicately. Ikarim watched him, impressed. He wondered if his brother had a natural knack for the work, or if he had been taught by their father. Ikarim parted his lips to ask about their parents but before he could say anything, Eliakim spoke. "We found her falling from the sky."

"What?" Arteus asked, a brow raised in confusion.

"Greta," Eliakim replied, his eyes trained on his work, never once rising to meet either Arteus or Ikarim's. "She was falling from the sky. We caught her. She was so breathtaking that we thought her a fallen angel, what with her beautiful blonde hair, long white dress, and a pair of wings. For the longest time, she did not talk or eat. She did nothing but cry. And one day, she snapped." Eliakim finally looked to his brother. "She chopped off her hair and used alchemy to change the color. She changed her name and became ruthless. Almost done," he added, to the Strong Arm.

Arteus' gaze was on the ground.

"How did you know who I was?" Ikarim asked, a change of subject for Arteus' sake as Eliakim finished up.

The scruffy man put the syringes and vials away, then closed the case of remaining infusions. He finally met his younger brother's gaze. "We've been keeping tabs on you."

"That sounds like something a mercenary would say..." Arteus muttered.

"What do you mean?" Ikarim asked, ignoring his friend's tone but secretly hoping the Strong Arm wasn't correct.

"After you and Dad went up, Mum and I returned home. The plan was to wait for Dad to gather enough money to send for us, but he returned without you. Mum was devastated. Dad did everything that he could to find you, and eventually he did, when *Doktor* Gesselmeyer came to the Lands Below. Dad talked to him."

"He never told us that..." Arteus said.

Eliakim shook his head. "No, Dad told him not to."

"Why not?" Ikarim demanded.

Eliakim put the case of infusions away then stepped past Ikarim, walking away without answering. Ikarim frowned before he followed closely as the Captain made his way to the kitchens.

"Why not?" he repeated.

The scruffy blond man exchanged a few words with the cook.

"Eli! Answer me!" He shouted, fists clenched, not caring whose attention he grabbed among the rest of the crew. But Eliakim was silent and still, his back to his brother. Why was he purposely avoiding the conversation? Ikarim deserved to know. "Is it a mercenary thing?" Ikarim spat, not wanting to say it, but finding it necessary.

Finally, Eliakim turned around, his blue eyes hard.

"You're dodging answers," Arteus said from behind Ikarim, anger in his voice as well. "Pretty suspicious for someone who was keeping tabs on us."

Eliakim huffed. "It's not a mercenary thing."

"Eli..." Ikarim said with a sigh. "I spent my entire life thinking I would never see you again.

Then there was a possibility, and *Doktor* Gesselmeyer just kept silent about it? I find that hard to believe. Why can't we just go get them and bring them aboard? We can live at *Doktor* Gesselmeyer's mansion..."

"Dad didn't want *Doktor* Gesselmeyer telling you because you had a good life up there, little brother! He didn't want you coming back to what our home had become!" he exploded.

Ikarim blinked in the sudden deafening silence. He didn't understand why his brother had kept so tight-lipped about it, but there was something else about what he had said that bothered him—scared him, even. "What..." he started, a lump in his throat. "What has our home become?"

Eliakim's irritation shifted to sadness, and he turned around, beckoning the mechanics to follow. He led them to a cozy recreational room with plenty of cushioned seating built into the walls and leaned against a long pool table sitting in the middle of the room as he picked up one of the wooden balls. "Sit down, you're going to need it."

Ikarim gulped and did as his brother instructed, taking a seat next to a small bookshelf full of literature in various languages, while Arteus' seat of choice was near a shelf containing a fife, concertina, and viola.

"The Carronade hit five years ago."

Ikarim's eyes shut as dread washed over him. The worst-case scenario was that his parents were dead, and he really didn't want to think that.

"Mum was the first to change and progressed far more rapidly than Dad. *Doktor* Gesselmeyer heard about the Carronade firing and came for research. Dad found him and pleaded with him to help Mum. When he followed Dad home and saw a broken frame with the family portrait, he recognized you, so he was adamant to help. Despite the danger, *Doktor* Gesselmeyer made weekly trips to try and slow Mum's change. When that wasn't working, he tried to find a way to reverse it entirely. He had Greta—Mags—work extra hard to create more infusions for us, and he would return with samples of the haze to try and understand it."

"That's got to be where he would always travel to," Arteus mused. "And why he would return worse for wear."

"There is only a small window of time before the haze starts affecting people," Eliakim said. "It affects everyone differently."

"Are you affected?" Ikarim asked.

Eliakim glanced down for a moment, seemingly pondering his answer. Ikarim frowned. Was he going to keep his answer to himself, again?

"I was," he finally answered, looking back up to his brother.

"You were?" Ikarim and Arteus said in unison.

"I was cured," Eliakim admitted. "Greta's infusions reversed the effects of the haze."

"If it cured you..." Ikarim started.

"Then why didn't it work on Mum or Dad?" Eliakim finished. "Because the change affected me the least. I was quicker to cure."

"Why was it so hard for you to say all of this earlier?" Arteus asked.

"Because saying 'hello, little brother, I haven't seen you in years! Oh, by the way, Mum and Dad are hazed' seemed like a really bad conversation starter."

Arteus said nothing, which surprised Ikarim. The bright, metallic shimmer of a triangle sounded throughout the ship, and Eliakim cast a sad smile to the duo before he pushed away from the billiard table. "Soup is on."

They followed him to the dining area, which was decorated with frames of various airships. Tables were set up on both sides, leaving the center free. They grabbed bowls of steaming *sauerbraten* and sat at one of the tables while Eliakim took a bowl to Magaliana, leaving both men to eat their roast stew in silence with the crew of the *Fang*.

Ikarim tried to process everything that his brother told them, from finding Magaliana to what happened to their parents. He wondered what he could have done for things to go differently and hated himself for not asking more questions whenever Gesselmeyer returned from his 'errands'. He felt utterly helpless.

Eventually, most of the crew finished their meal and returned to wherever they came from. Eliakim finally returned. Arteus cast him a concerned glance, to which he simply replied with a sigh and shake of his head. It seemed Magaliana would not be joining them.

"How did you find the Techno Mage?" Ikarim asked, breaking the silence.

"Ah, that was Greta's magnificent idea," he grinned. "The Techno Mage only gives you an audience when you have something he needs in exchange, so we got the message through that I wished for double the amount of the reward for finding Greta's body. Of course, he came running at the mention of his bride-to-be being alive."

Arteus glowered jealously into his empty bowl. Ikarim quirked a brow, impressed by the plan.

"Of course," Eliakim continued after taking a few bites, "we expected an ambush, so we brought along some friends. Greta says it's unlike him to have a large crew with him, but we figured that he must have really wanted her back..."

He finished his food while Ikarim's mind went a million miles per second. That was a lot of information to take in. He looked at Arteus, whose scowl had shifted into a pout. The sulk remained even after the Captain took his bowl away.

"Come on, I had some additional cots set up in the sleeping quarters. I'll lead you there."

He led them to the sleeping quarters and stayed until both men were settled.

"Can you take me to Mama and Papa tomorrow?" Ikarim asked.

"I have a pretty tight schedule I have to keep to."

"Please, Eli..." Ikarim quietly begged. "I need to see them."

"What's more important than letting your brother visit with your parents?" Arteus asked.

Eliakim turned to the Strong Arm. "Minus the fact that it's very dangerous to go down into the haze for any period of time, we're on the *Faugregir*'s trail."

Arteus blinked. "You know where the mythical ship is?"

"No, but we're so close that I can taste it. We can't turn around," he started, and Ikarim's face fell, "but I can arrange a secondary ship to take us, if you wish," he quickly added.

Ikarim nodded. He knew he interrupted his brother's plans, but he was kind enough to give in. He had to sort through all the information he had received anyway, though he wondered why he was chasing the mythical ship when everyone clearly saw Jocephus fall to his death.

"Goodnight." Eliakim turned around and made his way out of the sleeping quarters.

"Thank you, Eli. For everything."

Eliakim paused at the entrance and turned to look at his little brother. He gave a single nod of acknowledgement before he moved on and disappeared from sight.

"If Mags sleeps in his quarters, I wonder where he sleeps," Arteus mused out loud.

"Wherever the hell he feels like sleeping," came an annoyed grumble from another cot—one of the crew from the *Fang*. "He's the Captain."

Arteus gave a sheepish expression before he settled into his cot. Ikarim did the same, and since his naps aboard their stolen ship had been short-lived, he was very quick to fall into a dreamless sleep.

CHAPTER 41

Ikarim and Eliakim left shortly after break-fast, while Arteus stayed behind to help where needed. Ikarim appreciated the Strong Arm's offer to give them some space and alone time to connect. They were well on their way to England in the Lands Below aboard a small ship from Eliakim's fleet when Ikarim, breaking the silence, finally spoke up.

"Your German is quite impressive," he said, recalling the ease with which he switched in between both languages the previous day.

"I'm proficient in twelve languages," Eliakim said. "Helps me to know when my contractors are trying to pull fast ones on my team. And your English is horrible," he added with a chuckle. "But I suppose it's to be expected, growing up with the Germans and all that..."

"Why did you become a rogue?" Ikarim asked. He wanted to know why his brother chose the less-than-honorable route in life, as thankful as he was that he hadn't outright chosen piracy instead. "What do Mama and Papa think?"

Eliakim became serious once more, and it took him a moment to reply. "I wanted to take Mum and Dad to the Upper Lands. The quickest way to do it was to offer my services to the highest bidder. They didn't approve, at first—especially Mum—but they eventually came to terms with it as long as they didn't know about the details."

Ikarim fell silent as his gaze dropped, his heart heavy. He had definitely been granted a great life by being adopted by Gesselmeyer.

Eventually the Captain spoke up once more. "You're going to have fifteen minutes. That's pushing it, I should really only give you ten. I can't guarantee how your body will react to anything longer. The effects of the haze will definitely start attacking your genetic makeup."

"Understood." Despite all his military training, he was scared, nervous, and determined all at once, along with a few other vastly different feelings and emotions.

"We're almost here." Eliakim grabbed a nearby case and opened it, revealing a few vials of infusions and syringes. He placed one vial into the body of the needle and brought it to his left arm, stabbing himself and injecting the infusion. Grabbing another syringe and vial, he

331

turned to Ikarim. "I won't lie, this won't feel good."

He stabbed his brother in the arm. Ikarim hissed and winced as liquid fire spread out from his arm to his whole body. For a brief moment, he thought that the rogue Captain had slipped him some poison instead. That's it. He was done for.

Eliakim pulled the needle out and clapped his brother on the back, bringing his thoughts back to the present. Ikarim grimaced as he rubbed his arm. Shouting orders to his crewman to gently lower the ship, the Captain headed to the hatch and picked up the huge ladder, tossing it over.

Once they descended past the clouds, Ikarim's eyes went wide: Everything was in shambles, like the whole place had been suddenly deserted and left to crumble.

"After you," Eliakim said.

His attention was all over the place once on the ground. He just could not believe his eyes.

"Quickly," Eliakim urged, rushing ahead.

He led Ikarim to a home in ruins, half of its walls destroyed and crumbled. He wondered how his parents were even still living in such a place, but Eliakim stepped past the debris as one who had done it hundreds of times before, until he reached a hidden door in the floor. Pulling the handle, he revealed a hidden staircase.

"They live in the basement. Go, I'll stand guard here."

Ikarim nodded and treaded carefully down each step, the wood creaking beneath his weight no matter how careful he was. The basement was a mess once he reached the bottom, with piles of junk everywhere. He knew that he had to be quick, but his heart raced in wonder at what was around the corner.

"Eli? Is that you?" came a man's voice.

"No." Ikarim's answer was shaky, the tone of his voice high-pitched in fear and excitement and dread.

"Who are you?" asked the man. "What do you want from us?"

Ikarim turned the corner to see a stick-thin figure with one arm sitting in a rocking chair, alarm in his features. His stringy salt-and-pepper hair quivered when he trembled, and Ikarim couldn't tell if it was from fear, or a side-effect of the haze. Next to him was a bed with a thin, white sheet covering what appeared to be a sleeping form.

Speechless, Ikarim took slow, careful steps toward the man, who squinted at him for a long time before his eyes went wide.

"What's wrong?" asked a frail-sounding woman in bed. "Who is it?"

"Hello, Papa," Ikarim finally managed to say, with a quiver in his voice. "Hello, Mama."

His mother gasped out his name, while his father covered his mouth with a shaky hand.

Ikarim rushed forward, dropping to his knees in front of his father, who leaned forward, grabbing Ikarim by the shoulders to pull him into a hug. His mother extended a frail and bony hand to her son, who took her hand in his. His eyes welled with tears. "I can't believe you are both still alive..."

"I will be for a long time yet," his father said with a sigh. "I seem to have been cursed with long life in this crippled state. Your mother, well... she doesn't have very long left."

"That's going to change," Ikarim said as he pulled away. "Pack lightly, we're taking you with us. We'll bring you to safety. Eli was cured, so we can cure you, too, if we can get you out of the haze!"

Ikarim's father shook his head sadly. "We can't."

"You...?" Ikarim blinked, confused. "What do you mean you can't?"

"Your mother can't get up."

"I'll carry her!" Ikarim moved faster than his father was able to retort. Pulling the sheet away from his mother, he snatched his hand back as if a snake bit him. From the waist down, the woman was nothing but a tangle of bones. In fact, she wasn't lying on the bed at all, but rather on a pile of her own osseous matter.

Ikarim's father sighed. "Your mother can't get up. We've tried. She is rooted into the ground pretty deep. She must stay here, and I am not leaving her."

"Mama..." Ikarim was lost. He did not know what to do.

"Ike!" Eliakim called out, footsteps quickly pounding down into the basement. "There's not much time left, we need to leave." He then added "Hello, Mum. Hello, Dad," with a smile as if absolutely nothing horrific was going on.

"Hello, my sweet angel," their mother weakly replied.

"There's nothing we can do," Ikarim's father said. "It's far too late. Go on, it's alright. We've made peace with it." Ikarim still felt horrified, like a lost little child. His father grabbed one of his hands and squeezed. "We're proud of you, son. We've always been proud of you. We're sorry we did not request to see you sooner, but we figured you could go your whole life without seeing this."

"Ike!" Eliakim urged.

Ikarim's eyes stung from the welling tears. He clamped them shut and took a large inhale before he turned to his mother. Exhaling, he opened his eyes and smiled gently at her, though the sadness was evident. Covering her back up with the white sheet, he made sure she was comfortable before he leaned in and kissed her forehead.

Standing back up, he turned to his father in the rocking chair, who extended out his only arm for him to take. Ikarim grabbed his father's arm but leaned in and hugged the crippled man tight. Then he pulled away without a word and rushed toward his brother, following him back up the stairs without looking back.

Back aboard the small ship, Eliakim coiled the ladder. "Follow me, I need to give you another infusion for—"

Ikarim pounced on the Captain. One hand gripping his brother's throat, he pushed him over the edge of the hatch. "How could you just stand by and watch as if nothing happened?" Ikarim bellowed. "How could you not do a thing to help?"

"For Christ's sake, Mum is a *tree*!" Eliakim tried to yell back despite his throat being crushed.

The other two crewmen aboard the ship rushed to their Captain's aid, aiming and cocking their weapons at Ikarim. Eliakim held up a hand to halt them, then gave an exasperated look to his brother. Ikarim finally pulled his brother back inside, where Eliakim stumbled and gasped for air. Ikarim raised his hands near his head, not wanting to get shot. Threatening the life of a rogue Captain was probably one of the stupider things that he had ever done, and he suddenly realized why Arteus was always quick to anger.

"You could have tried..." he said.

"We did try!" Eliakim spat. "You're not the one who had to live with the haze, Ikarim! You're not the one who had to watch Mum's health decline so quickly! You're not the one who had to fend off the haze-rats from stealing every possession we've ever owned, or from killing Mum and Dad! You're not the one who had to live with the decision that Mum was never going to make it even if we tried, so she gave up her treatments to her hazed son! Do you think I wanted all of this? Don't you think that I tried everything in my power to change this?" Eliakim's anger dissipated into sadness. "To fix this?"

He instructed one of his crewmen to quickly fetch the infusions and to give himself and Ikarim a dose. Unable to say or do anything, Ikarim simply allowed his eyes to drop in silence. Eliakim was right: He couldn't judge what his brother did or didn't do, could or couldn't do. He had managed to do everything he could with the information he had at his disposal at the time.

Ikarim flinched from the injection and could have sworn that there was hostility in the administration, but he did not fight it. In all fairness, he probably deserved it. He finally looked back to his brother, whose eyes were shut as he took his dose. "I'm sorry."

Opening his eyes, he glowered at his younger brother. "I like to think that I'm a pretty laid-back Captain, but if you *ever* do that again, brother or not, I will toss you overboard without a second thought." Eliakim stormed away, followed by his crew, leaving Ikarim alone. He felt horrible, and his brother's words were entirely justified. He found himself once again relating to Arteus, completely understanding how the man wallowed in his depression after punching him.

Ikarim made sure to stay out of his brother's way the remainder of the trip back to the *Fang*.

CHAPTER 42

They reached the *Fang* by evening. Ikarim still felt horrible about attacking his brother the way he did. He figured he still needed to keep his distance, but he broke the silence before they disembarked. There was something he needed to do.

"Eli..." he tried quietly and continued once the Captain turned around to look at him, "I need to return home." When his brother shook his head and parted his lips to speak, Ikarim was quick to interrupt. "I can take the ship myself, you don't have to come along."

"Absolutely not."

"Eli, I need to go back to the library. I need to research what the Carronade is. I need to look through *Doktor* Gesselmeyer's notes. Please," he begged. "I want to try and help Mama and Papa."

"There's nothing we can do, Ikarim!" Eliakim hissed. "Please drop the subject—"

"Listen. You might have done everything in
your possibility while you were living it, but Art
and I have lived with *Doktor* Gesselmeyer the
longest. We might not look it, but we have
learned a few things from him. Even Mags—
MAGS!" he said, his eyes wide in sudden realization. "I need to speak with Mags!"

Eliakim looked to his brother as if he could-
n't keep up. He shook his head. "You are dizzy-
ing, brother, but I'll ask Greta. Follow me."

Ikarim's heart fluttered. Finally, he'd get to
see Magaliana! He followed his brother to the
closed doors of the Captain's quarters, where
the man pulled a key from his belt and unlocked
the door. Cracking it open, he turned to Ikarim.
"Stay here."

Ikarim blinked, taken aback, as the Captain
disappeared into the room, shutting the door
behind him. So, he wasn't going to be able to see
her after all? He was almost offended.

Eliakim opened the door once more, arms
full of books and scrolls, which he handed to his
brother. "When next we dock for supplies, you
can return to Germany for your research. In the
meantime, these are the notes I took each time
Doktor Gesselmeyer visited, and here are some
books that you might find something useful in."

"Thank you."

Ikarim caught a glimpse of Magaliana in the Captain's quarters before his brother closed the door. She sat in a chair with her feet propped up on a thick, wooden desk, a book in hand. Their eyes met for a moment before she was hidden from sight once more, separated by the door. Ikarim was alone.

He wanted to barge into the Captain's quarters so bad. He missed Magaliana with all of his being, but he didn't realize just how much that was until they made eye contact. He missed her so much it hurt. He just wanted to hug her, to hold her and never let go.

He forced himself to turn away. It seemed like Eliakim wasn't in a hurry to request help for him. Making his way to the entertainment room, he sprawled everything onto the billiard table and began his new quest.

Crew members came and went. Ikarim had gone through five scrolls and one book, and was well into skimming the second one when Arteus walked in with a lantern. "What are you doing?"

"Research."

"Clearly. What kind of research?"

Ikarim slammed the book shut, sending dust flying. Slowly closing his eyes, he rubbed them, irritated and exhausted, before finally answering. "I'm trying to find information on the Carronade... And so far, I have nothing."

"Does this have something to do with your visit to your parents?" Arteus asked as he grabbed the viola from the shelf and sat down.

Ikarim nodded and looked to his friend. "I need to go back home for *Doktor* Gesselmeyer's research. Eli was supposed to ask Mags for help, but I haven't seen him emerge from his quarters since I left him hours ago."

Arteus absentmindedly plucked the strings and paused at his friend's words, a flash of jealousy in his features. "I haven't seen him either, sorry," he mumbled as he resumed plucking.

"It's fine."

"Do you want help in your research?"

"No, I'll continue in the morning. Thank you for the offer, though."

Arteus nodded and stood up, putting the instrument away. He helped Ikarim carry the scrolls and books back to their cots and fell asleep pretty quickly. Ikarim laid in the cot, his mind going over the events of the day. It was going to be a long night.

CHAPTER 43

Ikarim awoke with the crew but was quick to retreat to the entertainment room once he scarfed down his breakfast, pouring himself into his research for another few hours. He needed to find something, anything on the Carronade. He took it upon himself to help his parents, despite what everyone had already done. There just had to be a way.

Eliakim eventually came to check on him, lounging leisurely on the cushioned benches. "So?" he asked. "How's the research going?"

Ikarim continued to flip through pages. "Your notes are remarkably interesting. The books, not so much."

"Well," Eliakim shrugged, "I tried..."

"I know." Ikarim finally tore his eyes away from the book and looked to his brother. "Did you ask Mags to help? You never came back, and I figured that—"

"That I forgot?" Eliakim smirked. "I did ask her."

"And?"

"And she refuses to help."

"What...?"

"Listen, she does what she wants. And I wouldn't blame her: She's been through a lot."

Ikarim glowered. "Is that your excuse as well?"

"No," his brother replied as he stood back up. "I'm the Captain, that's different."

Eliakim walked away, leaving Ikarim on his own once more. Realizing that he was glaring at nothing in particular, he shut his eyes and sighed. He knew Magaliana had been through a lot. He couldn't possibly imagine what she went through while he and Arteus were in the military, but to be so cold to not want to see or speak to them after everything they had been through together? Grumbling in frustration, he opened his eyes and went back to his research.

After another hour, something in one of the books caught his attention. His body stiffened and his heart skipped a beat as he focused on the few paragraphs he had just read.

"Eli!" he called out loudly as he finished reading. "Eli!"

Ikarim grabbed the book and rushed out of the room, climbing the stairs to the main deck two at a time as he continued to call for his brother.

He found Eliakim rushing toward him with a perplexed look on his face. "What's wrong?"

"It's from a mythical ship!" Ikarim said, out of breath, as he shoved the open book into his brother's face.

Eliakim caught the book and arched away from it, confusion still apparent in his features. "What are you—?"

"The Carronade! The Carronade is from a mythical ship!"

"The *Faugregir*?" Eliakim wondered out loud.

"I think so!"

"Does Greta know there was a Carronade aboard the *Faugregir*?"

"Wait, Mags was on the *Faugregir*?" It was Ikarim's turn to be confused.

"Yes," Eliakim replied in an obvious tone. "She lived aboard it with the Techno Mage. How did you not know this?"

Ikarim frowned and parted his lips to reply something snarky when Arteus rushed toward them. "What's going on?!"

"It's okay, Art," Ikarim said as he placed a hand on the man's shoulder. "I just... I found something."

"What?"

"The Carronade might be from the *Faugregir*."

"And Greta was aboard the *Faugregir*," Eliakim added.

When Arteus' eyes widened, Ikarim turned to the Captain. "You have to let me see Mags."

"No."

"Why not?" Arteus asked, anger in his voice.

"Because it doesn't work like that," Eliakim replied.

"It does work like that! You open the door and let us inside!"

"For somebody who loves her as much as you seem to," Eliakim drawled, "you sure don't have a lot of respect for a lady's privacy."

Arteus' eyes hardened and he raised a clenched fist toward the Captain. Ikarim yelled out for his friend to stop, but his arm continued. Eliakim dodged with ease as Ikarim gripped onto Arteus' shoulder, desperately trying to pull him back. A few of Eliakim's crewmen rushed to aid their Captain, and Ikarim quickly tried to diffuse the situation before things got worse.

Unfortunately, Arteus attempted to strike again.

"Art, stop! You promised I would only have to say it once!"

Arteus' eyes widened and he paused just before a few of the rogues tackled him to the ground.

"It's okay!" Ikarim called out to them before he turned his attention to his brother. "It's okay, he's done. He won't do it again, I promise."

Eliakim glared daggers at his brother for the longest time before he nodded to his crew to release the Strong Arm. As soon as he was free, Arteus jumped to his feet, hands raised by his head as a sign that he really was done.

"Get out of my sight," Eliakim spat as he spun around.

Ikarim bounded after his brother. "Eli, please. I know that Art and I are screwing up your ship. I'll take him with me back home when we dock for supplies and we'll be out of your hair soon, I promise. But please... Let me speak with Mags."

Eliakim sighed and slowed his pace, eventually coming to a stop. He turned to face his brother, his expression calmed. "It's not up to me, Ike. If Greta wants to grant you an audience with her, then by all means. But if she says no, I won't make her."

"An audience?" Ikarim repeated. "What, is she a queen now?" When Eliakim's eyes hardened into a glare again, Ikarim conceded. "Alright, alright. I'll ask her for an audience."

"Have fun with that," the Captain said as he walked away. Ikarim watched him for a moment before he turned and headed toward the Captain's quarters.

He approached the door quietly, almost afraid to disturb her. Slowly reaching for the handle, he tried to open it: The door was locked, just as he suspected. With his heart threatening to beat out of his chest, he softly knocked.

There was no answer.

He knocked again.

Still nothing.

"Mags?" he said, moving inches away from the door. "Mags?" he tried again, a little louder. "Greta? It's me, Ikarim." Still nothing. "I need to speak with you."

"No," came her simple reply, finally, from the other side.

Ikarim blinked in surprise. "Please, Mags... It's important."

She did not reply. He sighed and shook his head. So, he had to ask for an audience with her, was it? Biting his tongue and clamping his eyes shut, he tried again. "Mags... Greta. I wish to re-quest an audience with you."

"Request denied."

Ikarim's hands formed into fists as his eyes shot open. Why was she being so difficult? How badly was she hurt that her entire attitude com-pletely changed? He hurt for her. Placing his palms against the door, he leaned his forehead to the wood and shut his eyes. "Mags... I found out... I found out that the Carronade is aboard the *Faugregir*. Eli says that you were aboard the mythical ship. Do you know anything about it?" She didn't answer. "Please... I need you to tell me what you know. And if you don't know any-thing, I need you to help me. My parents... They were hazed. That's where *Doktor* Gesselmeyer was disappearing to. He was trying to help my parents. He cured Eliakim, Mags. Eli was hazed, too, and he's better now, thanks to your infusions. Please. Please help me cure my parents..."

Magaliana still did not reply. Ikarim sighed and turned around to leave, but he just couldn't. He leaned his back up against the door and slid down to the ground.

"I miss you," he said eventually. "Art misses you. We're going crazy without you. We tried finding you ever since Captain Keenan separated us. We never stopped looking for you. When we got your wedding invitation, well..." He remembered how crushed he was at the news, and how devastated Arteus immediately became. Both their hearts broke that day. "We were relieved that you were still alive... And that you were happy. Your happiness was all that mattered, Mags. But when you fell off the ship..."

He felt the tightness in his chest all over again as the image of the Alchemist falling to her death replayed in his mind. If his heart had broken at the news of her wedding, it had shattered into a million pieces when he thought he would never see her again. Trembling at the memory, he exhaled a shuddered breath.

"We never stopped hoping that you would be found. We even joined the military with the intent of finding and killing the Techno Mage. We never stopped thinking of you. Never. And now that we know that you've been alive this whole time..."

She still hadn't said anything. Was she even listening? Ikarim was pouring his heart out. Was it all for nothing?

"It's killing Art to be in such close proximity to you and not be allowed to see you. It's... It's killing me, too. What I wouldn't give for a hug, Mags, you have no idea. I want revenge. I want revenge on the world for separating us. But in the meantime, I'll settle for revenge on the *Faugregir*. Help us destroy it. Help us destroy the Carronade and the mythical ship. Help us avenge your parents' death and my parents' suffering... Help us avenge Eli, even though he's cured. He shouldn't have ever had to deal with what he has. You shouldn't have ever had to deal with what you have, either."

Ikarim stood up. He looked at the closed door, placing his hand upon it once more, as if he could somehow send his love through the surface and into the room to her.

"Whatever your decision, I'll support you. We both will, Art and I. But if you do decide to get revenge, promise that you won't do it without me. I need my revenge as well."

He released the door and walked away.

"Ike!"

He turned around just in time to catch Magaliana as she lunged into his arms. He hugged her so tightly that he was afraid to crush her, but he didn't want to let go in case he never got the opportunity to hug her ever again. They remained in each other's arms for what seemed like forever when Magaliana finally moved and looked up at him. "I have an idea."

CHAPTER 44

Magaliana approached Eliakim at the helm, ignoring the crew as they watched her in silence with curious expressions. She knew they were not used to seeing her out in the open aboard the *Fang*, as she was usually always locked up in the Captain's quarters.

Even Eliakim looked surprised before his features shifted to concern. He frowned in Ikarim's direction, but she quickly spoke before he could reprimand his brother for whatever reason. "I need the current map, the current destination coordinates, a broadcaster, sand, water, and bottles for infusions."

Eliakim blinked, then looked to his brother. Ikarim shrugged. The Captain's gaze fell back on Magaliana and he nodded at her strange request.

"I'm also going to need all of it placed in a private room. Your quarters," she added.

Eliakim looked to his brother again, as if expecting an explanation, but Ikarim was just as clueless. His gaze fell back to Magaliana. "Yes, Ma'am," he said with a smirk.

Magaliana stepped over to the edge of the deck as the Captain ordered his crewmen to gather the requested items. Even Ikarim went to fetch some of them. Resting against the gunwale with her eyes on the horizon, she wondered if her plan would work or not.

The thudding of rapid footsteps pulled her from her thoughts, and she swiftly spun around to face Arteus.

"Mags!" She flinched at the name. "I overheard that you were out of your self-induced solitary confinement, so I had to come and see you." He reached for her hands, but she took a step to the side. The Strong Arm frowned. "Mags, what's wrong?" Worry was even clearer in his features when she raised her palms outward as a signal to not come closer to her. "Mags...?"

She was no longer Magaliana. She did not wish to be Magaliana. She did not want to be associated with a name that brought back too many painful memories and negative emotions, a name that someone whom she thought loved her once called her.

She was different now. She was Greta Kretschmer, and she was no longer the weak damsel-in-distress. She had hardened. "My name is Greta now."

"But you'll always be Mags to me..." Arteus replied, tentative.

"No. I never want to hear that name again."

"Mags..." he started, then caught himself, "Greta, I... I'm so sorry that I've failed you."

If the scrawny man wasn't held up by his cybernetics, she was sure that he would have crumbled to his knees. She closed her eyes and shook her head. "You didn't fail me," she whispered as she tried to keep herself together. "It wasn't your fault. You didn't know."

"You have no idea how much we went through to try and find you..."

"Oh, I know..." she chuckled to hide a sob. "Ike told me."

She felt Arteus' cybernetic hand touch her cheek and her eyes shot open. He was inches away from her. His fingers found their way to her chin, gently lifting her head as he leaned in. Her breath caught in her throat, but she couldn't take a step back as she was already up against the edge of the hull.

"Art," Ikarim interrupted. Magaliana let out a quiet sigh of relief and saw the pain and sadness in Arteus' eyes as he turned around.

It was wonderful to see him again. She did miss the man that she considered a brother, but she had never loved him. She was never able to tell him that because she felt so helpless during his low, depressive episodes and never wanted to be the cause of them.

"Here are the destination coordinates—what's going on?" Eliakim asked as he slowed to a stop.

Magaliana cleared her throat and stepped past Arteus, briefly catching Ikarim's glance as she approached the Captain, taking the coordinates from him.

"Are you alright?" he asked quietly.

She nodded as she looked at the coordinates, her heart racing. "Have the crew continue on past these coordinates. The *Faugregir* won't necessarily be above land."

Handing the Captain back the map, she whispered her thanks and glanced up and back to the horizon. She knew Eliakim waited and expected her gaze to meet his, but she didn't comply. She was aware that he cared for her in much the same way Ikarim and Arteus did, so she simply stepped forward and walked away toward the Captain's quarters.

All the items that she requested had been delivered. After setting everything up onto the desk, Magaliana began to pace in what little room there was left, growing more nervous with each step. She hadn't replicated the spell since before the wedding. Occasionally, she paused and breathed deeply. She didn't want anyone knowing that she was a wreck.

"What do you need us to do?" asked Arteus from the other side of the door.

His voice startled her. She didn't know how long he had been there, but now that he was, she figured that a little faith wouldn't hurt.

"Hope that the first part of my plan works," she replied, not very confident.

"I believe in you. I know of no better Alchemist."

Magaliana caught herself smiling and immediately dropped her gaze and got to work. She then shut her eyes and cleared her mind.

She created her fire and snuffed it out. From that, she created the water. It almost felt like second nature to her. Grabbing the bowl of sand, she poured the water into it and kneaded the sand. A flash of Jocephus guiding her with his own hands flitted through her mind, and she choked.

"Mags!" Arteus called out, concerned.

"I'm fine," she insisted as she cleared her throat. "I'm fine." Shaking her head to clear her mind again, she continued.

Do you feel that, Dame? She heard him whisper into her ear, from out of nowhere. She twitched, and a shuddered breath escaped her as she clamped her eyes shut tight and continued to work at the wet sand.

You must knead it exactly right. Magaliana gritted her teeth from the memories. It was severely distracting and very unwelcome.

"There..." she found herself saying, just as Jocephus did, when she felt the difference in between sand and clay.

But it was too much. Her eyes shot open and she shoved everything away from herself as she tried to escape the ghost of her memories, knocking many things to the ground. She felt dirty. She did not want the memories of Jocephus to touch her or to whisper in her ear. Wiping at her arms and ears in a panic, she began fighting off whomever had grabbed a hold of her as they began to squeeze lightly and calmly shush her.

"It's okay, it's okay!" It sounded less and less like Jocephus. "It's just me..." said Ikarim.

Magaliana stopped fighting in his arms, trembling as she hyperventilated. She tried to be tough and strong like she made her new namesake out to be, but all she wanted to do was cry. She fought it hard; she was strong and vicious Greta Kretschmer, not weak little Magaliana Wiegraf.

"You can let it out, Greta," Ikarim said. "Let it out, it's just us. It's just Eli, Art, and myself. Nobody else needs to know."

Magaliana realized that the three of them had burst into the quarters during her panic attack. Collapsing into Ikarim's arms, she violently sobbed. He gently pulled her down to the ground and held onto her tight as she released months of pent up emotions.

It took her a long time to settle down. Nobody said a word the entire time she cried, and she realized Arteus and Eliakim sat next to Ikarim and herself. Though they all appeared pitifully helpless, she appreciated their silent support more than they would ever know.

"We understand if you don't want to try again..." Arteus finally said.

She softly pushed away from Ikarim and dried the tears from her face. "I have to. If we want our revenge, I have to."

"What do you need us to do?" Eliakim asked, as Arteus had before.

Magaliana shook her head. "There's nothing you can do. Not unless you're all secretly alchemists..."

Arteus stood up and began picking up the fallen tools and ingredients. Eliakim got to his feet as well, holding out a hand for her to take. Accepting it, he helped her up. Magaliana approached the items on the desk, setting everything back up. Inhaling and exhaling deeply, she began to focus once more. Once the three men left her alone in the room, she tried again.

She made fire, covered it, then brought the water to some sand. Kneading it, she took deep breaths as she tried to keep focused and keep Jocephus out of her mind. Her hands trembled and she gritted her teeth as she continued to work.

"Come on, come on..." she whispered.

She felt it: The sensation that let her know the sand was ready to become clay. She continued to grit through it until she formed a ball. Releasing a shaken breath, she held it in her palm and stared.

Pay attention...

Magaliana twitched and glared at the clay with a very unladylike cuss. She wanted Jocephus out of her head. She hated the memories and wanted them gone and forgotten. Swallowing hard, she shut her eyes. She needed to prove to Ikarim, Arteus, and Eliakim that she could do it by herself. She needed to prove it to Jocephus. She needed to prove it to herself.

Inhaling and exhaling deeply, her eyes opened as she flexed her left palm. The clay hardened and shined, turning to brass, then to bronze. She then placed her right hand over the top of the hardened glob.

Are you ready? She heard him whisper in her ear.

"Leave me alone!" Magaliana screamed.

She firmly pressed her hand into the bronze. She could feel the Techno Mage press his hand into hers just as he had done each time he walked her through it.

"Stop!" she cried. "Just stop!"

"It's alright, Greta!" came Eliakim's voice from the other side of the door. They were still there.

"We're here for you!" Ikarim added.

"We won't let him touch you!" Arteus said in turn.

Her emotions fluctuated as their voices drew her back.

Gritting her teeth together so tightly her jaw hurt, she pressed harder into the resistant bronze orb, imagining herself crushing Jocephus' hand. She felt the bronze begin to crumble in between her palms and imagined the look of horror and pain on the Techno Mage's face at what she was doing to him. But then a flash of Jocephus flinging her off the edge of the airship flashed in her mind; she screamed and flailed as she tried to push the memory away.

The fine powder from the crumbled bronze ball in her hands dispersed through the room. Another flash of Jocephus as he shot her mother made her collapse. She physically felt somebody touch her.

"Don't touch me..." she said, but she still felt the hands upon her. "I said don't touch me!" she screeched, pulling a small gun out of her belt.

She was very quick to point and shoot. The gunshot startled her back to reality.

Arteus and Eliakim were in front of her, with fear and surprise in their features. Ikarim was at her side, hands on her shoulder and arm. Arteus had one hand on her wrist, the other on the gun in her hands. Both mechanics had managed to point it away, but was it too late?

She heard Ikarim gasp as his brother shut his eyes, bringing a hand to the side of his neck.

"Eli?" she whimpered, trying to free herself from both Ikarim and Arteus. Once released, she rushed to the scruffy man. "Eli?" she repeated, panicked. "Eli, I'm so sorry..."

Eliakim gulped hard and raised his other hand to pause her in her words. "Let's just say that it was a close call. Any more to the right, I wouldn't be standing here."

Ikarim pulled his brother's hand away, revealing that the bullet had grazed him. Magaliana was relieved, but profusely apologetic about it.

"I'll live," he reassured her. "I'll get bandaged up later. Just try not to shoot anybody next time," he smirked weakly.

"Those memories again?" Ikarim asked.

She nodded. "I can't get him out of my mind. Every time that I try the transfiguration, I just... keep thinking of him. I'm doing horribly. I'm failing you all."

"You are not." Arteus placed her gun on a shelf, away from her. "You're doing what you can, given everything that you've been through. The fact that you got this far alone is quite impressive."

"I can't do it," she sighed, turning around. "I just... I can't do it."

"You can do it. We have faith in you. Do you want to know who has the most faith in you?"

Magaliana looked to Eliakim, then to Ikarim, wondering if it was one of them. Arteus took her hand and placed it on one of his cybernetic arms. Her eyes followed, and when they rose to meet his, he smiled.

"I do. Because without you, I wouldn't have this."

"You had that before me," she said, dubious. "*Doktor* Gesselmeyer made those for you."

"Not the cybernetics, the infusion." He dug one of his fingers inside his hand and pulled at the small wires that coursed with Magaliana's blue alchemy. "This is all you. This makes me the Strong Arm that I am."

"Any alchemist can do that. It's simple."

"Not for me. I'm not an alchemist, but... I know that once upon a time, this wasn't simple for you, either. You learned it... And mastered it."

He wiggled his finger and moved some of the wires until he only touched one. His cybernetic finger hooked around it and he pulled hard.

"Art!" Ikarim gasped.

Magaliana's eyes went wide. Arteus had managed to pull out a decent size of wiring from his cybernetic arm. He was quick to grab both ends of the broken wire and tie them together to keep the alchemy inside before his arm became temporarily paralyzed. The rest of the blue liquid inside his cybernetic veins spilled out onto the ground.

He wrapped the vein around her wrist with his good hand. "You'll master this new alchemy spell. And whenever you doubt yourself, whenever you see unwanted memories of the Techno Mage... Just look at this. Remember that I'm an idiot for doing this, but I wanted to prove a point."

Magaliana had tears in her eyes, but she managed a giggle and hugged Arteus. "Thank you." She looked to Ikarim, who smiled in turn, then to Eliakim and his bullet-grazed neck. "I'm so sorry, Eli..."

"Get back to work," he replied with a smile.

Magaliana pulled away from Arteus and turned back to her items. Arteus, Ikarim, and Eliakim all helped her set back up. When they stepped away to leave her to her transfiguration, she called out to them.

"Wait!" she said. All three turned around with raised brows. "Please... Please stay. I thought that I needed privacy, but what I really need is... Is you. All of you."

There was silence as the three men looked to one another.

"You heard the lady..." Eliakim said.

They all turned around and spread out in what little room there was left of the Captain's quarters. Magaliana shut her eyes, inhaled deeply, and exhaled, focused.

She created her fire. She created her water. She even created the clay. And when she doubted herself, when she thought that Joce-phus would show up in her mind, she looked at the infusion wire around her wrist. She even gave a faint smile. Once the clay solidified and turned to bronze, she held it between her palms and crushed it, almost with ease. But then there was a flash.

She remembered Jocephus' fingers as they gently dug in between hers as he pulled her hand away from her left palm. She released a shud-dered breath at the memory and looked at the dust in her hand. She snatched her fingers closed around the dust as she trembled.

"It's alright," Arteus said. "It's alright, we're right here."

Determined, Magaliana grabbed a bottle with her free hand. She placed her hand over top of it and turned her hand sideways.

Open your hand, she heard Jocephus say. She growled, then whined.

"Open your hand!" Ikarim cheered. "You can do it!"

She held her breath and bit down onto her tongue so hard she bled. When her lungs couldn't handle it anymore, she exhaled swiftly, panting as she struggled to open her hand... But she did it. The fine powder spilled into the bottle and turned into a green liquid once it touched the glass. Magaliana exhaled and fell to her knees as she sealed the bottle. The three men rushed toward her, cheering.

"You did it!" Arteus exclaimed.

"Well, there's one. I still need two more," she confided.

"That's okay! Now that you've done it, you can do it again and again, and never have to think about him ever again."

Magaliana nodded and got back to work on the two other bottles. Arteus was right—it didn't take her nearly as long, and it wasn't as hard to do. Every time she thought that a memory of Jocephus might cross her mind, she thought of what she had accomplished just a few minutes prior. Proud of her accomplishments, she pushed on. Eventually, the other two bottles were complete.

CHAPTER 45

"Green, huh?" said Arteus as he inspected the bottles.

Magaliana nodded. "It's alchemy in its purest form."

She had needed some much-deserved fresh air after her recent trial, so she had found her way to the bridge. Her friends followed her and for once, she didn't mind.

"That's amazing," Arteus whispered. "Do you think I can have some for my cybernetics?"

"Not right now," Ikarim answered, his attention on his work. "Pretty sure these ones were made for a plan."

"I'll make you some later, I promise," she said to the Strong Arm. Her eyes travelled to Ikarim. "How goes it?" She had tasked him with trying to get a signal from the broadcaster. He had tinkered with it and placed one of the infusions inside the battery to give it more power and reach.

A strange hum sounded over the broadcaster, and everyone fell silent as their gaze fell to the object.

"There," she quickly said. "That's it. Follow that, and it'll take you to the *Faugregir*."

"How do you know?" Eliakim asked.

"I remember there being a strange hum aboard the ship when I was there. I figured it was worth a shot."

"It's genius," Ikarim agreed.

"What are the two other bottles for?" Arteus asked.

"Part two and three of the plan," Magaliana grinned.

Eliakim took the helm and adjusted course based on how loud the hum became. They all took turns keeping an ear out for the signal on the broadcaster in case they had to change course.

Hours passed. Magaliana made infusions for Arteus, while Ikarim repaired the damaged wires in his cybernetic arm. Eventually, they reached thick cloud coverage.

"I can't see a thing!" Eliakim hissed. "This is dangerous."

"It's alright." Magaliana stood next to him. "There will be plenty of time to adjust course once we pass it. We're almost there. I can feel it."

As if on cue, they passed through the clouds. The clearing was so crisp, it almost seemed like a dream. The men gaped at the breathtaking view, while Magaliana gave a bittersweet smile; it was a beautiful sight, but it brought back nothing but bad memories. Now that she knew that it was associated with the Carronade, it needed to be destroyed even more.

"What are those?" Arteus pointed to something that moved on the ground.

"Those are part three of the plan," Magaliana said. "They're golems. They are all over. There's even a cemetery for them on one of the floors."

"What's part two?" Ikarim asked.

The *Fang* was unwelcomed. Fire sounded nearby as cannons shot in an attempt to knock them out of the sky. Magaliana turned to Arteus and took one of the bottles from him. "This is part two."

Uncorking the glass container, she flicked her wrist out over the hull. The green liquid spilled, but quickly crystalized, growing wider into a beehive pattern. The cannonballs crumbled, along with each crystalized hexagon they touched.

Arteus, Ikarim, and Eliakim stared in amazement.

"The shield won't last forever, so best hurry up," she urged.

Eliakim sailed his ship as best he could toward the surface of the *Faugregir*.

"There," Magaliana pointed out. "There is the way in. Before you get there, I need to jump down and reach that golem there." She pointed forward.

"Take the ladder," Eliakim instructed.

The shield caught more cannonballs as Magaliana looked to Arteus, who seemed unsure.

"Art, help her! Eli and I will catch up!" Ikarim said.

The Strong Arm quickly ran off toward the ladder, picked it up, and shoved it over the edge of the ship, dangling in the air. Magaliana climbed over the edge and quickly descended, followed closely by Arteus.

"We're not going to make it!" she called up to him. "The golem is too slow, and the *Fang* is moving too fast!"

Arteus sighed from above. "Come grab a hold of my neck."

"What?"

"I... I have a really stupid idea. I don't know if it will work, but it's worth a try."

"I'm not sure I'm into stupid ideas..."

Arteus climbed down until he was on the opposite side of the ladder from her. "How much do you trust your own alchemy?"

"I trust it..." she said, tentative.

"Then trust that your alchemy will save us from my stupid idea."

He grabbed Magaliana's wrist and released the ladder entirely. Magaliana shrieked and tightly wrapped her arms around Arteus' neck as they fell through the air, convinced that she was going to die. The Strong Arm had lost his mind and taken her with him.

"Hold on..." Arteus instructed. "Here we go..."

He hit the ground a few feet away from the golem so hard that the earth exploded beneath him. Magaliana screamed at the force of the impact, then heard Arteus hiss as they tumbled.

"We're going to fall off the edge!" Magaliana shrieked.

Arteus unwrapped one arm from around her and reached out for the railing along the edge. He grabbed on and cried out from the sudden stop thanks to his cybernetics, but Magaliana was flung away from the momentum. Screaming, she reached out and caught his hand just in time before falling over the edge. Kicking her feet in the air, she looked down and immediately regretted it as she saw how far the surface of the ocean was.

"You were right," she scolded in between gasps for air, "that was a very stupid idea!"

"Hang on, I'll swing you up. Are you ready?" he asked.

Her eyes went wide. Of course she wasn't ready! "For the record," she shouted, "I also think *this* is a stupid idea!"

"You can thank me later!"

Arteus slowly swung Magaliana like a pendulum and instructed her to let go once she got to the top. Before she could question him, she hurtled upward. Screaming, she let go of Arteus as he propelled her over the railing, landing on her back with the wind knocked out of her. Quickly trying to regain her bearings, she turned over and crawled to the Strong Arm. "Give me your hand!"

Arteus held out one hand and she pulled him up enough that he was able to climb the rest of the way. The Strong Arm parted his lips to say something to Magaliana but instead looked past her, his eyes wide. Glancing over her shoulder, she quickly spun around to find the golem slowly raising its long arm, winding up to smash them.

"Art, quick, I need that bottle!" she said before they dove out of the way, the construct crushing the railing.

"I don't have it!" Arteus said as they both scampered to their feet.

"What do you mean you don't have it!?"

"It must have fallen out during our landing!"

Magaliana cussed in German as the idol prepared itself again. This was it. The end. She had hoped to live a little longer, at least long enough to destroy the Carronade. Clamping her eyes shut, she shielded her face...

Nothing happened.

Opening her eyes and peeking up past her arms, she saw their attacker was blocked by the golem she revived from the cemetery. Her pleasant shock only lasted a few seconds as she wasted no time at all and traced symbols into the palm of her hand, then darted toward them.

"Mags!" Arteus gasped. "What are you doing?!"

"Plan three-and-a-half!" she called back. "And my name is Greta!"

She dove through the chaos of both battling constructs, managing to reach the attacking golem's leg. Placing her palm onto it, both idols stopped moving, their eyes glowing green like her hand.

"You're controlling it..." Arteus said as he caught up. "But how?"

Magaliana grinned. She did it! Her victory was short-lived, however, as gunshots ricocheted off both constructs' bodies, startling her. They were being shot at by the approaching ground crew of the *Faugregir*. Arteus fired back with his own pistol, while Magaliana dropped to the ground behind one of the idol's legs, tracing symbols into the earth.

"What are you doing?" the Strong Arm asked.

Magaliana didn't answer. She didn't have time to explain. She only hoped that what she was attempting would work. Slamming her hand down into the center of the new transmutation circle, energy shot out and through the ship. The previously-battling golems turned and swung at the crewmen, sending them flying.

"You can control them?!" cried Ikarim as he and Eliakim ran full speed in their direction to help.

All the other golems began helping as well, and soon the crew of the *Faugregir* turned their fire onto the new enemies.

"I... I was going to try it with the third vial, but we lost it when we landed. I didn't think that I could do it without the infusion..."

"You're the new Techno Mage," said Eliakim. "With him gone, you're the new master of this ship."

Magaliana looked at her hands in disbelief. With that kind of power, she could unite the Upper and Lower Lands!

No. She shook her head with a determined frown. The only thing she wanted to use her new powers on was destroying the Carronade and the ship. And that's what she intended to do.

Magaliana had an idea. She rushed off, followed closely by her friends.

"Where do we start?" Ikarim asked.

"I was given full reign of the ship... Except for one area. I say that's the perfect place to start."

Magaliana led them inside. Every crew member from the mythical ship was busy fighting the golems and rogues from Eliakim's crew, so it would be relatively easy to get to the lift... Or so Magaliana thought.

A bloated creature jumped out before they reached the platform, pointing a large grenade launcher at them and snarling from a head that was nothing but massive incisors and insect-like eyes. Ikarim and Arteus shot at it and continued shooting even after it fell limp to the ground.

"What the hell is that thing?!" Arteus cried in disgust.

"The hazed," Eliakim answered. "There are hazed people aboard this ship."

Magaliana did not ever remember hazed men aboard the ship, but she really didn't spend her time anywhere other than the cemetery.

"Come on," she said as she stepped past the patchy creature. "This way."

She led them down as far as they could go, fighting their way past more of the hazed, until they reached the level Magaliana was previously not allowed on, at the very center of the ship, where a squid-faced hazed being guarded a pair of thick doors. Eliakim, Ikarim, and Arteus took it out with ease while Magaliana looked for a way inside.

Her fingers ran over the intricate designs, and her eyes darted over the cog wheels as she tried to find how to open the doors.

"Would this help?" Eliakim asked.

Magaliana shot her attention toward him, musing over a dark screen and lever mounted onto the wall. Ikarim rushed over to study the lever, while Arteus looked for something to turn the screen on. Tapping it did nothing.

Approaching the lever, Magaliana pulled it, but nothing happened. Frowning, she reset the lever then crossed her arms over her chest, deep in thought. If she were Jocephus, how would he open the door to the safely-guarded core?

"Greta..." Eliakim said gently.

When her gaze travelled back to the Captain, she noticed that his eyes were locked onto the screen next to her. Her attention darted to the screen, which held a slight greenish tint to it. When she took a step back, it disappeared. Curious, she stepped toward it, again. The glow returned. Reaching for the screen, her eyes went wide as her hand passed through the solid screen as if it weren't there at all. Arteus gasped; hadn't she just watched him tap a solid surface?

"There is something at the back," she said. "It feels like a button."

"Should she press it?" asked Arteus.

"Considering hers is the only hand able to pass through the solid surface, I would say yes," Eliakim replied.

Magaliana pressed the button. The entire room glowed green for a second as the vines began to bubble with the green alchemy. Magaliana pulled her hand back, startled, as the group all glanced around. But nothing else happened.

Eliakim pulled the lever, and the cogs on the doors turned and churned and opened. Arteus tried the doors, but they were still somehow locked.

"Hold on," Ikarim walked toward the heavy brass doors. He pointed to a cog indentation that was previously hidden. "Do you have a key?"

Magaliana shook her head. "No, but I can probably make one. Give me a minute."

She walked up to the doors and inspected the cog indentation. She then quickly drew a few symbols into her hand. It glowed white for a moment, and she placed her palm up against the indentation, waiting a few seconds before she pushed. A large vibration occurred on the other side, and the doors slowly opened.

"You never cease to amaze me..." Eliakim said in awe as the doors opened and allowed the suffocating humidity from the other side to seep through.

"Ugh, what the hell is this stuff, it's disgusting!" Arteus said as they walked past the slimy tendrils and followed the hallway until they reached a gigantic dome.

"What is this place?" Ikarim asked.

"Welcome to the inside of the Carronade," came a voice.

CHAPTER 46

A figure slid out from behind a control panel, covered in horns and spiky bones. Recognizing the markings over the tattered body, Magaliana swiftly pulled out her gun, cocking and aiming at the man with a loathing glare.

"Don't move, Joss," she growled.

"What happened to you?" Eliakim asked, revolted.

Jocephus looked at them in resentment. "I fell right above the freshly hazed Hoia-Baciu forest. Instead of dying as I should have, I became like my beloved. My transformation was surprisingly quick..." he added, glancing to the spikes on his arms.

"Your beloved?" Magaliana wondered—then it clicked. "Lady Juliet was your beloved?"

"She is my wife, actually," he corrected. Magaliana glared even more.

"Who is Lady Juliet?" asked Arteus.

"She was an inventor and the best Alchemist I had ever had the pleasure of knowing. One of her experiments went wrong and she had a near-death experience. Except that she never died. She became... this," Jocephus said as he gestured to everything around them. "To her, alchemy and technology belonged together. It was not a matter of social status. I loved her so much that I created the *Faugregir* for her. Alchemy and technology. Magic. I then created it around her, and then the ship became her. And the haze... It's her excess energy. Her excess alchemy. Whatever it touches becomes like her. And I must bring her back those who were hazed so that she can use them as food. Fuel. Life cycle coming full circle, so to speak. I won't let you touch her. I won't let you harm her."

"If you are still married to Lady Juliet..." Magaliana spoke, a quiver in her voice, "Why did you ask for my hand as well?"

Jocephus chuckled. "I never loved you, *Dame* Magaliana, I was only making you my bride so I could have somebody of equal power to mine to revert Juliet back. And you were putty in my hands."

A gunshot echoed through the chamber, and Jocephus stumbled backward. "My name is Greta!" Magaliana screamed and pulled the trigger again, and again, and again, until her friends all tackled her, grabbing her wrist and wrestling the gun away. Jocephus collapsed, blood pooling around him, mixing in with the puddle of alchemy.

"Let go of me!" she screamed, her vision red.

A high-pitched shriek of anger came from inside the dome. Everyone quickly covered their ears just as it shattered. There, black eyes opened and sharp fangs bared, stood the hazed Juliet, tentacles lashing out angrily at the intruders.

Magaliana was dumbfounded. She recalled the Techno Mage's reaction to the portrait, how sad he seemed when he looked at the beautiful woman's picture. She hadn't left him. She hadn't refused him. She had been aboard the mythical ship the whole time. And that woman looked nothing like the enraged creature before them. Jocephus had nearly used her to revert the monster back into his beautiful wife.

"Mags!" Arteus shielded her, swinging his arm out to prevent her from getting whipped by one of the appendages.

Before she could lash out and scold the Strong Arm for using her old name, another feeler shot out and wrapped around his cybernetic arm. Magaliana ducked out of the way and unsheathed her sword. The hazed woman was on a rampage for her dead husband, and unfortunately, there were hundreds of tentacles, and only four of them.

Magaliana slashed off as many as she could,

but they just kept coming. Ikarim and Eliakim were doing their best to shoot at Juliet, though she deflected them, making it near impossible to directly hit her. Arteus crushed and shredded the appendages as well as he could, but Juliet proved overwhelming.

"We sure could use that hybrid gun of yours, Art!" Ikarim called out.

"You were with me!" Arteus quipped back. "You could have grabbed it, too!"

"Just keep attacking!" Eliakim hissed at them.

Suddenly, Magaliana heard a beautiful voice, soothing, melodic, euphonious. Ikarim and Eliakim dropped their guns while Arteus ceased fighting. Before she had time to react, tentacles entangled around her wrists and pulled her arms up while a rather large and slimy tendril slithered about her waist, crushing her. She struggled to break free but couldn't.

The siren call was beautiful and haunting all at the same time. For a moment, the men all stared at Juliet before Arteus finally took a step toward her.

"Art!" Magaliana hissed. "What are you doing?"

The Strong Arm didn't answer. He continued to move toward the hazed woman in some sort of trance. Ikarim and his brother did the same.

"Ike!" she called out. "Eli! Snap out of it!"

The three men slowly moved toward Juliet.

Magaliana growled and struggled more, but with each move, the appendage about her waist tightened painfully.

"Art! Ike! Stop! Don't listen! Cover your ears! Eli, please!"

They wouldn't listen. Panicked, Magaliana flailed more until she realized her legs were free. Kicking her heels together, she lashed her feet out at the tentacle about her waist, slicing it with the hidden blades in the toes of her boots. Juliet released her midriff and Magaliana took in a much-needed gulp of air. Launching herself backward, she kicked at the tendrils that still held her wrists hostage and dropped to the floor. Jumping to her feet, she slashed at the tentacles whipping about, wondering why the siren's call wasn't affecting her. That's when she saw it.

The transmutation circle glowed brightly in her palm, despite gripping her sword tightly. That was it. Jocephus wasn't affected, and it wasn't due to his love for the creature; it was because he was the Techno Mage. And because Magaliana had mastered the ability, she was immune. Gritting her teeth, she rushed past Arteus to get to Juliet first.

She wasn't going to allow the monster to claim her friends. She had had enough: Enough of the *Faugregir*, enough of the lies and deceit, enough of being taken advantage of, enough of being hurt. The mythical ship and Carronade needed to be taken down, and with her friends in a trance, she was going to be the one to do it; she had to be the one to exact everyone's revenge.

She lunged at Juliet with her sword extended, stabbing the hazed woman through the mouth. The siren's call immediately ceased. Magaliana dragged her blade down, splitting Juliet's form in half down to her belly.

The creature twitched violently from cadaveric spasms as Magaliana pulled her sword away, turning to the men as they blinked away their fog, only to fall to her knees as a powerful tremor shook the core and the whole area began to rumble and crumble.

"Without Lady Juliet sustaining the *Faugregir*, it's falling apart. We have to get out of here, quick!" she said.

They easily managed to escape the room, rushing to the lift. Magaliana hopped onto the platform, followed closely by Eliakim. But just as Ikarim was about to step on, the ceiling collapsed atop him and Arteus, sending them below level.

Magaliana screamed.

CHAPTER 47

Ikarim opened his eyes as the ground rumbled about him. He looked around. What just happened?

"Are you alright?" came a struggling voice.

Ikarim turned his attention toward the voice to see Arteus crouched amidst debris, struggling to hold up a large boulder from crushing them.

"Art!" Scampering to his knees, he paused once he noticed that there was a large hole next to him, revealing the ocean too far below. The Carronade, the core, was embedded into the bottom of the floating isle of a ship, and it was crumbling beneath them. He tried to help Arteus with the boulder, but it weighed too much, and his effort was meaningless.

"I can't keep it up," the Strong Arm grunted. "It's too heavy. I might be able to if I still had some alchemy in my right arm, but..."

Ikarim noticed the leak running down his friend's cybernetic arm, damaged from the fall. "Is your arm paralyzed?" he asked. Arteus gave a swift nod. "Don't give up on me, Art..." Ikarim said, panicked, looking around and trying to figure out how to help. He spotted an opening near the top, a small cavity that he might be able to squeeze through... but then what would happen to Arteus?

Their surroundings shook violently, and Arteus sank a little deeper beneath the weight of the boulder. Ikarim was forced to slink down a little closer to the ground.

"Leave!" Arteus yelled to his friend.

"I'm not leaving you!"

"Just leave! We don't both have to die. Tell Mags... Tell Greta that I love her. Always have."

"Art..."

The ship quaked once more, and Arteus cried out in pain, then in surprise as the stone beneath one of his legs crumbled away, causing the cybernetic limb to slip and dangle in the air as the Strong Arm dropped further into the ground. Ikarim was forced to lay flat on his stomach.

"Ike, go!" Arteus bellowed, panic clear in his voice.

The ground trembled violently and the boulder moved, but instead of crushing them, it was picked up and tossed aside. Surprised, both men glanced up at the opening to see an iron golem and Magaliana peering down at them. The construct lowered both of its arms toward them.

"Climb on! Quick!"

Ikarim scrambled to his feet and rushed around the hole to Arteus—who had finally regained movement in his arm—and helped him up and into the golem's large hand.

He was definitely glad to see the Alchemist, but his heart skipped a beat when he realized that his brother wasn't with her. "Where is Eli?"

"He went to fetch the ship. Quick! Follow me!"

Both men jumped out of the large hands, following Magaliana through the floors of the *Faugregir* toward the lifts. Ikarim was a little nervous to board the platform after the last time he tried, but he didn't have time to hesitate. Once at the top, they rushed to the docks.

"Eli!" Magaliana called out.

"Landslide damaged her!" Eliakim bellowed from the helm. "She runs, but we're stuck!"

"Climb on board!" she ordered Ikarim and Arteus. "Quickly!"

Ikarim followed the Strong Arm to the rope ladder but turned his attention back to Magaliana. A transmutation circle glowed about her feet and she seemed to be trying really hard to control something while a few of the golems approached.

"Go!" she screamed to Ikarim.

Suddenly, the ship moved. The rocks from the landslide melted away into muddy water. He mounted only one step of the ladder as a handful of the massive constructs pushed the airship. The muddy water rushed toward Magaliana like a tsunami wave, but she seemed unafraid.

"Eli!" Ikarim bellowed.

The ship continued to glide forward on the wave. Ikarim gritted his teeth and leaned out, reaching for Magaliana. He only had one shot at this.

"Grab on!" he told her.

The Alchemist raised her hands and grabbed onto Ikarim's arm as he snatched her by the waist. Struggling, he was slightly envious at how Arteus made it seem so easy aboard the train. Holding the woman tightly, he let Arteus pull them up and aboard.

"I can't get her in the air!" Eliakim called out.

Ikarim's eyes found their way to the rapidly-approaching edge of the *Faugregir*. "We won't make it..."

"Everyone hold on to something!" Eliakim ordered.

The *Fang* faltered as it attempted to lift off from the mythical ship, then finally floated down toward the ocean. Behind them, the *Faugregir* crashed into the water, resulting in a gigantic ripple of waves which caught the *Fang*, knocking the crew down as it lunged the ship forward with incredible speed. They rode the wave until it crashed, leaving the damaged *Fang* partially buried on land, stranded quite a distance from the shore.

His heart racing, Ikarim got to his feet as Eliakim bellowed orders to his crew. He glanced about for Magaliana, finding her staring out toward the ocean as the remainder of the *Faugregir* crumbled into the water, turning into an island at best.

Arteus rushed over to her, asking if she was alright. She nodded. Ikarim walked up to the both of them as the crew of the *Fang* scrambled about. He placed a hand on Magaliana's shoulder as he looked out into the distance as she did.

He had mixed emotions about the whole ordeal; on one hand, he was glad that the Carronade was destroyed. That meant that nobody else would endure what so many—including his parents and brother—had to go through. But on the other hand, the Carronade could be used for good. Filled with Magaliana's pure alchemy, they could have cured the effects of the haze on everyone.

CHAPTER 48

Everyone helped get the damaged *Fang* back in semi-working order. Ikarim put his mechanic skills to the test on more than one occasion, but compared to everything he had previously endured, it was nothing to complain about.

"Might want to make yourselves scarce," came a man's voice as Ikarim and Arteus finished up. "The Imperium and the Royal Guard are on their way to the scene of the crash as we speak."

Ikarim turned to see Eliakim and Magaliana approaching. He then looked to Arteus. "We did sneak away, after all. We'll get Court Martialed and fined for desertion... We've probably earned jail time as well."

"Care to join my crew?" Eliakim asked. "We sure could use a Strong Arm and a mechanic..."

"I can't. I need to face responsibility for my actions. Perhaps they'll let me off lightly; I did just help destroy the *Faugregir*, after all. But after that... I need to return home."

"I know what you're thinking," Arteus said. Ikarim turned to his friend with a raised brow. "You want to go through *Vater*'s notes. You want to see if you can cure your parents."

"You know me too well," Ikarim smiled. "You can stay with the *Fang*. You don't have to turn yourself in... You've sold the shop, there's really nothing left to do but join the rogues."

Arteus shook his head. "I can't let you do all that research on your own. And I definitely can't let you turn yourself in on your own. Besides, you wouldn't have been caught up in this mess if it weren't for me."

"I definitely agree that I've surpassed my adventure quota because of you," Ikarim jested. Arteus laughed.

Ikarim's gaze fell back to Magaliana, who remained silent next to Eliakim. Her eyes had grown softer now that Jocephus and the *Faugregir* were out of the way. Deep down, however, he knew the answer to his next question, but he asked it anyway. "Will you come home with us?"

She glanced at Eliakim, who watched her, then shook her head as she looked back to Ikarim. "No. I... I need time to myself. That was

Mags' life. I am Greta now. This is where I belong."

Ikarim nodded as he approached, his arms open in request for a hug, which Magaliana happily obliged. Ikarim closed his arms around her and shut his eyes, inhaling and exhaling deeply. He knew that she needed time to process everything that just happened, everything she was supposed to have already come to terms with before Jocephus dropped another bombshell on her.

"Promise you'll keep in touch?" he asked.

"I promise," she replied with a smile.

Ikarim smiled back and released Magaliana, who then tentatively approached a pouting Arteus. She wrapped her arms around his waist and the Strong Arm froze, but soon wrapped his arms around her as well. He knew his friend would always love the Alchemist but wondered if he had finally come to terms with the fact that they would never be together.

Ikarim turned to his brother to find him reaching out. With a smile, he clasped his hand around his brother's forearm.

"The *Talon* and the *Tusk* will escort you back to *Doktor* Gesselmeyer's mansion."

"Thank you," he said, then added, "take care of her, Eli."

Ikarim released his arm as Magaliana had stepped away from Arteus, finding her way back to Eliakim's side. The Captain looked at her with a soft smile, and Ikarim noticed that familiar, love-struck look in his brother's eyes that both he and Arteus had. He smirked and shook his head some, wondering if the Captain knew what he was getting himself into. Unrequited love definitely hurt.

The scruffy man looked back to Ikarim with a grin. "She'll be just fine."

"We can rebuild it, you know..." Arteus said, quite randomly. "The *Faugregir*," he specified. "We can rebuild it. With Greta's pure alchemy, your amazing mechanic skills..." Art's attention tore away from the horizon and turned to Ikarim. "Think about it!"

Ikarim chuckled and waved goodbye to his brother and to Magaliana before he turned to embark onto the *Talon*, Arteus by his side.

THE END

TRANSLATIONS

German

Dame ['daː.mə]: Lady (noblewoman)

Deutsches Kaiserreich [dɔɤtʃ 'kai̯ɐrai̯ç]: The German Imperium (empire)

Doktor ['dɔktoːɐ]: Doctor (scientist)

Fünf ['fʏnf]: Five

Gulden ['gʊldn̩]: Gold coin (currency)

Guten morgen ['guːtən 'mɔʁgən]: Good morning

Herr [hɛʁ]: Lord (lowest title of German nobility)

Hurensohn ['huːʁn̩ˌzoːn]: Son of a bitch (personal insult)

Kapitän [kapiˈtɛːn]: Captain

König ['køːnɪç]: King (monarch)

Laufmaschine [laʊ̯f maˈʃiːnə]: Running machine (two-wheeler principle of the bicycle)

Nein [nai̯n]: No

Norden ['nɔʁdn̩]: North

Panzerbüchse ['pantsɐ 'bʏk.sə]: Armored rifle (anti-tank)

Prinz [pʁɪnts͡]: Prince (monarch)

Sauerbraten ['zaʊ̯ɐˌbʁaːtn̩]: Braised beef (food)

Schleswig ['ʃleːsvɪk]: Sleswick (town/second military conflict over the Schleswig-Holstein region)

Sechsundvierzig ['zɛksʊntˌfiʁts͡ɪç]: Forty-six

Sieben ['ziːbən]: Seven

Und [ʊnt]: And

Vater [ˈfaːtər]: Father
Verrückter [fɛɐˈʁʏktər]: Madman

<u>Portuguese</u>
Príncipe [ˈpɾ̃ĩ.sɨ.pɨ]: Prince (monarch)

ABOUT THE AUTHOR

Raine is Canadian, born and raised, and constantly moved in between Ontario and Quebec with her military family. She moved to Michigan, USA, in 2004, where she currently still resides with her husband and son.

She has always had a vivid imagination and loved reading and writing from a very young age. She took courses in Children's Literature through ICL in Illinois, and published her New Adult Steampunk debut in 2020. She has participated in NaNoWriMo for over a decade and is currently a Municipal Liaison for the Detroit region.